THE
DISCOVERY

Center Point
Large Print

Also by Dan Walsh and available from Center Point Large Print:

The Deepest Waters

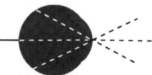

**This Large Print Book carries the
Seal of Approval of N.A.V.H.**

THE
DISCOVERY

DAN WALSH

CENTER POINT LARGE PRINT
THORNDIKE, MAINE

Library of Congress Cataloging-in-Publication Data

Walsh, Dan, 1957–
The discovery / Dan Walsh.
pages ; cm.
ISBN 978-1-61173-696-0 (library binding : alk. paper)
1. Large type books. I. Title.
PS3623.A446D58 2013
813'.6—dc23
                                                    2012047909

To Cindi, my "Claire,"
and to my first grandson,
Caden Alexander Mosier.
So glad God has added you to our family.
Already you have given us
a treasure of memories;
we can't wait to make many, many more.

1

I remember . . . I was supposed to be sad that day.

Everyone was sad. It's always sad when a legend dies. Our family was gathered in Charleston to read his will.

Gerard Warner's novels sold in the millions. He'd won the Pulitzer Prize. Several of his books had become blockbuster movies. I remember reading interviews with some of the celebrities who'd starred in those movies. Talked as if they were friends with my grandfather.

I knew instantly they were lying.

They didn't know him. None of them did. He wouldn't have let them.

To his adoring fans, Gerard Warner remained an enigmatic, elusive figure his entire career. He wouldn't even allow his picture on his own book covers. Every time a new novel came out, TV producers and talk show hosts made their appeals —again—wanting to be the first to interview him. He only said yes to print interviews. Even then, no pictures. And absolutely no questions about his personal life allowed.

Still, Gerard Warner's books flew off the shelves. They were that good.

I called him Gramps.

"You're smiling, Michael."

I looked over at my beautiful wife, who was holding tightly to my hand, her blonde hair lit up by the sun. "Can't help it, Jenn. I love this place." It's hard not to love a slow walk down Broad Street in Charleston, especially in October. Pick any street in the old downtown area. I loved them all. The cobblestones of Chalmers, the courtyards along Queens. The iron gates and grand staircases on Church Street, the tilting townhomes on Tradd.

I loved the magnificent plantations beyond the city limits that had survived the Civil War. My grandfather had taken me on tours of every one. The exquisite gardens and ponds of Magnolia Plantation. The stunning tunnel of live oaks leading up to Boone Hall. The rolling green lawns and gardens of Middleton Place resting quietly along the banks of the Ashley River.

Charleston was my grandfather's favorite place in the world. For the last decades of his life, he called it home, wrote some of his best work here. He made me love it too. So many memories for me.

Memories with him.

"I don't think anyone else in your family will be smiling," Jenn said. "Your sister Marilyn certainly won't. I forgot to tell you, she called when you were in the shower. Umm, can you slow down a little?"

"Sorry." I always did that, walked faster when I

got excited. Jenn said it took her three steps to match two of mine.

"She didn't want to leave a message," Jenn continued. "And she seemed kind of tense to me. Do you think she's nervous about the will?"

"Maybe, but it's not about the money." We stopped at the corner of Church and Broad to let a carriage go by. The tour guide turned down Broad, drew his passengers' attention to the steeple of St. Michael's up ahead. I looked up. A beautiful building. "Remember, my grandfather talked to each of us individually before he died." We crossed the street. "Didn't want there to be any tension in the family about who was getting what. My dad and Aunt Fran will get half the estate. The four of us grandchildren get an equal slice of the second half."

"I do remember you telling me that. So what's bothering her?"

"Marilyn's tense because of this ancestry thing she's obsessing over."

"I thought you said she gave that up," Jenn said.

"No, I said she *needed* to." I exhaled some frustration. "She's spent a ridiculous amount of time trying to solve some mystery involving my grandfather. I keep telling her to let it go. Every time she'd bring it up to Gramps, I could see how much it bothered him. But she'd just keep poking and prodding him." I inhaled the aroma of fresh garlic bread as we walked past the open

9

door of an Italian restaurant. "You smell that? Let's come back here when we're done."

"I'd love that. So, what's Marilyn after? What's the big mystery?"

Jenn and I had only been married a year. We lived near Orlando, a seven-hour drive from here. She'd only gotten to spend time with my grandfather a handful of times. "She thinks he was hiding something."

"Hiding what?"

"I don't know. That's what she said."

"I know he shunned the public eye," Jenn said. "But a lot of famous people do."

"She's convinced it's more than that."

"He seemed really nice to me," she said. "Every time I talked with him, he had the kindest eyes."

"He was an amazing guy. I'm not talking about his books, but just being around him, doing ordinary things. I think he was the most honorable man I've ever known. Which is why this thing Marilyn's doing makes me so mad."

"What's she trying to do?"

"She says she's just trying to put our family tree together. A bunch of her friends started doing this a few years ago, some kind of social thing. They each researched old family albums and letters, looked up things on the internet, then met once a month over coffee to share what they found. Everyone else dug up plenty of stuff, but apparently our family tree stops with my grandfather."

"Really?"

"Now don't you get started."

"I'm not, but you've got to admit, that is kinda strange."

"C'mon, Jenn."

"What? I'm not implying anything. It's just, I think it would be fascinating, looking into your family's history. But really, Michael, most people would expect to hit a dead end a few more branches back than the grandfather level."

"Can we drop this?" I looked across the street, not at anything in particular.

"You're getting edgy."

"I am not." But I was.

Jenn suddenly stopped, jerked my arm a bit. She led me back a few steps, toward the large shop window of an art gallery.

"Oh, Michael, look at that."

We just stood there. It was beautiful. A fireplace-sized painting of a low-country marsh at sunrise. Palm trees swayed to a slight breeze. A large mossy oak drifted over the water. In the foreground, larger than life, a majestic blue heron surveyed the entire scene, his eyes fierce and penetrating. The whole thing as colorful and detailed as if Audubon had painted it himself. I remembered that blue herons were my grand-mother's favorite birds. I looked down at the price. Eighteen hundred dollars.

"Maybe they have it in a smaller print size," she

said, looking up at me with those big brown eyes. She knew I couldn't resist that look, made me want to give her half my kingdom. "How much you think we'll get from the will?" she asked.

I hadn't told her how huge my grandfather's estate was, nor how dramatically I expected our lives would change in an hour or two. "We'll just have to wait and see," I said, easing her away from the window. "But I have a feeling we may just stop in here on the way back to the hotel and wrap that bad boy up."

We resumed our pace down Broad. She squeezed my hand. She liked that answer.

At that point, I felt pretty sure our part of the estate might be enough to break free from my day job at the bank to take a stab at another passion I shared with my grandfather, besides the city of Charleston.

I wanted to be a writer too.

The thought occurred to me just now to add the words "like him," but that would be an absurdity. I could never write like him. Compared to him, my best efforts were like the refrigerator drawings of a child. But Gramps never let me think that way about myself. He told me once, "You got it in you, son. I can see it. Something God gave you. So don't get hung up trying to be like me. Do what you can do. Find the road you want to take, see where it leads you."

When we reached Meeting Street, we stopped. I

spun us around to see the whole of Broad Street facing east toward the Old Exchange Building. "Now look at that, Jenn. You realize people from George Washington's time shopped in these same stores? Washington himself danced at a ball in that building at the end of the road." I turned her to the right and pointed at St. Michael's church across the street. "He went to church right there in the spring of 1791."

"That's really something." She spun us around to face the right direction. "How much farther to the law office?"

"Two blocks on the left. It's in this gorgeous old three-story house, built in 1788."

"Two more blocks? We should've taken the car, Michael."

"Jenn, it's such a beautiful day."

"And I'm in heels."

2

"That's it?"

My sister Marilyn's remark sliced through the joyful, almost euphoric mood enjoyed by everyone else. We were all sitting—every adult member of our extended family—around the plush conference room of Bradley and Dunn, Attorneys at Law. I may have been the only one who heard her, and that was only because I'd been dreading the possibility she'd make a scene. Except for Marilyn, the rest of us were properly stunned by the enormity and benevolence of my grandfather's will.

I was nearly in shock. Each of us had become instant millionaires.

I looked over at Jenn. Didn't recognize the look on her face. Several notches above pure amazement.

Despite Marilyn's obvious annoyance, tears welled up in my eyes. Not so much at the thought of my newfound wealth but at the magnitude of my grandfather's generosity, and the obvious care and thought he'd put into the words read just now by Alfred Dunn, the firm's senior partner. No legalese here; the words had been clearly penned by my grandfather's own hand. I could almost hear his deep, gentle voice, as if he were sitting in his favorite armchair, reading us a chapter from his latest book.

"I'm sorry, Mr. Dunn," Marilyn continued, "but that can't be all my grandfather wrote."

I glanced around the room. Everyone else sat back in their burgundy leather chairs, trying to take it in. Marilyn alone leaned forward, elbows on the mahogany table.

"Excuse me?" the elder Dunn replied, turning toward her. In such a large firm, his presence at the table was an obvious concession to the huge probate fee from the estate.

"There's got to be something else my grand-father gave you for us. A letter he wrote or a video. That can't be all."

"Marilyn . . . please." My father spoke up.

"I'm sorry, Dad. But Gramps promised me."

"What are you talking about, Marilyn? Promised you what?" my cousin Vincent joined in.

I sighed and took a sip of a latte offered when we came in.

"Not here, Marilyn. Not now," my father said.

"When, Dad, if not now? When are we all going to be together like this again? Thanksgiving? Would that be a better time?"

"Mrs. Jensen," Mr. Dunn said, using Marilyn's married name, "I'm not sure what you're referring to. I went over your grandfather's will with him . . . in person. This is exactly what he wanted said and the way he wanted this moment to proceed. There is nothing else besides the will itself. Are you unhappy with what he left you? I was under the impression he'd met with each of you beforehand, to avoid any . . . unpleasantness at this moment."

"No, as far as the money goes, I couldn't be happier. I'm not talking about the money."

"Then what?" Vincent asked, barely restraining his anger. "You don't seem very grateful to me."

His attitude matched the look on everyone else's faces, including mine, I'm sure. "It's about this family tree thing," I said. I took another sip of the latte.

"What family tree thing?" Vincent clearly had been spared her obsession.

"Marilyn, can't you just drop this?" my mom said. "What difference does it make now?"

"It makes all the difference in the world to me, Mom. Gramps promised he'd clear up all the secrets after he died."

"Secrets," I said. "I doubt he said that."

"I don't know the word he used," she said. "But that's what he meant. At the picnic back on Labor Day, he said I could stop asking him all these questions, because everything I wanted to know would come out after he died. I said, 'You promise, Gramps?' and he nodded his head."

"He was probably just trying to get you to back off," I said.

"He was not. Gramps wouldn't do that. He wouldn't promise something just to shut me up."

She was right, he wouldn't.

Marilyn finally sat back on her chair, tears welling up in her eyes.

"It sounds like you were almost waiting for Gramps to die," Vincent said, "so you could solve your little mystery."

"It's not like that at all," she said.

"Sounds like it to me too," I said.

Marilyn pulled her hands up to her face, started massaging her temples.

"All right, guys," Aunt Fran said. "You know that's not true."

"Well, everyone," the elder attorney said in a strong tone, "sounds like you have other family matters to discuss. I will leave that to you for a later time." He had turned in his chair to face all of us. "Perhaps at dinner. I've arranged a catered buffet at Mr. Warner's home here on Legare Street. And there's something else. As I mentioned after reading the will, because his novels are still in print and new editions are being printed as we speak, the affairs of Mr. Warner's estate have not concluded today. His estate will continue to grow. We have been told by his publisher to expect a new resurgence of interest in his works, as is often the case when a writer of his stature dies. Before his passing, our firm worked with him on an equitable arrangement to disburse future royalties to you as they become available. It was Mr. Warner's wish that from this point, you would all get an equal percentage of those funds, after our expenses are deducted."

Even more money. It was crazy. Jenn was squeezing my hand so hard, I couldn't feel my fingers.

The last thing the attorney said, before sharing some superlative observations about my grandfather, was to ask us to see his secretary before leaving his office. She had some form for us to fill out, indicating whether we wanted any new funds to be mailed to us by check or by direct deposit into our bank accounts.

I looked around the room. Everyone else's attention was focused on Mr. Dunn. But not Marilyn's. She stared at a silk fichus tree in the corner, lost in thought.

What was wrong with her?

3

"Michael, I have a confession to make."

"You do?"

Jenn and I were strolling back to the hotel. I didn't think she minded that she was in heels anymore. We even made a few stops along the way. Bought that big low-country painting to put over our fireplace, then grabbed some fettuccine alfredo at the Italian restaurant we'd passed earlier on Broad.

"Yes," Jenn said. "I only married you for your money."

"Okay, was it for the money I was making when you married me, or the money we just found out about an hour ago?"

She laughed. "It's too crazy," she said. "Are we really millionaires? Did that really just happen?"

We stopped at the intersection, nodded to an older couple walking by arm in arm. Us someday,

I thought. "I didn't know we'd get that much, but I suspected it would be pretty big."

"Pretty big," she said. "Michael, we have twelve hundred dollars in our savings account."

"Which is why I just put that eighteen-hundred-dollar painting on our Visa. Wonder how long it will take to get the money in our bank account."

"I heard the secretary tell Vincent it would be there by tomorrow afternoon."

"No way."

"Yes . . . Michael . . ." She couldn't finish her sentence. She giggled, smiled some more, and shook her head in disbelief.

"Well, guess we can check out of the hotel in the morning," I said.

"Why?"

"We can move into my grandfather's house over on Legare Street. It's ours now."

"Is that for real?" she asked. "I didn't really understand that part."

"It is most definitely for real. That's why I got less cash than the other grandchildren."

"I was wondering about that," she said. "I'm not complaining, but I was surprised at how much less."

"Jenn, that house is worth close to two million dollars, even in today's market. I asked Mr. Dunn about it when you were talking with my mom. Gramps had them get an appraisal then deduct that much from my portion, so we all got an equal amount." It still hadn't sunk in. I was talking way too matter-of-factly about this. "Getting that house means more to me than the money. It's priceless. You remember it, don't you?"

"Of course I remember it. I fell in love with it the first time I saw it."

"Jenn, you realize what this means?"

"You can write your book now," she said.

"And do it in the same place my grandfather wrote his books for the last thirty years." Just then it dawned on me . . . that's what he had in mind all along. He knew how much I loved that house, and this town. He had never once asked me if I wanted it for my inheritance. He just knew.

"The whole family is supposed to meet over there in a few hours, right?" she said.

I looked at my watch. "Yeah, at 6:00 for the dinner. Mr. Dunn said it was my grandfather's idea. Give us all a chance to chat and reminisce awhile before we go our separate ways."

"So . . . that place, that incredible house . . . it's really *ours?* Just like that?"

"Just like that. Mr. Dunn said he'd give me the keys at dinner, and also the keys to a safe deposit box at my grandfather's bank, where the deed and title are sitting safe and sound."

"There's no mortgage?"

"It's free and clear."

"I have a house," she said.

"You have a house . . . actually, way *more* than a house. You have a historic landmark, fully furnished with nineteenth-century period antiques. Every single one handpicked by my grandmother."

"Incredible," she said.

We walked in contented silence for a while. I thought about how happy Gramps and Nan must be at this moment, together again. Their love for each other had spanned almost sixty years. It was, at times, an odd thing to behold. Usually when I'd see older couples together, they'd seem comfortable with each other; many times I'd observe them eating a meal at a restaurant, barely saying a word the whole time.

But Gramps and Nan were a couple in love, right to the end. Their passion for each other at least matched my own for Jenn. But they'd had a depth of intimacy far beyond our reach. An intimacy forged over time, granted to a select few. Sometimes I'd catch them stealing glances at each other that seemed to convey entire conversations. I never saw them walk together when they weren't holding hands. They still preferred to sit together, and without fail, Gramps's arm would instantly wrap around Nan's shoulder, like he was some teenage boy at a movie.

Gramps had told me something very encouraging the first time Jenn and I visited him, a few months after our wedding. We were drinking iced tea in the courtyard by the fountain. "You chose well, Michael. I can tell. I'm a good judge of these things. She's going to make you very happy. Like Nan made me. Nan would have loved Jenn right off if she were here. Take good care of that young lady, all your days."

That was my plan.

I looked over at Jenn as we turned the corner at Church Street. Her eyes looked all around, taking in the sights of this beautiful city. Maybe trying to envision herself now as one of its citizens, living in the prestigious historic district itself.

It seemed perfectly right that my grandfather should live here, the reward of a long, successful life. But how did I . . . *we* . . . rate this distinction? We walked past yet another large, majestic home on Church Street. I couldn't process the fact that its owner was now my neighbor.

It got me thinking about our new home on Legare Street. One of Charleston's famous Single Houses. Gramps's was built in 1868, just after the Civil War. The town lots in the old walled city were long and narrow, so the homes had to be also. Most were two floors, some three. A Single House, by definition, was just one room wide. The more money you had, the wider the room. Each house had a long, covered porch that ran front to back, called a piazza. The same porch repeated above on the second floor, held up by white pillars spaced evenly across the front. To add privacy, a solid front door was added on the first-floor porch, facing the street.

Legare Street, like most in the historic section, was designed for carriage traffic. Barely two lanes wide. Many of the homes were on the small side, but here and there you'd find a huge mansion built on double- or triple-sized lots. My grandfather's house—our house—was somewhere in between, built on a double lot. It was two stories, with a decent attic for a third, and had neat little dormers poking out the south side.

The house and driveway occupied the entire left side of the property. A garden courtyard filled the right side, bordered by a brick wall, head high and covered in ivy. A tall hedge set just inside that wall extended a few feet above it, creating even more privacy. Really, except for the ornamental iron gate stretched across the driveway, the whole property was enclosed and obscured from prying eyes.

Just the way my grandfather wanted it.

His favorite thing was the massive live oak in the far corner, which spread its thick limbs in every direction, covering the property in shade. At the courtyard's center was the angel fountain, old and weatherworn. Water trickled down from the angel's bugle into a circular pool. You could see most of this through the windows in my grandfather's study, the last room on the ground floor.

I was seeing it all now in my mind.

"What are you thinking about?" Jenn asked. We had reached the door to our hotel.

"I still can't believe he left it to me."

I didn't expect it, but tears welled up in my eyes.

4

Two hours later, the whole family was at the house on Legare Street. We'd just eaten a wonderful dinner, a full buffet of low-country cuisine, spread out on tables in the courtyard. Perfect temperature. Pleasant music playing softly in the background, old forties love songs in honor of Gramps and Nan. The sun had set, but there was still a dab of light left in the day.

Everyone was in high spirits. How could we not be? Oddly enough, that included Marilyn. She seemed fine now, like nothing had ever happened. Jenn and I were sitting next to my cousin Vincent and his wife, Abby, sipping some high-end coffee from the island of St. Helena.

"So, Michael, you going to write that book you've been talking about the last few years?" Abby asked.

Jenn answered for me. "He is, from the same desk their grandfather wrote all his." She was so happy saying it.

"You going to use Gramps's old typewriter?" Vincent said.

I laughed. Gramps had never switched to a computer. "No, I think I'll stick with my laptop. But I'll keep it on a shelf nearby for inspiration. Worked pretty well for him." Vincent's eyes reflected concern. "What are you thinking?" I said.

"Nothing."

"C'mon, I know that look. It's why I always beat you at poker."

"It's just . . . how do you follow an act like that? Gramps was, you know . . . a megastar."

Abby made a face at Vincent. If I got it right, that face told him he was a total idiot for bringing that up.

"Michael's not going to try to be like his grandfather." It was nice of Jenn to come to my rescue, but it didn't help. "He's going to write the way he writes, find his own voice. Right, Michael?"

"That's the idea," I said.

"I'm sure you'll do fine, great even," Abby said. "I heard your grandfather bragging about one of your short stories last Christmas. He really thought you have talent."

"Maybe you could write his biography," Vincent said. "Might be a good place to start. You'd have instant name recognition. It'd probably be a bestseller, especially if it was written by his grandson. Everybody's curious about the great and mysterious Gerard Warner."

"I don't know, Vince."

"You know somebody's going to write it," Vince said. "Might as well be family, someone who'd do it right."

Apparently, Aunt Fran was listening in. "Say, Michael. That's not a bad idea. And it would be a nonfiction book, so no one would be drawing comparisons."

That didn't help, either. Jenn reached over and grabbed my hand. She was feeling my pain. Just then I noticed my mother get up and walk to the fountain. Marilyn joined her.

"Hey, everyone," she called out.

About half the family stopped and turned.

"Hey, y'all, can I get your attention just a minute."

Now the rest turned to listen.

"I know this celebration's probably going to start winding down soon," she said. "Most of us will be heading home tomorrow."

"Except Michael and Jenn," Vincent yelled out. "They're home right now."

Everyone laughed.

"Well, let me get this out before they tire of our company and put us out by the road," she said. "Marilyn and I had a nice long chat after things wrapped up at the attorneys' today. She's got something she wants to say . . . well, I'll shut up and let her say it." Mom stepped aside.

"Okay, everybody," Marilyn said, stepping into her spot. "You know what's coming. I'm sorry I was such an idiot this afternoon. I want you to know how sorry I am if I spoiled the moment for anyone. I love Gramps so much, and I . . ." She was getting choked up. "Today was so special. Gramps was so good to all of us, his whole life. I don't want any of you thinking I'm not grateful for all he's done. Not just now, but . . . you know what I mean."

She took a deep breath. "I guess I'm just going to have to let go of this family tree thing I've been going after these past two years. But . . . doesn't it bug any of you that we don't know a single thing about how he and Nan met, or who his folks were, or . . . I'm sorry. Look at me, doing it again. Anyway, I am sorry." She stepped off to the side.

There were a few awkward seconds, then my father walked into the spot vacated by Marilyn. "Hey, everyone, let's let Marilyn off the hook on this. Took some guts to do that." He started to clap gently. We all joined in, till it almost reached the volume of something you'd hear after a nice birdie putt.

"And before anyone takes off," my dad continued, "let's say a toast to my dad and mom." He held up a champagne glass. "To two wonderful lives well-lived." He looked like he had more to say, but he started choking up. We all held our glasses up, then the courtyard filled with the sound of glasses clinking together.

I looked over at Marilyn. She wasn't smiling.

I just knew . . . she wasn't about to give this up.

5

The next day Jenn and I were still at our hotel. A week ago, she had protested when I'd made the reservations. It was too expensive. I told her we'd certainly be getting enough from my grandfather's will to afford a few days of comfort. Obviously, I was right.

Now I was ready to check out and move into our *new* house, but she wasn't. I looked over at the keys Mr. Dunn had given me, then over at Jenn sitting at the desk in our hotel room. She had just made a convincing case for staying in this expensive hotel one more day.

As Gramps had pointed out before he died, I had married a good woman and it would be stupid not to listen to her.

"Now, Michael, you're going to help me when we get over there, right?"

Jenn's voice brought me back to the present. Apparently, I had started shaving. I looked at Jenn through the mirror; she was still sitting at the desk, writing a checklist of things we needed to do for the house. The adult thing to do. "Of course, I will," I said. "You think I'm going to goof off and let you do all the work?"

"Not goof off, but you do get distracted easily, and there's a lot there to be—"

"I'm going to help you, Jenn."

She looked up at me. Guess I said it with an edge.

"Michael, since I'm heading home in a few days, we've got a lot to get done in a short amount of time. When's the art gallery delivering our new painting?"

"Eleven-thirty, but I could call and make it later."

"Maybe you should; then we won't be so rushed. The first thing on my list: we need to buy some new sheets and pillowcases. I loved your grandfather, but . . . didn't he die in that bed?"

I hadn't thought about that. Something else I hadn't thought of was Jenn not being okay with us moving into the house so quickly and leaving our lives in Florida behind.

Like our jobs. Well, her job anyway.

My bank had just been taken over by a large Canadian outfit, and I didn't care what they thought of me. I was probably on somebody's hit list anyway. But Jenn liked her job, cared about the people she worked for. "I have to give them at least two weeks' notice," she'd said last night when we talked this over.

So we agreed that after another day or so, she'd head home, work her last two weeks, and I'd stay here, get the house ready. Gramps had been in his late eighties, so there was probably a lot that needed tending to.

After I finished shaving, Jenn walked up behind me and hugged me around the waist. "You doing okay?"

I turned around and hugged her back. "Sure. I'm not happy about the idea of you leaving me for two weeks, but—"

"No, I mean about the book thing. I felt bad about what Vincent said last night, about you getting lost in your grandfather's shadow."

Vince hadn't actually said that, as I recalled. What Jenn just said sounded worse. "It's okay, it's not like there's anything I can do about it. No matter how good I am, I'll never be as good as he was, and—"

"Don't say that."

"Jenn, I'm just being realistic. You inherit things like a big nose and high blood pressure, not the ability to write like that."

She laughed. "I don't know, famous singers often have kids who can sing."

"But they're never as good."

"That's not true."

"Okay, name one megastar singer whose child or grandchild became just as good or just as famous."

30

She pulled back a little to give it some thought. Clearly, she was drawing a blank.

"I've got two names for you," I said. "How about Julian Lennon and Ben Taylor?"

"Who are they?" she said.

"Exactly."

Later that morning, our shopping all done, we drove the handful of blocks to our new home on Legare Street. Really, except for the weight of our shopping bags, we could have walked the distance. It was that close.

My grandfather's house—*our* house—was just past the Tradd Street intersection. Almost the entire street was shaded, either by the homes built right to the edge of the sidewalk or by the rows of palmetto palms and oak trees lining the homes set back from the road.

As I drove slowly down the street, Jenn said, "This is ridiculously charming."

I pulled up to our narrow driveway. A couple in their early twenties stood by the sidewalk, peeking through the wrought-iron gate at our courtyard, engaged in a favorite Charleston tourist pastime: gawking. Jenn and I used to do the same thing when we'd visit my grandfather, just walk all around the neighborhoods, admiring the homes, the courtyards and private gardens. I remembered occasionally getting caught by residents pulling into these incredible homes.

"See that, Jenn? Gawkers." I pointed to the couple. They hadn't seen us yet. "Watch this."

"Don't, Michael."

I pushed the remote button. The iron gate rumbled to life, then creaked as it opened, startling the couple. They stepped back and gawked at us as we drove through.

"You're terrible," she said, then smiled and waved at the pair.

"Just having a little fun." As I got out of the car, I waved also as the gate closed and they hurried by. Didn't want to be a snob. It took us three trips to carry all our purchases into the foyer. We'd bought a tad more than bed linens, and it felt good to be able to turn Jenn loose on a shopping spree. But now we only had fifteen minutes before the art gallery folks delivered our painting.

"I'll put all this stuff away, Michael. You go get the mantel ready for the painting over the fire-place."

"Got it." I stepped to the left through the doorway into the living room. It didn't take long to finish my task. The wall over the fireplace was already empty. A big portrait of my grandparents used to occupy the space. It had been given to Aunt Fran in the will. I moved a few knickknacks off and put them on nearby tables. I expected to find the mantel caked in dust, but it was clean.

So were the knickknacks. The tables I put them on were clean too. Completely free of dust.

I walked around the room, did a little spot-check. The whole room was neat and tidy. Even the wood floors, peeking out from the large oriental rug, were polished and shiny. I couldn't imagine my grandfather having the strength to keep things this nice, and then I remembered.

Helen.

He'd hired a housekeeper shortly after Nan died. That meant . . . Helen still came around. "Say, Jenn." I walked through the foyer, through the dining area, and into the kitchen. Jenn was on her knees, had the pantry doors open, and was filling up boxes with things neither of us would ever eat, especially me. "You remember Helen?"

"What?"

"Helen, Gramps's housekeeper."

"No."

"You notice how clean this place is? The living room would pass your inspection."

"Well, we don't need a housekeeper," she said, staying on task.

I had a feeling she'd say that. "Don't you think you might like to have someone clean the house for you? It's a big place. Not like we can't afford it now."

She turned to face me. "Michael, I don't want some strange woman I don't know cleaning my house. I'll do it, and you'll help me."

"What about Helen?"

"I don't know. I'm afraid we'll have to let her

go." She set a can of beets in the box beside her.

"Let her go?"

"Yes, what else can we do? See if her phone number is someplace, like on the fridge."

"Me?"

"Michael . . ."

I sighed.

"C'mon, Michael. You can do this."

"But she's an old woman, Jenn. What if this is her only means of support?"

"Well, maybe we can give her some kind of severance pay."

"How about this . . . I let her know we're not going to need a housekeeper, but she could stay on for these two weeks. You know, give her two weeks' notice. Then we'll give her some kind of severance pay. She'll be gone before you get back."

I walked over to the refrigerator. Sure enough, there was an index card under a palm tree magnet with Helen's name written across the top. I slipped it out and saw her phone number along the bottom. In the middle was her weekly schedule.

I looked at my watch. She was coming here at noon.

"Say, Jenn."

6

Noon came and went, and no Helen.

I waited about an hour, then called and left a voice mail, just after the art gallery people had left. Our new painting was now mounted over the fireplace. It suited the space well. The colors even matched everything in the room. Jenn had a knack for that sort of thing. We were about to head out and grab some lunch when the phone rang. Not my cell but the phone in my grandfather's house. We stopped at the front door. "Should I answer it?"

"It's probably somebody calling for your grandfather," Jenn said. "Maybe they don't know he died. Or maybe it's Helen."

I walked to the nearest phone, which was on a small antique table in the hall next to the stairs. We'd have to add "disconnect the landline" to our to-do list.

Jenn walked into the living room and sat in the nearest chair. "It never takes just a minute," she said, smiling.

"Hello?"

"Hi, this is Rick Samson. Who am I speaking to?"

Rick Samson, my grandfather's literary agent. I

was immediately intimidated. He was the man I hoped to call whenever I finally did get my first book written. "Hi, Mr. Samson. This is Michael Warner, I'm—"

"Michael," he announced. "I know who you are. You're the one I wanted to reach."

I looked over at Jenn, put my hand over the phone, and mouthed the words "Rick Samson" to her, pointing at the receiver. She didn't get it. "You wanted to reach me, Mr. Samson?"

"Please, call me Rick."

"Okay, Rick. You know you called my grand-father's house."

"Sure I did. I spoke with Alfred Dunn, your grandfather's attorney. He told me it's your house now. And here you are."

"Here I am," I said. "I'm kind of surprised you know who I am . . . how *do* you know who I am?"

"Your grandfather talked about you a lot in the last year or so."

"Really?"

"He thought you could be quite a writer some day."

"I'm . . . I'm honored that he'd say that." Something stirred in my emotions.

"Well, that's how I know who you are. I wanted to call and talk to you about a possible book deal. Is this a bad time?"

A book deal? "We were just getting ready to head out the door. My wife Jenn and I."

"Jenn, I know who she is. Your grandfather talked about her too, said she reminded him a lot of Mary when she was young."

This also stirred something in me. I had to press to stay focused. "I can talk for a minute or two, but maybe you should give me your number, and I'll call you this afternoon." Everything in me wanted to head back to my grandfather's study, pick up the extension there, and hear everything this man had to say. I looked over at Jenn. She sat on the edge of her chair, clearly interested in the call.

"That's fine, Michael. Actually, you can find my number on your grandfather's desk. He used one of those old-fashioned Rolodex things."

"I've seen it."

"Don't look up my agency's name, use my name. The number he wrote there will get you past all my office staff. It's my personal line."

"Thanks, Mr. Samson . . . Rick." I gave him my cell number and told him to feel free to use it from now on. We exchanged a few more kind words, then hung up.

Jenn stood up, picked up her purse.

"Do you know who that was?" I said.

"No, but you look almost as excited as you did when you heard how much your grandfather left us."

"*That* was Rick Samson."

"Why do I know that name?" She opened the front door, moving us along.

"He's my grandfather's agent, been doing his book deals for years. He's huge in this business." I followed her out the door, turned, and locked it.

"Really?" Her face showed that she got it now. "He's the guy you were telling me about, right? The one you hoped might represent you when you finish your book."

"Well, I wasn't thinking he would personally. I'd take any one of the agents at his agency. All of them are A-listers."

"But he called you," she said. "He didn't have one of them call."

"You're right." We walked down the three brick steps. "He did. Rick Samson called me." Repeating it didn't make it feel any more real. It was too wonderful. Hundreds of would-be writers, maybe thousands, would give anything they owned to have anyone from his literary agency give them the time of day. I walked to her side of the car and opened the door.

"So what did he say?" she asked, getting in.

I got in and turned on the car. "He wants to talk about a book deal with me."

"No way," she said. "Really? Oh, Michael, that's wonderful!"

I clicked the remote button and watched the ornamental iron gate open in my rearview mirror. I looked at the gorgeous courtyard through the windshield, the exquisite Charleston Single House out my left window, the beautiful wife sitting beside me. Suddenly, a strong desire hit me. As I slowly backed out of the driveway, I shared it with Jenn. "This car is all wrong."

"What?"

"This car does not belong at this house."

"What are you thinking?"

"It's time," I said. "As soon as you fly home, I'm going to find the nearest Mini Cooper dealer and trade this old buggy in. Get that one we've been dreaming about the last few years."

"The blue turbocharged Cooper S?" she said. "The one that's all decked out, with the white roof and white stripes down the hood?"

"The very one."

"You'll do no such thing," she said.

"Why? It would look perfect in that driveway." I pointed as the iron gate closed.

"You're not going to buy it *after* I leave. We are going to go buy it together, before I leave, and I'm going to drive it every minute until I get on that plane."

There are so many great places to eat in downtown Charleston. This time we picked Tommy Condon's Irish Pub. Can't go wrong there. It's got all the ambiance you'd expect in such a place. Even the live music is worth listening to. I finished off some fish-and-chips and Jenn ate half of her Irish Cobb salad. The conversation was light and fun, alternating between the fact that we could actually afford to buy a new Mini Cooper and the book deal conversation I'd be having this afternoon with Rick Samson.

I already had two or three novel ideas roughed out. I wondered which one he'd want to start with. It would be amazing to write a book, whichever one, knowing it was already under contract. Who gets an opportunity like that? Just after I paid the bill, my cell rang.

"Is it him?" Jenn asked.

I didn't recognize the number, shook my head no. "Hello?"

"Is this Michael?" A woman's voice, older.

"Yes it is."

"This is Helen, your grandfather's housekeeper. You probably don't remember me."

"No, I do, Helen. I remember you. We didn't get to talk at the funeral, but I saw you there."

"I'm so sorry for your loss. Your grandfather was the most amazing man. A complete joy to work for."

"Actually, that's why I called earlier."

"Yes, I got your message."

"I saw your schedule on the refrigerator." I paused, trying to think of a nice way to say this.

"I guess I forgot to take it down," she said. "I came in a few days ago to clean for the last time. I hope everything was satisfactory."

"It was very nice, spotless, actually."

"Thank you. I only worked for him a few years, but . . ."

"So, are you . . . no longer coming over?"

"I guess you didn't hear. Your grandfather, bless his heart, I mean, I didn't expect it at all. He set something up with his attorney and gave me a severance package that commenced the day after he died. The most amazing thing."

I should have figured my grandfather would take care of her too.

"He put some money in an annuity that will keep paying me what I was getting paid until I'm old enough for Social Security. That's just a few years from now. With that and what I've been able to save, I won't have to work again. Isn't that something?"

"I'm so happy for you," I said. "He was incredibly generous, to all of us. I guess you heard he left me the house."

"I knew that was coming. He talked to me about that a number of times. You need someone to work for you? I know some great friends who do that for a living. I could make some calls. One or two I have in mind would do an excellent job for you, good cooks too."

"That's very kind of you, Helen, but I think we'll just take care of things ourselves. You enjoy your . . . retirement."

"Oh, I will."

We hung up. I looked over at Jenn. She had

pieced together our conversation. "No Helen," she said.

"Nope. Guess I'll have to fend for myself while you're gone."

"Somehow I think you'll survive," she said. "Let's go to the grocery store. I made a list back at the house."

"How about first I get on my phone here, and we find out the nearest Mini Cooper dealer?"

Jenn smiled. "Did you make sure the money's in our checking account?"

I smiled. "Jenn, let me show you. I looked at our balance before we left. There's an obscene amount of money in there, more than I've ever seen." I got on the internet and logged into our account. "Here." I held the phone up so she could see.

"Michael, that's just crazy," she said, staring at the screen.

7

It was late afternoon. Jenn and I had returned to our new home on Legare Street with an antique lamp. An authentic 1860s white, opalescent coin dot oil lamp to be more precise (at least I think that's what the antique dealer said). It was far less a prize than what I hoped we'd be bringing home.

42

We had a blast at the car dealership, looking over the inventory of Mini Coopers, and test drove one like the one we wanted. Smooth ride, great pickup, incredible sound system. Problem was, it was red. Had the white roof, white stripes down the hood, but it was shiny and red.

I would have been happy with it. But I knew, for Jenn, the dream was the blue one. The Charleston dealer didn't have a blue one fully loaded. But he promised he'd have it here in two days. Jenn was heading back to Florida tomorrow to start her last two weeks at work. We reminded ourselves that such disappointments hardly amounted to anything close to suffering. As we drove off the lot I remembered an antique lamp Jenn had her eye on the day we came into town. But it cost six hundred dollars.

That day, way out of reach.

I looked over at her now, holding it on her lap, rubbing the bottom half with her palm. "I know exactly where I'm going to put it. On that table in the foyer, next to the phone."

"It'll look great there." Of course, she knew I knew nothing about such things. But the lamp said "I love you" and that I felt bad she wouldn't get to drive the Cooper for two weeks. The iron gate closed as we got out of the car. "Why don't you take care of the lamp, and I'll get the groceries in the house?"

She walked around the front of the car, holding

the lamp, and gave me a one-armed hug. "I love you," she said.

"Love you too."

I popped open the trunk and stared at the grocery bags. My cell phone rang. I looked at the caller ID. Rick Samson. I couldn't believe Rick was calling me again. I was supposed to call him, planned to right after I put the groceries away. Was Rick Samson actually pursuing me?

"Hey, Michael, is that you?"

"Yeah, Mr. Samson, it's me."

"You forgot—"

"Actually I was just about to—"

"—to call me Rick. I know I'm an old guy, but we can still be friends, right?"

I laughed, probably a little too hard. "Sorry, Rick. I was just about to call you. We were out running errands. Just got home, so—"

"No problem. I've got an appointment that's going to eat up the rest of my afternoon. Thought I'd try and reach you before it got too late. Got a few minutes?"

He *was* pursuing me. "Sure, uh . . ." I looked down at the groceries; there was some milk and frozen things in there. I wondered how long we'd be talking. What was it, ten bucks worth? Heck with it. "I've got time. You said earlier you wanted to talk about a book deal." I leaned back against the rear fender.

"I did. I've been talking with your grandfather's

publisher. As expected, sales are way up on his books. Seems like a great time to get something out quick. I'm assuming your grandfather left you enough money to quit your day job."

"Already have, didn't even need to give two weeks' notice."

"Great. So you're free now?"

"Free as a bird. I've been thinking about this since your call earlier. Jenn and I even talked about it over lunch."

"So she's on board? Good. 'Cause if we do this thing, we're going to need you to get right on this, work some long days to put something out soon. I can keep the interest alive between now and the book's release with some promo ideas we're working on. All his fans will really eat this up. I'm sure of it."

It sounded exciting, but my novels wouldn't even be in the same genre as my grandfather's. I wasn't expecting to catch many of his fans, certainly not a majority. "So . . . why do you think it will do so well, Rick? Is it just the name recognition, the family tie?"

"That's just a small part of it. But it's a serious plus, don't get me wrong. I'm thinking about flying down my best ghostwriter, help you get this thing done quick."

This thing?

"It'll be your name on the book, and you can write as much of it as you want, pick the parts that matter the most to you. But this guy is fabulous. He'll interview you, read a bunch of things you've written, and before you know it, he'll be writing just like you. It'll be so close your own wife won't be able to tell the difference."

This was beginning to sound very strange. "What kind of time line are we talking about here?"

"I'm thinking eight weeks, tops."

Eight weeks, I thought, to write a full-length novel? Guess I would need some help. But I couldn't imagine how that would work. Jenn wouldn't be too happy having some strange guy here day and night writing a book with me. And I wasn't too keen on having a ghostwriter writing half of my first novel. "You really think my grandfather's fans will want to read one of my books?"

"Are you kidding, Michael? You've got the grandson of a literary legend writing a book about his grandfather . . . especially someone as elusive and mysterious as he's been all these years . . . I mean, I don't even know much of his story, and I've been working with him over twenty years."

"What?"

"I'm assuming you guys know all about his personal life, the stuff he's always kept hidden from the public. I'm not talking about dirty secrets. Your grandfather seemed squeaky clean. I'm talking about, you know, the family stories.

How he and your grandmother met. The kind of questions he'd never answer in all those interviews. A book like that coming out now, we'd sell a hundred thousand, maybe a million."

This was awful, just awful. "So, you're not interested in hearing about any of my novel ideas?"

"What? Your what?"

"Novels, books. Stories I've made up in my head." I wanted to say, like my grandfather wrote, but didn't. Because they wouldn't be like my grandfather's books. They'd be my books. Books nobody would ever want to read.

"Oh . . . I see." A long, awkward pause. "Well, Michael, I'd be open to that, maybe after this. I can almost guarantee, you write a biography about your grandfather and you'll have a huge audience ready to hear anything else you have to say. Even if you kept a fraction of his fans for yourself, you'd still have a bestseller on your hands. So what do you think? How about I get a contract written up and overnight it to you. And you can start doing some research, start organizing things in your head, collecting old photos, maybe think up some interview questions to ask your family members."

Awful. I was feeling almost sick to my stomach. Why didn't I see this coming? "Can I think about this for a while?"

"Sure, it's a big deal. I don't want to steamroll

you here. You give it a few days, talk it over with your wife. I'll get the contract written up, start a conversation with my ghostwriter, see how quickly he can get on board. How's that sound?"

"Fine, Mr. Samson, I—"

"Rick, remember."

"Right, Rick. I really do appreciate you thinking about me for this project." *What am I saying? I do not.* "I'll get back to you real soon."

"Good. You do that. And seriously, we get this thing together, I'll get one of my best agents to get back with you on one of your novel ideas. I promise."

One of his agents . . . that was something anyway. "Thanks, Rick."

"Gotta go, Michael. Keep in touch."

We hung up. I picked up the bag with the milk in it. Another with frozen vegetables. I turned toward the front door. There was Jenn standing in the doorway. She knew something was wrong; I'm sure it was all over my face.

If I was going to do this thing, I'd need to call my sister Marilyn and get her help.

I really didn't want to do that.

8

I was depressed. For so many reasons, I had no right to be.

And that depressed me more.

Jenn and I had just finished a fabulous dinner. She'd warmed up some of the leftovers from the catered dinner with my family, compliments of Bradley and Dunn. We were sipping coffee while sitting in a pair of Adirondack chairs out back. My grandfather's favorite section of the court-yard, which wrapped behind the house, out of sight from the street. The temperature was a mild sixty-seven degrees, low humidity. A slight breeze wafted over the brick wall and across the yard, moving the tree branches ever so slightly as well as serving up an aroma of night-blooming jasmine from a few houses down.

The historic house sitting directly behind me was mine and mortgage free. A small fortune was sitting safely in our checkbook. A blue, decked-out Mini Cooper S was on order. Beside me sat Jenn, looking gorgeous. What in heaven's name did I have to be depressed about?

"You don't have to do this, Michael. It's not like we need the money."

I set my coffee down. I can't talk unless I can

move my hands. "I know, Jenn. But I'm wondering if maybe I should. Both Vincent and Aunt Fran suggested the same thing the other night. Marilyn would be thrilled. She'd probably do anything I asked just to be a part."

"But you don't want to do it," Jenn said. "Not even a little, I can tell."

I sighed. She had a point. "I don't see how you say no to someone like Rick Samson. You should've heard him. He is seriously jazzed about this. If I could do it, I'm pretty sure he'd have me on a huge book tour, traveling all the big cities. I'd be on talk shows and radio interviews. I'd go from being a complete unknown to best-seller status in a matter of months. That's a crazy opportunity to walk away from."

"Is all that stuff something you'd even want to do?"

"Someday, yeah. But I was hoping it would be because of my own novels. Maybe not the first or second book, but . . . someday. I figured being the grandson of Gerard Warner might open a few doors, then I'd have to keep them open myself, because people would see my writing deserved the attention."

"Well, you can still do that. It would just take longer." She reached over and took my hand. "And that's not a problem. You've got the time."

She was right. I had nothing but time now. All the time in the world. So what was the rush?

"There's something else I've been thinking about."

"What's that?"

"The research for something like this. Rick's assuming my family knows all the things about my grandfather he never wanted to talk about in public. But we don't. I never cared about any of that stuff. He was just Gramps, she was just Nan. I mean, I could write about all kinds of family stories, favorite Christmases, how we spent the Fourth of July. But I don't even know how my grandparents met or where he was born."

"Apparently, Marilyn couldn't find out any of those things either."

"Right. I think they'd be expecting that in a book like this. Biographies usually start with the person's birth. Gerard Warner, the early years."

"I have an idea."

I looked over at her. Man, I hated the fact that she was leaving tomorrow. "What's that?"

"Maybe after I fly home, you could do some exploring. Up in the attic or maybe in your grandfather's study. People don't usually throw out their old things. You know, old photo albums, love letters, birth certificates. When my grandmother died a few years ago, my folks found five boxes of stuff they'd never seen before. They had a blast going through it all."

It was actually a great idea.

"Why don't you do it?" she said. "See where it

leads? I'm sure Marilyn will give you anything she has."

"I'm sure she will. But let's don't call her just yet. I'm not even sure I—"

"Michael, don't worry about that. It's not like Marilyn and I talk all the time and it might slip out."

"You're right. It's just, I'm not even sure I want to do this yet, even if I did find a ton of old goodies."

"Then don't make a decision, either way. Just take it one step at a time. Pray about it. Think about it. When did Rick say he needed an answer?"

"He said take two or three days."

"Well, take them then. We don't have to decide anything now."

"All right," I said. I reached for my coffee mug, took a smooth swallow, and leaned back in my chair.

"There's another decision I'd like to talk about," Jenn said. She had a mischievous look in her eyes and sat forward in her chair. "A totally different subject."

"Okay . . . do I need to brace myself?"

"No, silly. It's a good thing . . . a really good thing."

"I could use a really good thing about now."

"You know I'm going back to Orlando to work my last two weeks."

"I did know that," I said, smiling.

"Well, I'm also going to make a list of things I want to bring back. I think I'm going to give most of it away. There's very little in our apartment that compares to anything in the house."

I didn't see where this was going, but sometimes Jenn did that—got offtrack when she had something big she wanted to talk about. "Is this still about the 'really good thing'?"

"Okay, I'll just say it. After my two weeks are over, I was thinking . . . I don't see any reason why I need to rush back here and find a new job."

"No, I agree with that."

"So . . . how about . . . we start our family, start trying to have a baby?"

"Really!" I was almost shouting. I'd been wanting to start having kids for months.

"Really," she said.

"Jenn, I would, that would be . . . definitely. It's a perfect idea."

She stood up, still holding my hand. "And I was thinking . . ." She pulled me to my feet. "We could start trying tonight."

I wrapped my arms around her, and we kissed. Holding hands, we walked down the brick path toward the house. I stopped a moment. "Don't you want to get the coffee cups?"

"They can wait till the morning," she said.

I smiled and we walked some more.

Suddenly, my depression had completely disappeared.

9

Jenn was in the air now, flying the friendly skies back to Orlando. And I was spending the rest of the day in our new home, alone.

At the airport, I'd finally convinced her there was no way I could live without her for two weeks in a row. I'd said, since we're millionaires now we could probably afford a couple hundred dollars to fly her back to Charleston for the weekend. I knew she'd say yes because she loved me and wanted to be with me as much as I wanted to be with her. So I ignored the fact that she'd given in only after I'd reminded her that if she came home, she could drive the new Mini Cooper all weekend.

I closed the car door and fiddled with the keys, trying to single out the one to my new front door. As I walked up the front steps, I took a moment to admire the covered veranda running the full length of the house. Two finely trimmed topiaries stood on either side of the door, boxwoods, I think. Their healthy days on earth were numbered, now that I was their master. A dark green set of wicker furniture spread out to my left, the perfect place for evening coffee and conversation. To my right, a wicker dinette set, with a round glass table and a silk floral centerpiece.

On their own at the far end of the porch, two white-painted rockers sat angled toward each other, like a couple wishing some time alone from the crowd.

How did I rate coming home to something like this?

As I closed the front door, the grandfather clock just inside the living room began to chime, informing me it was now 3:30 p.m. The clock was a fine piece of furniture, one of my grandfather's favorites. I wasn't sure I could get used to it sounding off every quarter hour, day and night. I set my keys down on the foyer table and immediately gave myself to a little project I wanted to accomplish before dinner.

I still hadn't decided whether to write the book about my grandfather but thought I should at least search the house like Jenn had suggested, to see if Gramps kept any boxes of old memories lying around. Of course, the attic was the place to start.

Ascending the winding stairway to the second floor, I admired the amazing trim work in the handrail, in the stairs themselves, even on the circular medallion surrounding the light fixture suspended from the ceiling. I crossed a short landing and opened the door leading to the attic. This was a more basic stairway with steeper steps. Plenty of natural light came down the stairwell from the attic dormers. Gramps had turned the front half of the third floor into a nice guest bedroom, mostly in sky blue. Jenn and I had stayed there on our second visit.

I cleared the final step, which opened right into the guest room, kind of a loft effect. I still felt like I was standing in someone else's guest room. I felt that way wherever I went in the house.

A door on my left opened to the back half of the floor, the unfinished attic. I opened it and fumbled for the light switch. A stack of boxes blocked most of the light coming in from the far dormer. I left the door open as I stepped inside, and soon my eyes adjusted enough to see.

The only boxes in plain sight were those blocking the window, so I started there. Twenty minutes later, I had nothing. Except I could see better now that I'd moved the boxes out of the way. They were filled with household goods—a bunch of old plates, pots and pans, musty linens and bedspreads. I continued snooping around, looking high and low for more boxes, anything that might help me write this book about my grandfather.

I covered every square inch of space and didn't find a single photo album, a single box of old letters, a single container holding records of any kind. I sneezed a lot, which was pretty much all I had to show for my effort.

As I closed the door and started down the stairs, I remembered something. The pirate trunk. A Victorian-era wooden trunk at the foot of the bed in the main guest bedroom. Years ago, Nan had said they bought it because my grandfather thought it looked like something a pirate would use to bury treasure.

I hadn't thought of the trunk before, because I already knew what was inside. She'd shown it to me herself before she died. "This is where I bury my treasures," she'd said with a girlish smile. It was full of family photo albums. Over a dozen of them. But none of the early years, none of Gramps and Nan as children or even while they were dating. In the earliest pictures, they were already married.

Marilyn had confirmed this fact herself, in one of our many exasperating conversations a few months ago. She had sneaked upstairs to search the trunk on my grandfather's last birthday. She'd come downstairs totally disappointed. But what if my grandfather had added some things to it since then? Maybe just before he died.

I hurried down the last few steps and across the hall. The bedroom door was already open. I knelt down and lifted the trunk lid. It creaked eerily, the way pirate trunks should.

Inside, it looked exactly as I remembered. Two stacks of neatly arranged photo albums filled most of the space. My guess was that Marilyn had been the last one here, and she'd put everything back the way Nan had left it years before that. A number of smaller boxes had been tucked along the sides. I lifted them out, but they were pink and flowery; nothing my grandfather would use.

I opened them anyway. They were filled with postcards. I scanned the dates, none older than twenty years. I spent the next thirty minutes lifting and thumbing through the photo albums. I could have spent hours there, reliving the memories. But I had seen them all before. I didn't see a single picture or find a single document that shed any light on my grandfather or grandmother's existence prior to a few years after they married.

This had never bothered me before.

After putting everything back as carefully as I could, I closed the lid and stood up.

It bothered me now.

10

I walked down the stairs, my mind awash with troubled thoughts.

I hated what I was thinking.

Every memory of my grandfather had only ever been positive. More than that, they were pleasant. I had never thought of him as being secretive or vague. I couldn't recall him ever dodging a question I'd asked him or changing the subject. It was just the opposite; he'd fill the next ten minutes telling some wonderful story.

But then, I had never asked him the kinds of questions Marilyn had.

I walked through the dining room into the kitchen and poured a glass of iced tea, this question burning in my brain: *Who doesn't have pictures of their wedding day?*

It was Marilyn's voice asking one of the many irritating questions she tossed at me when this subject had come up. She'd pointed out that Gramps and Nan had gotten married in the forties. All her friends' grandparents had lots of black and white photographs of their wedding day, and dozens of others during their dating and engagement years. Most even had pictures of themselves as children.

Why didn't Gramps and Nan?

Right now, it seemed like a good question.

Why didn't they?

For that matter, why no wedding license or birth certificates? They should be there too. Yellowed and frail, torn at the edges. And why no love letters? Theirs was a wartime romance; people back then wrote dozens of such letters to each other. Did my grandfather even fight in World War II?

I always assumed he had. His books were filled with action and suspense scenes, many set in times of war. He certainly wrote like someone with firsthand knowledge of danger and dying and the intensity of human combat. But as I thought about it, I couldn't recall having a single conversation about his own war experiences. Why had I never asked about it? It had never occurred to me that he wouldn't answer me straight if I did.

It just never came up.

I walked back to the dining room table and picked up my laptop. I had a strong compulsion to write something, anything. I needed to clear my head before my mind fell down the stairs into total discouragement. "Gramps, you are still my hero," I said aloud as I made my way to the back of the house to his study.

Was he a criminal, a felon running from the law? Had he killed someone? Did he—

Stop.

I had to stop listening to Marilyn's conspiracy theories. I walked through the doorway to my grandfather's study. "Watch your step" went through my head. He'd said it every time I'd walk into his office over the years.

It was the only add-on room in the house. It had floor-to-ceiling bookshelves on either side. The top three shelves on the left held first editions of all his novels, put there by Nan. The rest contained books he'd bought for research. Come to think of it, this room by itself was probably worth a fortune now.

But the first thing you noticed entering the study wasn't the bookshelves. The whole back wall was filled with windows, the classic nine-over-nines famous throughout Charleston, which looked out over the most private section of the courtyard behind the house. There were the Adirondack chairs Jenn and I had sat in the other night. Centered beneath the windows was my grand-father's desk.

My desk now.

And there, centered on the desk, was his famous typewriter. A vintage Remington Rand portable, made in the 1940s. A smooth flat black finish, simple, effective. Hit a key, hear a clack, type a letter.

I flashed back to a memory from when I was twelve or thirteen. I had come by myself to stay with Gramps and Nan for a week that summer. But I'd been warned, Gramps was on a fixed deadline, so he'd have to write every afternoon. We'd spend the morning together, but after lunch, he'd disappear into his study until dinnertime. I remembered standing by the counter nearest the study door, the smell of beef stew and fresh baked bread filling the kitchen.

"Would you like to get him?" Nan said. "Dinner is ready."

"Should I knock?"

"He won't hear you."

"I can knock hard." I listened through the door, heard the click-click, clack-clack of the Remington Rand clear as a bell.

"I'm sure you can," Nan had said. "But it's not

61

the sound of the typewriter I'm talking about. When you open that door, you'll see Gramps's body sitting right there at his desk, hammering away on that thing. But his mind will be in another world."

And she was right. She'd instructed me to approach him gently but firmly. To tap him on the shoulder a few times and talk to him like I was trying to wake him from a sound sleep.

I looked down at the Remington Rand now, remembering how fascinating it was to watch him work. I leaned over and rested my hands on the keys. Without thinking, I typed "t-h-e."

"The," I said out loud. *"The?"*

That's what I came up with? T-h-e? Who was I kidding? I would never be able to write like him. I sighed. It would take a lot more than living in his house and sitting at his desk to become a good writer.

Staring at this typewriter every day didn't seem like a good idea now. It would probably intimidate more than inspire me. I looked to my right and saw the carrying case sitting on a shelf by itself, the case he put his typewriter in when he traveled. It wasn't a Remington Rand case but a fancy hand-carved wooden box. Guess he had it specially made or something.

I decided to store the typewriter in there instead of leaving it out. At least it would still be in the room, and the case would keep the dust off it. I reached for the box and lifted it up, surprised to find how heavy it was, like it already had a typewriter inside. As I set it down beside the Remington Rand, I felt something shift inside. It was definitely not empty. I flipped the two brass latches and opened the lid.

I was staring at what appeared to be a fairly thick manuscript tied together with two pieces of twine. And an old leather journal. I picked up the journal first and flipped through it. Only the first few pages had any writing; the rest were blank. I instantly recognized my grandfather's handwriting.

I pulled out his chair and sat down.

I set the journal aside, picked up the manuscript, and leaned back on the chair.

The paper was slightly yellowed with age. My hands began to tremble as I read the handful of words centered on the title page. Obviously, typed on the Remington Rand sitting before me.

AN IMPOSSIBLE LOVE
BY GERARD WARNER

I could hardly believe my eyes. I knew every book my grandfather had ever written.

In my hands, I held what appeared to be a fully typed, unpublished novel by one of the greatest authors of our time.

11

"Jenn, you're not going to believe this."

I had to call her. I'd already tried a half dozen times as soon as her plane was scheduled to land. But she hadn't picked up. It was killing me.

"What's the matter? Is everything all right?"

"Everything's fine. You just get in?"

"I'm walking through the terminal now."

"Jenn, I found the most incredible thing."

"Pictures of your grandparents? I told you, people don't throw out—"

"No, not pictures. Actually, that hunt was a total waste of time."

"You didn't find any?"

"Not a single one. Marilyn was right. But listen, this is something else, something way better."

"What is it?"

"A manuscript, Jenn. A book my grandfather wrote that he never published."

"What?"

"I'm holding it right now. It's sitting on my lap."

"A finished book?"

"I think so. I have to read it to make sure, but do you realize what this means?"

"Sounds pretty big."

"It's *huge*. Way bigger than the biography idea."

"Hold on," she said. "I have to go down the escalator. You can keep talking."

"Gramps's last novel was over three years ago. Do you realize the impact of discovering a brand new book he's written, and what publishers might pay to get something like this now, a few weeks after his death?" As I said this, it sounded crummy, even to me. Like I suddenly didn't care that he had died.

"I'm guessing quite a lot. Say, Michael, maybe I should call you after I get my bags and get settled in the rental car."

I really wanted to keep talking this over with her. "All right. You figure about thirty minutes?"

"I think so."

We hung up. I walked out to the kitchen to refill my iced tea. And to clear my head. Carrying the glass back into the study, I stopped just inside and stared at the manuscript lying on the desk. It was an astounding find. Seeing it there, beside the typewriter . . . I realized Gramps had written it right here, in this room, on that little machine. I looked at the wooden carrying case on the edge of the desk, and it suddenly dawned on me.

He had meant for me to find it.

Sometime shortly before he died, Gramps had set this up so that I'd discover this unpublished manuscript in that wooden box. When he'd left the house to me, he knew I'd want to write in this study. And he also knew when I did, I'd be using my laptop, not his typewriter. He could have put the typewriter in the case himself. But he left it out, centered on the desk, knowing I'd put it back in the wooden carrying case.

And when I did, I'd find it, his last novel.

His last, unpublished novel.

I stood over it and noticed again the slight yellowing of the paper. That didn't make sense. I picked it up and thumbed through the first fifty pages or so. They were the same color. Maybe it wasn't his last novel. There was no date on the cover page. I sat down and untied the twine, then scanned the first few pages until I came to chapter one. Nothing there, either, about when he'd written this.

It didn't matter. The main point was, it was an unpublished manuscript. And Gramps had intended for me to find it, *after* he died.

But why?

I read the title again. *An Impossible Love.* Intriguing. I wondered what it was about. I immediately gave up the idea of digging around for more information for Gramps's biography. This was way bigger than that. I was sure Rick Samson would agree.

I wondered when I should call him, what I should say. Obviously, I'd have to read the manuscript first, make sure it was a completed book. That gave me an idea. I lifted it up again and went to the last page. Sure enough, there it was: THE END.

So it was complete. Still, I'd need to read it. That was job one.

I set the manuscript down and took a sip of iced tea. Wait a minute, what was I thinking? *I'd have to read it.* As if it needed my approval. I rolled the chair back from the desk a few inches. What had come over me? I *wanted* to read this. Not to assess its monetary value but because my grandfather had written it. Because I loved him. I didn't need any more money. He'd already given me more than I would probably ever earn myself in a lifetime.

He'd written this and, for some reason, had never gotten it published. And for some other reason, he'd set things up for me to find it after he died. He'd have to have known how valuable something like this was. Did he mean for me to get it published for him? It seemed obvious that he must. And if so, would he expect me to share the money with the rest of the family? With just the four grandchildren or my dad and Aunt Fran too?

If that were the case, why not just publish the book himself before he died and make it part of the estate?

None of this made any sense.

I smiled as I thought about it. Gramps's novels had always included an air of mystery in them. I wondered what Jenn would think about all this. As I set down my glass on a coaster, I noticed the old leather journal that was also in the wooden box.

The journal.

That's where I should start.

12

Jenn had called me back from the rental car before I'd gotten a chance to read my grandfather's journal. I filled her in on the details, including my confusion about what to do with the manuscript. She was as puzzled as I was. We agreed I should just read it over the next few days. Maybe a sensible idea would present itself by then. I almost felt like I should put it in a safe deposit box or something.

I was looking at the only copy on earth.

When I wrote almost anything, I'd back it up in two or three places. The ease of the digital age. I was looking at a stack of papers that could easily be worth a million dollars. But I guess if this house had made it through almost two centuries intact, and this manuscript had been here long enough to turn yellow, I could relax for a few more days.

I'd also told Jenn about the journal. Gramps had only written in a handful of pages. I told her I'd read it and summarize what it said the next time we talked.

The sun had begun to set. I reached across the

desk and pulled the little chain on the Tiffany lamp, which added a soft glow. I leaned back, spun the chair around, and rested my feet on a small leather ottoman, which my grandfather had set on the floor for this very purpose. It caught the light just right over your shoulder. I opened the journal to the first page.

I'd never known my grandfather to keep a journal, not in the traditional sense, like someone jotting thoughts in a diary. He'd always kept a little memo pad and pen with him, though. Saw him write little things in it more times than I could count. I remembered one time, maybe five years ago, we were hunting redfish near the mouth of Nowell Creek. I had just snagged a nice one. After he lifted it into the boat with a net, he got this look on his face, then yanked out that little pad.

"Gramps," I'd said, watching the redfish flipping about in the net at his feet. "What's up?"

"Saw a way to describe something in a scene I'm working on."

"About fishing?"

"No," he'd said, "about the way that redfish came back to life when he caught sight of this net. Gimme a minute."

He knew I wanted to be a writer, so when he put the pad back in his shirt pocket he said, "You need to get yourself one of these. Some of my best lines come at the worst times."

I pulled out my Pocket PC that I'd put in a ziplock bag so it wouldn't get wet, and said, "Already got one."

"Ever write in it?" he said.

I thought a moment. "Nothing worthwhile." Sadly, that was the truth.

It was still the truth.

I set his journal on my lap and began reading the first few pages. He'd written the dates in the space at the top. All the entries were written last month, in the two weeks before he died.

The first several entries were a collection of some of his favorite and final memories with Nan.

A cruise they'd taken on their last anniversary together in the eastern Caribbean. Picking wild blueberries on a hillside during a walk in southern Maine. Driving through Sedona, Arizona, at sunset. A simple conversation they had on those same Adirondack chairs in the courtyard, where Jenn and I sat last night. Nan told Gramps he was still her favorite author after all these years. Then there were some things Nan had said about heaven, in those last few weeks when her mind was still clear.

Each entry affected me. It wasn't the kind of writing I'd come to know in his books. It was much more personal. But his ability to make you see and feel what he experienced was just as strong. There was joy present as he spoke of the love he felt for Nan, the fun they had together. But I also sensed a pronounced loneliness, and heartache was evident on every page.

The last entry, just shy of two pages long, was different. That was obvious from the first few lines:

I am going to die very soon. I can feel it.

I haven't gone to the doctor to confirm this, and I don't plan to. Call it an old man's prerogative. He'd simply try to talk me into any number of painful and intrusive life-saving measures which, if I'm dying, won't prolong my life but merely cause it to end badly. I saw what they did to my beloved Mary, death by inches. I won't let them do that to me.

Why would I want to prolong my life anyway?

I've lived a full measure of years. I'm ready to depart this world the moment my Maker intends. I want to see Mary again, be with her. I've wanted that every waking moment since I last felt the warmth of her hand in mine. Four long years now.

So I will let this disease inside me have its way, whatever it is. Probably a cancer of some kind. It's not very painful, at least not now. I can still do all the things I need to do, a few I want to. From what I've read, this will continue until, at some point, my body begins giving way to the inevitable. When that happens, well . . . that's why they call it inevitable.

I'll just spend my last days on morphine, unless the Lord has a mind to take me quietly in my sleep. A few moments after that, I will be doing just fine.

So Gramps knew he was dying, had for some time. We weren't told exactly how he died, just that he died in his sleep. Guess he got his wish on that one. My dad and Aunt Fran had passed on having an autopsy done. It was clearly not foul play and neither cared to know the biological details.

I'm writing these last few pages for my family. More precisely, for my grandson Michael to find.

"What!" I said aloud when I read my name.

I trust he'll know what to do with it, and with the package I've left in my wooden box (which has its own story, and he'll find out about that too).

I knew it. Gramps meant for me to find the manuscript. What did he mean that he'd trust I'd know what to do with it? I didn't know what to do with it. I looked at the wooden box and wondered what he meant, saying it had its own story. How was I supposed to find out these things? I flipped through the rest of the journal.

No more entries.

So how was I supposed to know?

My will has already been written, and by now everyone should know what they're getting. I suspect they will all be very happy. They have a right to that happiness, for all the countless ways they have added to mine. Besides that, the Good Lord set things up so you can't take a single thing with you.

I know none of them will be nearly as happy as me. I expect to be holding my Mary's hand again, seeing and knowing things that have puzzled wise men for ages.

Do I have any regrets?

All the worst ones have been washed away by God's mercy. There is this one matter that has chased me the better part of my life. I've spent decades dodging its shadow. Since we're so close to the end now, it looks like I may succeed. But I don't believe it's fair, nor is it right, to allow it to chase after my family, once I have departed.

They have a right to know the truth.

I will leave it to them to decide what, if anything, to do about it.

Actually, Michael, I leave that decision to you.

I reread the last few lines three times. "Oh, Gramps, you're killing me." Some mysterious matter had chased him his whole life?

I've spent decades dodging its shadow.

What did that mean? And how would it now "chase after my family"? Marilyn would freak out if she read this. It seemed to confirm the worst of her conspiracy theories.

And why . . . I stood up and said it out loud: "Why, Gramps, would you leave the decision of what to do with all of this up to me? Why me?" I set the journal down next to the manuscript, turned out the lamp, and hurried out of the study, closing the door behind me.

This was just crazy.

I decided I needed to get out of the house for a few hours, get some fresh air, some good food. Talk to Jenn for a while. But I knew what I'd be doing right after that.

I'd come back home, dive into that manuscript, and read it front to back. Probably stay up late tonight and then get at it first thing tomorrow morning.

AN IMPOSSIBLE LOVE

by Gerard Warner

Chapter One

October, 1942

"Ben," she said, "what are you thinking? You've left the room again."

Ben Coleman looked up at Claire, then at all his newfound "friends" sitting around the lunch counter at McCrory's. How could he tell her what he was thinking? He was thinking he'd fallen hopelessly in love with her. He was thinking how impossible it was for them to be together. And he was thinking about why—two reasons came to mind. Both presented insurmountable obstacles. He looked into her beautiful eyes. "I'm just tired," he said, suppressing a sigh. "What did I miss?"

So many lies.

Starting with his name. It was not Ben Coleman. In the past two months, he had become aware of how heavy words become when you carry them alone. Lies spoken to someone you love were heavier still.

"Hank was just saying we should all go to the movies tonight," Claire said. "I get off at 6:00. What time's it playing, Hank?"

Ben looked at Hank Nelson, who stared at Claire with lovesick eyes. He always looked at her that way, and she never seemed to notice. But Hank didn't have a prayer; she was way out of his league. Most, if not all women, were out of Hank's league. "Starts at 7:00," Hank said. "I could swing by and pick you up."

Three others sat at their end of the counter. Hank's offer was clearly meant for Claire. "That's okay, Hank. I don't need a ride," she said. "So Ben, can you come?"

Claire Richards, her real name, looked right at him as she said this. Either he was totally off, or she felt something for him too. Like just now. She was almost asking him for a date. "What's playing?" he said.

"A war flick," Hank said. "*Secret Mission*, with James Mason and Stewart Granger. Didn't you hear me a minute ago?"

"Sorry, no. I didn't." A war movie, thought Ben. Even worse, a war movie about spies. Not the way he wanted to spend his Saturday night. But it would give him more time with Claire. He'd learned that her heart belonged to Jim Burton, her high school sweetheart, who was off fighting Rommel and the Nazis somewhere in North Africa. Burton was his first big obstacle. "Sure, I'll come," Ben said.

"Great. Barb and Joe, you coming?"

Barbara Scott was Claire Richards's best friend. She and Joe were engaged and planning to tie the knot the week before Thanksgiving. Sometime between then and Christmas, Joe would be shipping off to boot camp. "I don't know," Joe said. "I'm not really in the mood for a war movie."

Claire made a face at Barb.

"C'mon, Joe, it'll be fun," Barb said. She'd gotten the message. Claire wanted them to come, to make this a group event.

"I guess if you want to," Joe said. Barb leaned over and kissed him on the cheek.

Ben took the last swallow of his root beer float. He was beginning to like these things. The jukebox stopped playing. Hank stood up. "I'll get it."

"Put on Frank Sinatra," Claire said, *"Night and Day*, will you, Hank?"

Ben caught Hank making a face; clearly not what he had in mind. "Sure, Claire. You got it."

Ben liked Sinatra. In fact, he liked all the music he was finally getting to hear again these past two months. Bing Crosby, Glenn Miller, the Andrews Sisters. It had been so long since he'd heard good American music.

As soon as the song began, Claire said, "That was the last song Jim and I danced to before he shipped out."

"Aww," Barb said, "that's so sweet. I love this song."

"You love anything Sinatra sings," Joe said.

"True," she said. "True."

Ben noticed Claire's eyes when she talked about Jim. She never cried or showed any emotion. Even now, as Sinatra swooned into the chorus, she was just smiling away.

That had to mean something.

Claire looked at the clock on the wall. "I have to leave after this song, gotta clock in at 2:00." Claire worked at Woolworth's, just a few stores down on Beach Street, right on the corner of Magnolia. "Did you find a job yet?" she asked Ben.

"Not yet." Ben wasn't looking all that hard. He had plenty of ready cash. Really, enough for a lifetime. But eventually, for appearance's sake, he'd have to get one.

"Maybe while you're waiting, you can volunteer with the Civil Air Patrol," Barb said. "I started back in August. It's a lot of fun."

"Have you ever ridden a horse?" Joe asked.

"What?" Ben said.

"Horses, you know how to ride 'em?"

Ben shook his head. "Never been on a horse. Why?"

"The Coast Guard is looking for men who can ride. I wished I'd heard about this before I joined the Army. I could have been fighting Krauts here at home instead of shipping overseas."

"You don't ride horses," Barb said.

"Not anymore, but I used to all the time as a kid. We lived out near Samsula."

"Really? I never knew that."

"There's a lot you don't know about me," Joe said, reaching for her hand.

"A real man of mystery," Hank said in a mocking tone. "So what are they doing, these guys on horses?"

"Nothing you can do anything about," Joe said, referring to the fact that Hank was 4-F.

Hank looked down at the table, deflated.

"Joe," Claire said.

"That wasn't nice," Barb added.

"What? I wasn't putting him down."

Ben looked at Hank's thick glasses. They made his eyes pop out when he looked straight at you. He even had the big nose to go with the glasses, and with curly hair that piled high on his head, he looked like one of the Marx Brothers. "So what about these horses?" Ben said. "Not that I can join up, either. I'm 4-F too. Remember?"

"I forgot," Joe said.

Ben had told them he had a heart murmur when he first met them. He needed some reason to explain why he hadn't signed up like every other healthy, patriotic young American.

"Your problem isn't as obvious," Joe said. "No offense, Hank."

"It's all right," Hank said.

"Well," Joe said, "last month the Coast Guard decided to add horses to their beach patrols. You know, checking for more Nazi saboteurs coming onshore from those U-boats."

"That was wild," Hank said. "Four of them came in just south of Jacksonville back in June. The paper said they found guns, explosives, and a whole suitcase full of cash in the dunes."

"Well, they won't be sneaking any more Krauts in once this thing gets cooking," Joe said. "Each patrol's supposed to have horses and German shepherds, patrolling in shifts all night long. They won't make any noise or get stuck in the sand. Krauts won't even hear 'em coming."

"You sure you can't get reassigned to this?" Barb said.

"No, darlin'," Joe said, "already tried. The Army recruiter said what's done is done."

She formed her lips into a pout. Joe leaned over and kissed her.

"Well, Ben, I wasn't talking about joining the Coast Guard," Barb said. "I remembered about your heart. I'm talking about volunteering with the Civil Air Patrol. You've seen these watchtowers they've been putting up."

Ben nodded.

"Well, they train you as a lookout. You don't get paid anything, but it's a lot of fun. You sit up there scanning the skies for German planes and the ocean for U-boats, and call in anything you see."

"Have you ever seen anything?" Hank asked.

"Well, no U-boats, but lots of planes."

"Lemme guess," he said. "All ours."

"Yes," Barb said. "So far, but you never know . . ."

"I think we do know," Hank said. "Germans don't even have a plane that can fly across the Atlantic. Not yet, anyway."

"I'll think about it," Ben said. He wanted to change the subject. This whole conversation made him nervous. They were now talking about the second greatest obstacle to wooing Claire. If his real identity were known, Ben would be arrested, tried, and executed, just like six other German saboteurs had been eight weeks ago. They had been caught in June. Tried in July. Then strapped to the electric chair in August.

The Sinatra song ended.

"Well, gotta go," Claire said. She stood up.

Ben stood up too. "Yeah, I've got to head back over the bridge. I told my landlady I'd help her with a few things before dark." Another lie, but without Claire here, there was no reason to stay.

Claire stopped at the glass door and looked at Ben. "But you're coming back for the movie, right?"

"Wouldn't miss it for the world," Ben said.

As she waved good-bye and headed down the sidewalk, Ben watched her glide past the window. There it was again; she'd singled him out. Claire wanted him at that movie.

So, for her, he'd come back over the bridge tonight and sit through the stupid movie.

On so many rational levels, he knew Claire could never be his. But he didn't care. His whole life was up in the air now. The finely crafted plan that had landed him on the beach a little north of here in mid-August had been annihilated that very first night. Getting free of that plan, getting a chance to start his life over . . . that was the new plan. The only plan Ben cared about now.

Claire, he thought.

So many lies.

Chapter Two

The spy movie at the Daytona Theater was a wash, for the most part. No surprise there. British actors, a British plot, and loaded with propaganda. The Nazis were evil and incompetent, the Allies noble and intelligent. A predictable ending.

Ben didn't mind it, though. With the newsreels and previews, it had given him two full hours to sit next to Claire. During some tense scenes, she'd leaned up against him. Twice she'd grabbed his forearm instead of the armrest.

He also didn't mind how the Nazis were portrayed. He knew firsthand that they really were evil. And many he'd dealt with—some in positions of real authority—were seriously incompetent.

He wanted them to lose this war with all his heart.

It was dark out now. He stood at the center of the Broadway Bridge, looking west at the downtown area he'd just come from, such as it was. One main road called Beach Street ran north and south along a river that divided Daytona into two sections: the beachside and the mainland. That's how he'd heard the locals describe it. There were a few more streets that branched off from it, a few more on the beachside, but it was a small town. Like many others he remembered seeing in Pennsylvania, where he was born.

The thing he liked most was the absence of the color red. If this had been any downtown area in Germany, in any city, no matter what size, that's what you'd see. Red flags, white trim, black swastikas. Everywhere. It sickened him.

The downtown area here was lined with charming stores, diners, and the movie theater on one side, and on the other side of the street was a beautiful riverfront park, with peaceful walkways that wrapped around ponds and fountains. Flowers and shrubs abounded, along with stately palms.

You could only see such details in the daytime. The whole city was encased in darkness, except for a few dim lights glowing here and there. He turned and looked toward the beachside, which was almost entirely blacked out. Ben laughed at the absurdity of this. He wished he could tell someone. Hank was right. He might not see too well through those thick glasses, but he saw better than most of the leaders in this country on the issue. Not a single soul in America was in danger from the air. Every air raid warning, every air raid precaution that took place was a complete waste of time. The German Luftwaffe could barely keep its planes across the English Channel for an hour before they ran out of fuel. Ben doubted they would ever come up with a plane that could fly across the Atlantic.

The danger for America was from the sea.

Since the day Hitler declared war on the US in December, German U-boats had sunk several hundred Allied ships along the East Coast and in the Gulf of Mexico, many within sight of the shoreline. He'd been back in the US for nearly two months but hadn't read a thing about this in the newspapers. Why were American officials hiding this danger from the public?

He recalled what Barb had said in the diner that afternoon. She was so happy with herself, climbing her watchtower on the beach several days a week to keep an eye out for the enemy. She would never see anything but American planes, and she'd certainly never see a U-boat during the day.

As he stood there leaning against the rail of the Broadway Bridge, he remembered standing one night along the railing of U-boat 176, next to the deck gun, two days before his mission was set to begin. He'd come up to catch some fresh air. Two German sailors scanned the waters between the boat and the shoreline, hoping to spot the silhouette of an Allied cargo vessel sailing north. Liberty ships, they called them.

The trick was to patrol coastal waters just outside the shipping lanes. U-boats cruised slowly and quietly, parallel to seaside towns. Surprisingly, many towns left their lights on at night. When Allied ships passed between them, the city lights provided a perfect backdrop, allowing German spotters to easily see the outline of a ship, even though the ship itself had turned off its lights.

That night, Ben had witnessed this very thing. Both sailors had simultaneously spotted the Allied ship and sounded the alarm. The U-boat instantly shifted to battle stations. "Sorry, sir. You must go below now," Ben was told.

"Right, good luck," he said as he climbed down the ladder.

Good luck? Had he really said that? He'd wished somehow he could warn the Americans on that doomed freighter. But he was helpless.

He quickly dodged around the sailors hurrying to ready the torpedoes below as he made his way to his quarters. He and his team of three other men, all highly trained agents with the German Abwehr, were mere spectators on this vessel, confined to quarters whenever the U-boat went into battle.

Battle, he thought. This was no battle. It was a slaughter. Like firing a high-powered rifle at a lumbering cow grazing in a field. These Liberty ships never had a chance, nor any means to defend themselves. The first sign of danger American merchantmen received was the massive explosion erupting in the center of their boat, often splitting it in two.

Ben sat below in the crowded officers' bunk with his partner, Jurgen Kiep, a true believer.

"It's so exciting, don't you think?" Jurgen said. "I wish we could watch it from up there." He pointed topside.

"I got a glimpse of the ship's silhouette," Ben said, "before they sent me down."

"Well, that ship is going to be sent down," Jurgen said, pointing to the floor. "Any minute now."

Ben smiled and nodded, instantly regretting his feigned enthusiasm. He'd been forced to live this charade for almost six years, pretending to be a faithful, even passionate Nazi. Now, he was only a few days out from finally being rid of this albatross. The calluses that had crusted over his lies were already beginning to soften.

A few moments later, the submarine shuddered, the deep groaning sounds followed by the swoosh of the forward torpedoes releasing.

"Won't be long now," Jurgen said.

Ben sighed, then tried to conceal it. Both men sat in silence. A few minutes went by, then a deep bass sound. A moment later, another . . . *Boom.*

"They got her!" Jurgen yelled and jumped to his feet. "You hear it? Both torpedoes. She's going down."

Ben stood, forced a smile.

"Let's go," Jurgen said. "Maybe they'll let us up on deck. Must have been amazing to watch, don't you think?"

"Amazing," Ben said. He didn't want to see it. Those booms meant dozens of American men, some his same age, had just died. Others were clinging to flaming debris or drowning in the surf. *I am an American,* he said in his mind, walking a few steps behind Jurgen toward the conning tower. He knew he was making a choice, firming his resolve—

"Excuse me, young man."

"What?"

"May I get by? There's a car coming across the bridge or I'd walk around you."

Ben looked down at the face of a short man wearing an overcoat and fedora, a bit bundled up for the slight chill in the air.

"You weren't thinking of jumping, were you?"

"What? No," Ben said, smiling.

"Got girl troubles then?" he said, stepping by as Ben leaned up against the rail. "A man stands out on a bridge this long without a fishing pole, I figure he's either gonna jump or he's got girl troubles."

"You got it, sir. Girl troubles. No plans to jump. Too much to live for."

The man stopped. "So you shipping out soon, wondering if she'll wait? Lot of that going on. My boy went through that a few months ago. He's in England now."

"Well, that's not exactly my problem. I'm 4-F. The girl I love loves someone like your son, only he's in North Africa."

"Ah," the man said. "That could stick a man out on a bridge, I guess. If you don't mind me saying, hope she stays true to her young man in Africa, after seeing what my boy went through. But then I hope you find somebody else, just right for you." He waved, turned, and started walking toward the mainland.

"Good night," Ben said. He shoved his hands in his jacket pockets and started walking toward the beachside. Why had he told that man about Claire? He'd just blurted it out, like it was . . . the truth.

It was the truth.

And it felt good to say it. It had been so long since he'd said anything close to the truth. But it saddened him to think about what the man said, hoping that Claire would stay true to Jim Burton.

As he looked out over the water, he remembered she'd talked about Jim the day they met, that first week he'd come into town. He'd been heading into the diner at Woolworth's.

Lying there, blocking the entrance to the front door, was this big brown dog. He seemed friendly enough. Ben was about to step over him when the dog looked up and began wagging his tail. Ben bent down to pet him. "Hey, boy, how you doing?" As soon as Ben patted his head, the dog rolled on his side. "I see, you want me to scratch your belly."

He heard the front door open. Before he could look up, a woman shouted, "Oh no!" The next moment, a thick stream of water poured over his head and all over his clothes.

"Oh my goodness, I'm so sorry."

Ben rubbed the water from his eyes and looked up into the face of a beautiful young woman.

"I am so sorry," she repeated. "I didn't see you."

"I'm all right, really. It's just water." How could he be angry? She was so lovely.

"No, it's not all right. Let me go get a towel. You stay there, I'll be right back."

He stood and so did the brown dog. The girl returned with a white towel and began drying him off. She had the brightest smile and the kindest eyes. "I'm really okay," he said.

"I was just bringing a bowl of water out for Brownie," she said. "It's so hot out here."

"I'm all cooled off now." Ben smiled. "Is this your dog?"

"No, he's sort of the downtown mascot. I don't think anyone owns him." She finished drying Ben off as best she could. "I'm Claire, by the way."

Ben introduced himself, and they shook hands politely. He didn't want to let go of her hand.

Standing there now on the bridge, Ben still remembered the moment their hands first touched. She'd said she worked part-time at Woolworth's. He found out she got off at 4:00. Before she went back in, Claire insisted he allow her to make it up to him somehow. Ben suggested his honor might be restored if she met him for dinner when she got off work.

That's when Ben found out about Jim Burton.

But it didn't matter. Ben knew he had to keep seeing her, so he kept coming back to Woolworth's every chance he got. He'd found a seat in the diner that let him view the entire store. Over the next several weeks he'd come in for lunch or a cup of coffee and watch her as she went about her various tasks. As he did, his attraction and affection for her continued to intensify. Beyond her physical beauty, which had thoroughly captivated him, Ben was struck by how incredibly kind she was. Bringing water out to a thirsty dog on a hot day was just Claire being Claire. She treated everyone at the store the same way: her boss, co-workers, even grouchy customers.

He did his best to be discreet but whenever he'd see her, he couldn't help but stare. Once in a while, she'd notice him and smile or wave. Occasionally, they'd even talk, but she'd always keep a respectful distance. He never once felt the green light to ask her out.

A few weeks ago, she'd walked over to where he sat and invited him to join her and "the gang" down the street at McCrory's. That's where they hung out, she'd said. He thought it might be the beginning of something positive and instantly said yes.

Nothing came of it, however, except the opportunity to spend more time with Claire. That alone made it worthwhile. But she must have discerned his growing interest; she'd regularly insert little Jim reminders, like she had done that afternoon. But Ben kept seeing little glimmers of hope, like he did that afternoon.

Ben sighed, turned, and started walking down the bridge toward the beachside. He realized Claire would probably stay true to Jim Burton, even if she did have feelings for him. She was that kind of girl. Not just beautiful, not just a delight to be with and talk to. She was a nice girl, an honest girl. The kind of girl who would always do the right thing.

And Ben knew, he was the wrong thing for someone like Claire.

For so many reasons.

Chapter Three

After coming off the bridge, Ben walked the few blocks toward his apartment on Grandview Avenue. It seemed quiet for a Friday night. Few cars had driven by, and few people were out walking, all of them on the opposite side of the road. No more conversations. He turned the corner, saw his two-story apartment building ahead on the left. It was set one block back from the beach, close enough to hear the waves breaking when the wind blew in from the ocean, as it did tonight. A pleasant sound, but he wasn't quite ready to head down the beach for a night stroll.

Not after what had happened *that* night.

The memories were so real and terrifying that he was still having nightmares. But something Joe had said at McCrory's this afternoon forced him to face the fact that he'd have to go back there, to the place where he, Jurgen, and the other two-man team had landed onshore. And he'd have to do it tonight. Go back to the sand dunes, twenty minutes north of here, before the Coast Guard had a chance to get those new teams out patrolling the beaches at night with horses and dogs.

Ben turned off the sidewalk, ready to head up the steps to his apartment building, when he noticed his landlady, Mrs. Arthur, sitting on the top step, smoking a cigarette. Her hair was up in rollers and wrapped in a scarf. Her razor-thin legs stuck out the bottom of her coat, her feet resting two steps below inside thick woolen slippers.

"Evening, Mrs. Arthur. Nice night."

"Surely is, son. Coming in early for a Friday night, ain't ya?"

"Actually, I just came back for a moment to get the car. Then I'll be heading back out."

"Where you going?"

Mrs. Arthur was so nosy. If she didn't ask so many questions, he wouldn't have to add to his stockpile of lies. "A friend needs a ride. I've been walking a lot lately, saving up gas coupons. He's all out."

"That's nice of you, sharing yours like that."

Ben had all the book one ration coupons he'd need for this year and another set of book two coupons for next year. For food, gas, you name it. All counterfeit, but perfectly forged beyond detection.

"You boys going on some hot date?"

He laughed. "Nothing like that. Just giving him a ride to work." Where did he come up with this stuff? "Well, better get a move on, he's expecting me to pick him up in fifteen minutes."

"Drive safe," she said. "Everyone's got those dimmers on their headlights now. Hard enough to see at night as it is, without them things."

"I'll be careful." He passed her on the steps, opened the door, and walked into the dark hallway. His apartment was on the first floor, three doors down. Once inside, he flicked on the light switch and locked the door behind him.

He turned and looked at the door.

That lock was a problem. With a little effort, almost anyone could break in here. The dark hallway was another problem. This apartment itself was a problem. It didn't have nearly enough security. Not after tonight. He paid his rent weekly. He decided he'd pay it one more time but had no plans of staying here another week. He needed his own place, a place he could secure like a vault.

The apartment was just two rooms, a small kitchen/dinette area and a slightly larger bedroom, furnished with a chest of drawers, a stiff upholstered chair, and a lumpy bed. He walked through the kitchen into the bedroom, bent down, and opened the bottom drawer. He pulled out a cigar box, set it on the bed, and sat beside it.

Inside was a pistol, a stack of ration coupons, and a wad of cash, maybe two hundred dollars. Each of the German agents had been issued the gun as part of their training. It was an American Colt 45, standard issue for GIs. Ben was a crack shot with a pistol, first in his class. But that was using the Walther P38, a German pistol slightly bigger than the luger.

He picked up the gun and set the cigar box back in the drawer. As he shoved the .45 in the waistband behind his back, he said a silent prayer to a God he felt sure had stopped listening long ago. *Please, keep me from having to use this tonight . . . please.*

He reached into his pocket, made sure he still had his keys, turned off the lights, then headed out the door, locking it behind him.

Ben slowed his speed down to thirty-five miles an hour, the new patriotic speed, keeping an eye out on the left for High Bridge Road. The only road out here on this lonely stretch of A1A. Almost nothing to see but sand dunes on either side for the last ten miles. Rolling by on his right, just beyond the dunes, was the Atlantic Ocean.

He was glad to be closing the distance this time by car. That night, he'd walked the ten miles back to Ormond Beach, the nearest town, just north of Daytona. He'd picked High Bridge Road as his marker, so he'd be able to come back here later and find the suitcase he'd buried.

"Fifty by fifty." He repeated aloud the little phrase he'd memorized that night. Fifty paces south along the highway, then fifty paces west into the dunes.

He'd purchased this car, a black '35 Ford coupe, for two hundred dollars cash within a few days of coming into town. It already had an "A" sticker on the windshield. That was the basic ration sticker given to average Americans. The attendant at the pump would see the sticker and know to pump only four gallons of gas into the tank. An A-sticker American would hand him a week's worth of ration coupons. Ben easily overcame this obstacle. He had an unlimited supply of ration coupons so he'd just visit several stations in different parts of town until the tank was full.

The coupe was a nice basic car, nothing flashy. Also part of the training. Make every purchase decision with invisibility in mind. Be middle of the road, do nothing to stand out in a crowd.

The long walk into town that night in August was the reason he had to bury the suitcase. He couldn't afford someone seeing him walking down A1A carrying something like that. They might mistake him for a GI on leave, stop to offer him a ride. Or worse, a sheriff's deputy might spot him and pull over, likely with his gun drawn, to see if he was a German spy.

That could easily happen, especially after the fiasco back in June, when the first two teams of German spies had landed. One team landed south of Jacksonville, the other on Long Island near the village of Amagansett. A band of idiots and imbeciles, the whole lot of them. Not one a trained German soldier or Abwehr agent, they were picked mainly because they spoke English fairly well and had, at one time, lived in America. Their entire regimen of training was less than five weeks.

It was called Operation Pastorius, the brainchild of Walter Kappe, a German who'd lived in America during the 1930s and who tried in vain to create a legitimate Nazi party here from all the Germans who'd fled the Fatherland after World War I. Tens of thousands of them.

Like his parents.

Back in high school, Ben would hear them talk about Kappe, going on and on about his "German-American Bund" and all the wonderful things taking place in Germany now that Adolf Hitler had risen to power. Ben didn't take it seriously until one day in 1935 when he came home from school to find his parents packing.

"We are going back to the Fatherland, son," his father had said. "All is well again. Plenty of jobs for everyone. Isn't it exciting?"

Ben shook his head, trying to jar the memory from his mind. Too many sad thoughts if he got stuck there. His headlights picked the High Bridge Road sign up ahead. Fortunately, there were no cars in either direction. He decided to pull completely off A1A and park off High Bridge Road, as far as he dared without getting stuck in the sand.

He turned off the headlights as soon as he made the turn, pulled the car over, and got out. Good, the shadows from the dunes on either side cast the entire area in total darkness. He opened the trunk and grabbed a shovel.

As he walked toward A1A, headlights from an oncoming car flashed on the road up ahead. He jumped behind a cluster of scrub palms until the car sped by. He was probably being too careful, but that was okay. He remembered something his Abwehr commander had said: *"It is good for spies to be a little paranoid; being very paranoid . . . even better."*

It was a lesson those earlier teams back in June should have learned.

He stepped out of the bushes, thinking how ironic it was. Because of the depth of his team's discipline and training, he despised the arrogant Kappe and his men for their stupidity and incompetence. But because of his intense hatred for the Nazis, he was equally glad they had gotten caught. Ben decided he must exercise all the skill and cunning this third team had received to avoid capture.

And to avoid their fate.

He double-checked to make sure no cars were coming in either direction, then counted off the first fifty paces. He turned right, heading straight into the dunes as he walked out the next fifty.

He stopped and looked around, trying to regain his bearings. It was no use. Whether it had been too dark or he had been too nervous that night, nothing in this gully looked familiar. He was surrounded by the silhouettes of short rolling dunes, covered by scrub palms and sea oats. It all looked the same.

So he started digging. He'd have to hope his steps this time mirrored the ones he'd walked two months ago. Back then, using his bare hands, it had taken over an hour to dig the hole.

Within ten minutes, the shovel hit something solid. He tapped on it a few times; it was definitely not a rock. As he scraped the sand around it, he could tell it was flat and just about the right size. He tossed the shovel aside and laid down near the edge of the hole, cleared away more sand.

Finally, he felt the handle on the side. A few strong pulls and he freed the suitcase from its hold. He lifted it and set it beside the hole. He brushed off more sand then carried it back to the street. He didn't need to look inside; he and Jurgen had loaded it themselves before boarding the U-boat, and checked off everything inside. And he'd opened it before burying it here two months ago, when he took out some cash and ration coupons, just enough to hold him over till he came up with a better plan. But not enough to draw suspicion if he'd been stopped.

That was his greatest fear now, getting stopped holding this suitcase. There'd be no way to explain its contents. Besides the year's worth of ration coupons, there was over $175,000 cash.

Not counterfeit—real American dollars, in small unmarked bills, compliments of Herr Fuhrer.

He reached the edge of the dunes by the road and stopped, still cloaked in darkness. A car drove by, heading south toward town. He climbed up the dune on his belly and kept low until he broke through. But there were no more cars in either direction. He hurried back, grabbed the suitcase, and ran the final fifty paces toward High Bridge Road, feeling the same rush of fear and panic he had that night two months ago.

A few moments later, with the suitcase safely in his trunk, he hopped in the front seat and checked the rearview mirror. Another car passed on A1A, going north away from town. He sat a few moments more to catch his breath.

As he turned on the ignition, the memory that had haunted his nightmares these past two months floated into his mind. He tried to extinguish it, afraid if he let it play through, he'd relive it again tonight.

He knew why it came to him now. He was less than a hundred yards from another hole he'd dug in the sand dunes that night.

The place where he'd buried Jurgen's body.

Chapter Four

The tension Ben felt last night had dissipated, sometime between waking up and finishing his breakfast at McCrory's. He was still nervous about the suitcase in his trunk. He looked at his car through the window of McCrory's, like he could see his suitcase sitting there, right through the metal. Every few minutes, every time someone walked by on the sidewalk, he looked again. As if they could see it too. At least it was in the trunk; he didn't have to worry anymore about getting caught retrieving it.

"You want me to freshen that up?"

Ben closed his notebook and looked up at Miss Jane. He had no idea why she wanted to be called that, but she'd made quite a point about it. He pushed his coffee cup in her direction. "That would be great. Do you need me to pay my bill?"

She poured the coffee. "I'm fine, darlin'. I'm here through lunch. You can settle up whenever you're ready."

"I'm afraid I'm going to have to pay rent for how long I've been sitting here, Miss Jane."

She laughed. "Just take your time."

"I'll leave you a nice tip," he said. "That's a promise."

"Won't argue with you there, Ben." She walked away.

He opened the notebook again, a little project he'd been working on most of the morning. His cover story—his *new* cover story, not the one he'd been assigned by the Abwehr. He'd kept one of his Nazi commander's instructions. When creating your cover, use as much of your personal story as possible. Only lie in the essentials. The idea was, the more truth it contained, the less chance you'd slip up in casual conversation. Or under the hot lights of an FBI interrogation.

Of course, Ben wasn't too concerned about that now, since he'd abandoned the plan to sabotage American defense plants. Little chance he'd get caught now, especially since Jurgen was dead. Who'd interfere with his plans? The other two agents had left the beach that night, heading north. He hadn't seen or heard from them since, and didn't expect to. They'd have their hands full with their own mission.

To avoid what had happened to the earlier teams, the Abwehr commanders had decided the new teams should not even attempt to contact each other for six months. Use the time to settle in, blend in with the populace. Ben had a full four months until that point. But the way he figured, he would never see or hear from either of them ever again.

They didn't know where he was, had no means

of contacting him. When the time was right, the Abwehr plan called for both teams to use a series of coded messages in the classified section of selected newspapers. The other team would run their message four months from now, then look in vain for his. They would try again two weeks later, then two weeks after that. If a team failed to respond, the other team was to assume the worst and carry on with the mission as planned. But under no circumstances were they to try to make contact.

The Germans could not afford another embarrassing scandal.

Assume the worst, Ben thought. German efficiency and paranoia had guaranteed his freedom. The danger of getting caught had passed.

His big concern now was creating a cover story that sounded believable to Claire. She'd been asking a lot more questions lately when they talked. Deeper questions, the kind a woman asks when she's trying to get to know a man. He loved it. Except for the guilt that came later. He wanted so much to talk freely with her, to just be himself, tell her who he was. Including his past, especially the things that had forced him into this double life.

But he couldn't. It was too much information now, and far too risky.

He would lie to her about certain parts of his story but find a way for her to know the person he truly was inside. He could talk about his hopes and dreams, the things he wanted to do with the rest of his life. With her, if she'd have him. All of those things would be true.

"If you don't mind me saying, hope she stays true to her young man in Africa . . ."

The voice of the man he'd met on the bridge last night ran through his head. He took a sip of his coffee. Ben had nothing against Claire's high school sweetheart. He'd never met him. Poor guy was off fighting for his country, doing the honorable thing. And if Ben thought for a minute Claire was genuinely in love with the guy, he'd back off. Because that would be the honorable thing.

But he just didn't see it.

He took a last sip of his coffee then looked at his watch. He really needed to wrap this up. Claire and "the gang" were going to meet up at the Bandshell over on the beachside and spend the afternoon listening to big band music and maybe going for a walk around the amusement park. He closed his notebook and put his pen in his shirt pocket.

"Sure you don't want to stick around awhile?" Miss Jane said as he stood up. "About time for lunch."

"It's a tempting offer, but I got to head out, meet up with some friends." He brought the check to the register. "We're going to that USO concert playing at the Bandshell."

"I read about that in the paper this morning," she said. "Lots of Army girls moving into town. This place is going to be hopping in a few weeks. Well, you kids have fun."

He smiled and walked out the door, then stopped on the sidewalk and looked in both directions, eyeing the people. No one paid him any attention. But he wouldn't feel right until he had the suitcase stashed in a secure location.

He got in the car and instantly thought about Claire and how happy he was to be seeing her again. Somehow he had to get some time alone with her this afternoon, after the others had gone. He wished he could think of some way to make it happen.

Something that wasn't a lie.

Chapter Five

Claire loved October.

Even at midday the temperature was cool. The stifling humidity that had clung to everything throughout summer had tapered off and would stay that way until spring. The mosquitoes were gone. The sea breezes always picked up in the fall. Her family lived just two blocks back from the river on Ridgewood Avenue, so the sea breezes made it here quite often. They were blowing now, gently swaying the gray moss that hung from the live oak branches.

She could see over a dozen of these ancient trees from her front porch, where she sat on a rocker, drinking a glass of iced tea. The screen door creaked open behind her.

"Shouldn't you be getting ready for work, Claire?"

"Mother, you need to stop whatever you're doing and sit out here. It's so nice."

Her mother walked out and sat in the rocker next to hers, but just on the edge. "I just got back from the store. I need to put away some groceries."

"Want some help?"

"Don't you have to work?"

"I asked Mr. Morris for the afternoon off so we could go to the USO concert playing at the Bandshell."

"Your father was telling me about that this morning at breakfast. The *News Journal* had an article about it. Did you know the Army is setting up a training base here? For women? He said it will probably bring more work for his company. Thousands of girls have signed up from all over the country. They'll be taking over most of the hotels along the beach. They're even taking over the hospital."

"Really?" Claire said. "Why?"

"I guess they need the space."

"So we're not going to have a hospital anymore?"

"No, silly. The hospital said they're only using a fraction of their rooms, so they're moving to a hotel on Atlantic Avenue. The paper said they might just stay there the rest of the war."

"So all these girls are joining the Army?" Claire said. "They're not going to fight, are they?"

"No," her mother said. "That'll never happen. They'll be assigned different kinds of support roles and administrative duties. Like switchboard and radio operators. Some will learn how to drive and fix trucks. Can you imagine that? Women fixing trucks? The paper said some will even become pilots."

"Really? What kind of planes?"

"The same ones men fly in battle. But they'll fly them here, test them out, make sure they work before they ship them overseas. You're not thinking of joining—are you?"

"No," Claire said. "I'd never want to be in the Army. For one thing, have you seen the uniforms they make you wear? Some WACs came into the store yesterday. I think uniforms look great on men, but they look awful on women."

Her mother sat back on the rocker and closed her eyes. "This really is nice."

"Well, look, let me help you put the groceries away, and we can both relax here for a little while, at least till I leave for the concert." Claire set her *Look* magazine on a table nearby and sat up.

"You stay put," her mother said. "It's not that

much. Anyway, I have to make some telephone calls for the church choir, reminder calls." She looked down at Claire's magazine. "Oh, John Wayne," she said, eyeing his picture on the cover. "Does he have some new movie coming out?"

"I guess," Claire said. "A war movie called *The Flying Tigers*. You like John Wayne? I thought you liked Gary Cooper."

"I love Gary Cooper. I tolerate John Wayne."

"Does Dad know you love another man?" Claire said, smiling.

"Well, your father and I have an understanding," she said, standing up. "I go with him to John Wayne movies, and he goes with me to Gary Cooper movies."

"I see," Claire said. "That's a pretty big price to pay to see Gary Cooper."

"Maybe, but I'm willing to pay it." She walked back toward the screen door. "Speaking of the men in our life . . . have you gotten any more letters from Jim?"

This was a touchy subject between them. "No, Mother, I haven't."

"How many have you written him since the last letter he sent?"

"I don't know, maybe four or five. But he can't write that often. In case you haven't heard, we're at war."

"But Claire, your brother is overseas. I've talked with Brenda. He writes her a lot. Your father and I get more letters from him than you get from Jim."

Brenda was the wife of Claire's brother Jack. They had married last year a month before Pearl Harbor was attacked. "I don't know what to say, Mother." Claire sighed. "Jim's just not much of a writer."

"He wasn't much of a talker, either," she said. "You two dated your whole last year of high school. But I don't think we ever had more than two minutes of conversation. He was always polite, but that was about it."

"He didn't talk to you and Dad very much, but . . . he talked a good bit when we went out." Claire wished her mother would just let this go. She and Claire's father had made it pretty clear that they didn't think it was a good idea for Claire to promise to wait for Jim when he shipped overseas. They weren't even engaged.

"Well, I'm sure you know what you're doing." Her mother opened the screen door. "So who's going to the concert?"

"The usual gang."

"Does that include that nice-looking young man, what's his name . . . Benjamin?"

Claire looked over her shoulder at her mother, who wore a mischievous grin. "Ben's coming too."

"He seems nice," she said.

"Yes, Ben's nice. I don't know him very well yet."

"Will he be joining the military?"

"He can't. He's 4-F."

"Really? He looks fine."

"Something about a heart murmur. He said it wasn't anything serious but enough for them to turn him down."

"So . . . he's going to be staying here in town then."

"Yes, Mother. I suppose he is."

"What does he do for a living?"

"I'm not sure. Like I said, I don't know him very well yet."

Her mother walked in the house, then turned and talked through the screen. "You know who he reminds me of, a little bit?"

"No, who?"

"Gary Cooper," she said as she turned to walk away.

Claire smiled. She thought about it a moment.

He did look a little like Gary Cooper.

Chapter Six

Ben decided to walk to the Bandshell. It was only four or five blocks away. He grabbed his keys, put on a light jacket, and headed out the door. His landlady was locking the door to her apartment, the one nearest the front door.

"All dressed up, Mrs. Arthur. Going someplace special?"

"In a way," she said. "I'm heading off to church."

"On a Saturday?" he asked.

"Well, I'm not going to Mass," she said. "I'm going to confession. Are you Catholic?"

"No, my family is Lutheran." It wasn't a total lie, though his family had stopped going to church when they moved back to Germany.

"At my age, I don't ever miss Mass and I go to confession at least once a week. Gotta keep that slate clean." At Ben's puzzled look she continued. "Sins, you know. You tell the priest everything you've done wrong, tell God you're sorry, and he gives you absolution. You do your penance, and your slate . . . you know, your soul. It gets washed clean."

They stood at the bottom of the stairway. "Can you tell a difference?" Ben asked. "Do you feel . . . *clean* after doing it?" This was starting to feel much too personal.

"I do," she said. "Are you feeling like you need to go?"

"No, just curious."

"Well, I've got to get going," she said. "I'm heading across the bridge to St. Paul's. Can I give you a ride somewhere?"

"No, I'm going the other way."

"Well, you have a good afternoon."

"You too." He turned and started walking toward the beach. "Say, Mrs. Arthur." She stopped and turned. "The things you tell the priest. He can't tell anyone else, right?"

"What?"

"I saw that in a movie. A cop was asking a priest some questions about a suspect who'd gone to confession. The priest said he couldn't say anything they talked about."

"That's true," she said. "It's church law. Even the courts can't make a priest repeat anything he hears in a confessional. Everything I say in there is between me, the priest, and God. You should try it sometime."

"You said you're going to St. Paul's?"

"It's not far. Just head over the Broadway Bridge, turn right on Ridgewood. A few blocks on the left, can't miss it. But I'm not sure if there's a Lutheran church in town."

"Okay, thanks," he said.

As he turned the corner, he started to regret his conversation with Mrs. Arthur. What must she be thinking about him now? Probably trying to figure out what sins he must be guilty of, what kind of things might be bothering his conscience.

Well, it didn't really matter. He'd be leaving this apartment for good in a few days.

Ben could hear big band music playing well before the Bandshell came into view. He stepped up his pace along Atlantic Avenue. Up ahead on the right, he saw a Ferris wheel spinning slowly, all lit up. He was close. He started to run, trying not to collide with all the people walking in the same direction. Many of them women in uniform, the WACS. The USO concert was being held in their honor to welcome them to town.

There was the clock tower, in the center of the boardwalk area, where he was supposed to meet Claire and the gang. He hoped they had waited for him. He hurried down a stone stairway that connected the street level to the boardwalk, all the while keeping his eyes on the tower. As he drew near, his eyes searched the crowd, trying to spot Claire. There were a lot of people standing around the base, but he didn't see her or any of the others.

"Ben, over here."

Her voice.

"We're over here."

He walked around the tower's circular base and there she was, coming his way. Just past her were Joe and Barb, and Hank standing beside them, facing the Bandshell. "It's already starting, guys," he said, tapping his foot to the beat. "Hurry."

Ben recognized the tune, one of his favorites: Glenn Miller's "In the Mood." It had been out for several years already, but Ben had only heard it for the first time a few months ago. Special permission had been granted during his Abwehr

115

training. He'd loved it instantly, and so many of the other songs he'd heard. For years, the Nazis had forbidden almost all big band music in Germany.

Ben rushed to meet Claire. He wanted so badly to take her in his arms right then. She was so beautiful. She reached out her hand as she came close but then quickly put it down.

But he saw it. *She wanted to hold my hand.*

"I love this song," she said as they joined the others.

"Me too," Ben said. "The band sounds just like Glenn Miller."

"We'll probably get stuck in the back row now," Hank said in a whiny voice. He ran on ahead.

"Slow down, Hank," Barb said, "or we'll get separated."

No, run faster, Ben thought. Please.

But Hank slowed his pace, and they walked together across the grass and through the opening to the Bandshell. There were thousands already seated. Some had moved out into the aisles. Ben looked down the main aisle and saw the bandleader waving his baton in the center of the stage.

He stood for a moment, wanting to take it all in, but Hank quickly steered them to the right, the side closest to the ocean. There were four large seating sections, two on each side of the main aisle.

"The two center sections are full," Hank said. "But I see half a row open over here, halfway back."

"Look, people are dancing," Barb said. The wall surrounding the Bandshell was waist-high. On the other side, a wide concrete walkway ran for several blocks parallel with the beach. It had now become a dance floor. "C'mon, Joe," she said.

"You're on." They ran through an opening in the wall, found an open space, and started swing dancing.

Claire looked at Ben with pleading eyes. She wanted him to ask. What he said in reply felt like physical pain. "I want to dance with you so bad, but I can't swing dance."

"That's okay," she said.

"Well, I can," said Hank. "C'mon."

She looked back at Ben.

"I'll be okay," he said. "You two have fun."

Hank led Claire by the hand to a spot a few yards beyond Barb and Joe. The music played on. They danced. Ben watched, cringing inside as he leaned on the wall. They swirled around each other, holding hands, spinning in short circles. Their heads, arms, and legs in constant motion, perfectly in sync with every drumbeat and trumpet blast.

Ben could feel himself dancing inside. The music was made for it. It was absolutely a perfect song. He was a gifted athlete and had excellent coordination, but his saboteur training didn't allow such frivolity. Dancing was considered morally corrupt. Such hypocrisy.

He looked at Hank's face, which was on fire with joy. Of course it was. He was dancing with Claire. The saddest thing of all was that Hank was a good dancer. Great even. Ben looked around. Hank may be the best dancer out there. *How is that right?* Ben thought. *On any level?*

Finally, the song ended, ending also Ben's torture.

Everyone dancing and the thousands in the seating area clapped and cheered. Ben looked toward the stage as the bandleader bowed. He turned to face the band, tapped his wand a few times, and then . . .

"Chattanooga Choo Choo" began to play.

"C'mon, Claire," Hank yelled.

The torture continued.

Chapter Seven

The band ended the concert playing slow dance tunes. Barb and Joe stayed out on the makeshift dance area, on the other side of the coquina wall. Claire told Hank she needed a rest, which was true. But she knew he had feelings for her, and she had no intention of encouraging that by slow dancing with him. He seemed to take it okay.

It was so relaxing to be able to just sit there and listen to the music, the gentle ocean breeze cooling her down. But she found herself a little on edge, sitting next to Ben, and she didn't know why.

After the third slow song, the bandleader turned and faced the crowd. "Thank you, ladies and gentlemen. You've been such a wonderful audience. We'd like to especially thank all you young ladies here with the Woman's Auxiliary Corps, for your dedication and service to your country. Hopefully this will be the first of many more concerts for me and the band, here on this lovely stage right at the edge of the sea. I've selected for our last number another beautiful Glenn Miller song to honor our good friend the moon. About two hours from now, if you look to your right over the ocean, you'll see him rising up full and round from the horizon."

The band began to play "Moonlight Serenade." The soothing sound of muted trumpets and trombones, saxophones and clarinets filled the air.

Ben leaned close and whispered, "If you're too tired, I understand. But I think I could manage to dance this one without hurting you too badly."

She instantly nodded yes. He stood up and took her hand. She looked into his smiling face and dark brown eyes as she rose and followed. He led her to an open space and gently swung her into place. A few moments later, it was all she could do not to lay her head on his shoulder.

What am I doing?

"You dance very well," he said softly. "Not just now, but with Hank. The two of you stole the show."

"I never knew he could dance like that," she said, glad for the conversation. "He doesn't seem like someone who—"

"I know exactly what you mean," he said. "I'd give anything to be able to dance half as well."

"You're doing just fine," she said.

He squeezed her hand as he swung her gently in a half-turn. "Thank you. I did learn to slow dance a little."

"Who taught you?"

"My mom, before . . . well, several years ago."

"Where is she now?"

"She's . . . both of my parents died earlier this year."

The words stunned her—they were not at all what she expected to hear. "I'm . . . so sorry."

"Me too," he said. She thought she saw tears form in his eyes. He looked away. "I'll tell you about it sometime, but not now. I just want to enjoy this moment."

She followed his lead as he backed two steps into an open spot and turned her the other way. When he looked into her eyes, his smile had returned, and the tears were gone. He looked as if he wanted to say something but held back. Something deep inside her stirred; she wished she could comfort him.

They danced in silence a few moments. But he kept looking at her, and she didn't look away. She didn't want to. He seemed to be saying things with his eyes they both knew should not be said.

But she wanted to hear them. She looked beyond him. *It's just the music,* she thought. And the ocean, and the breeze. She looked back into his eyes as the song ended.

If only she knew what he was thinking.

Ben could hardly believe how things had turned out. Barb and Joe had plans to go out for dinner after the concert. Hank had to leave also. His aunt and uncle were driving up from Miami and his folks insisted he be there for dinner.

Ben was actually alone with Claire. And she seemed in no hurry to leave.

Most of the crowd had left the Bandshell. He and Claire followed many of them down the wide concrete walkway toward the amusement park. Claire gently corrected him when he'd referred to it as the boardwalk. Locals called it the "broad-walk," she said, since it was rather broad and made of concrete instead of wood.

They stopped for a moment to let the crowd thin out, leaned against the railing, and looked out over the ocean. Behind them, the sun was already setting. A string of pelicans flew by over the ocean. Ben watched amazed as they dove down, one by one, skimming one wing just inches above a wave. Just before it broke, the first bird tilted the other wing slightly and instantly rose back into the sky. At the same point, each of the other pelicans did the same maneuver, following right behind him. "Who teaches them to do that?" he said.

"I don't know," Claire said. "God, I guess. Looks like it would be so much fun."

"That has to be why they do it," he said. "Don't you think? I mean, it doesn't seem like something they have to do." Right then, it dawned on him; he couldn't remember the last time he did anything just for the fun of it. He looked at another odd sight on the beach, this one man-made. "I still can't get used to the cars, people driving on the beach. I've never seen a beach like this. It goes out so far, and it's so flat."

"It's really just like this at low tide," she said. "But low tide can last for hours here. And you're right, I think this is one of the few beaches in the world like this. They actually race cars here."

"On the beach?"

She pointed south. "Down by the inlet. They created a track there a few years ago. You know where the lighthouse is?"

Ben nodded.

"It's right around there. I don't think they're

racing this year because of the war, but I've watched a few of them with my dad a few years ago."

"You mean drag racing?"

"No, stock car races. Maybe thirty or forty cars at a time. They block off traffic and use the beach for one side of the track and Atlantic Avenue for the other. My dad said the straight part is two miles long, so they're really moving by the time they reach the turn. And it's so loud."

"I'd love to see that."

"Maybe next year you can, soon as this war is over. It's really exciting."

Ben didn't want to say this, but he didn't see the war ending by next year. The Nazis had far too many men, tanks, and planes. He wouldn't be surprised if it went on for years. "Maybe I could go with you and your father when they start racing again."

She smiled. "Maybe."

Ben turned and faced the Ferris wheel. *If pelicans can have fun,* he thought. "Ever been on that?"

"A few times," she said. "The view at the top is amazing."

"Want to go on it now? I'd like to see that view." What was he saying? It was too soon.

She looked at the clock tower. "I guess we have time to ride it once, then I probably need to head home for dinner."

"What time do you need to be home?"

"Five-thirty."

Before the others had left, Ben had agreed to drive Claire home. He was shocked she'd said yes. "My car's parked at my apartment on Grandview. It's only a few blocks from here. I promise I'll have you there by then."

"Then let's do it."

They walked past the clock tower. The Ferris wheel was just up ahead. He wanted so badly to reach out and take her hand.

"Mind if I ask you something?" she said.

"No."

"When we were dancing, you said your parents had died . . ."

"And you want to know how?"

She shook her head, seeming embarrassed for asking. "You don't have to talk about it if it's too painful."

It was extremely painful, but he wanted to tell her. At least as much as he could. "It happened six months ago."

"Six months. Oh, Ben, I'm so sorry."

"It was quite a shock. I still can't believe they're gone."

"Honestly, Ben, you don't need to tell me any more. I had no idea it was so recent."

"It's okay. I probably can't share too many details but . . . I want you to know." They walked past a shooting gallery. Ben smiled as he read a handwritten sign tacked above the original: "Practice Defending Your Country—Right Here!"

"Whatta you say, young fella?" the carnival worker yelled.

Ben looked at the man. Popping and pinging noises rang in his ears from four other customers firing away at an array of moving bunnies, swinging stars, and ducks rotating around a metal ring.

"Yeah, you. Whatta you say, young man? Only cost you twenty-five cents. Shoot down five in a row and win this nice big bear here for your best girl."

"We're kind of in a hurry," Ben said. "And she's not—"

"C'mon, twenty-five cents. I'll bet you can't even shoot four in a row. I'll let you have this bear if you can shoot down four targets."

Ben looked at the others he'd sucked in to the game. They were all shooting rifles. He noticed on the table in front of them two pistols. "How many do you have to hit if you use the pistol?"

"Pistols? A lot harder to hit moving targets with a pistol. I'll give up my bear for three in a row. Just three in a row."

Ben looked at Claire, tried to read if she was sending him any signals. She just smiled back at him. "How many shots do I get?"

"It's a six-shooter."

"Claire, would you like that bear?"

"Ben, you don't have to do this."

"Would you like it?"

She laughed. "What girl wouldn't?"

She was being sarcastic. "See anything else up there you like?"

"What?"

"Pick a second prize." Ben glanced at the man. He had a confused look.

"Okay," she said, "that tiger looks pretty cute."

Ben faced the carnival man. "Make you a deal, sir. If I get all six targets in a row, you give Claire here the bear and the tiger. Anything less than six, I get nothing."

The man smiled. "A wheeler-dealer, eh? You're on, son. Hand me a quarter and step right up." The man looked at Claire. "Young lady, you might want to turn away. I guarantee this won't be pretty."

"I'll take my chances," she said.

Ben walked over to the table. The other four shooters must have heard Ben's challenge. They all stopped to watch. He picked up the pistol, eyed the targets, lifted the pistol, and fired six shots in a row, not a second between each shot.

Down went two bunnies, two stars, and two ducks. Just like that.

The man's eyes bugged out. He looked from the targets to Ben. "Would you look at that," he said.

Ben walked over, picked up the tiger and the bear, and handed them to Claire. "Have a nice day, sir," he said. As they walked away he looked at his watch. "It's up to you, Claire, but I think I can have you on that Ferris wheel and still back home in time for dinner."

She looked up at him. "Yes, I believe you can."

Chapter Eight

"Are they our chaperones up here?" Ben looked down at the stuffed bear and tiger sitting between them. They weren't moving at the moment; the Ferris wheel was stuck at the top of the circle.

"I guess they are," Claire said. "Don't you love the view? Makes me wish he would leave us up here our whole turn."

"I'd like that." They were facing south. Ben could see his apartment on Grandview Avenue. And all the way down to the lighthouse and the inlet. To the west, a very nice sunset was unfolding. He looked to the east, past the Main Street pier, out to the edge of the ocean.

"See those little lights out there?" she said. "Those are shrimp boats."

Ben knew this already. He tried to shut down a memory floating into his mind. An image of a shrimp boat through the U-boat periscope. So close, he could see the crew walking on the deck. The U-boat captain had invited him to take a peek. Then he said, "We wouldn't even need a torpedo for that one. Just the deck gun, pow-pow-pow, and down he'd go. But tonight, we spare them. We are hunting bigger game than shrimp boats."

"What are you thinking?"

"What?"

"You're staring off into space again."

Ben refocused on her eyes, then her lips. A much better image. "Uh, just thinking about what it must be like to be on one of those shrimp boats these days." Not a total lie.

"You mean because of the war?" she said. Ben nodded. "I've heard they're actually supposed to keep an eye out for German U-boats too." She turned to look back out over the ocean. "I wonder if there are any out there right now?"

"I doubt it. At least I hope not." He knew the one that had dropped him off wasn't anyway. Their next mission was somewhere in the Gulf of Mexico. "Hold on." The ride started again, pitching them forward a little.

"Ben—about that question I asked before the shooting gallery—"

He'd wondered if that would resurface again. "You mean about my parents?"

"I don't mind if you want to drop it. I just want to get to know you better. I mean, if we're going to be friends."

"A friend should know something as important as that," he said. He didn't mind that she used the word "friends." They were friends, and he honestly felt she had added that last part just to be polite. She was starting to feel something more than friendship for him. He was almost certain. The Ferris wheel swung them down at the bottom of the circuit, then lifted them up again. "I wonder how many more times we'll get to go around."

"Three or four more," she said.

Good, he would make this short. "Well, they were killed in a bombing raid."

She gasped. "Really? Where?"

He couldn't tell her where. It happened in Cologne, a large German city on the banks of the Rhine River. "We'd made a trip to Europe, to reconnect with some family."

"Oh, in London? I've watched the newsreels. It's so terrible what's happening there, all the fires, and the people being dug out of the rubble —I'm sorry, I shouldn't have said that."

"No, it's all right. I wasn't with them when it happened, thankfully. And I was told it happened quickly, that they didn't appear to have suffered." He wondered, was it a lie to let her think it was London? It couldn't be helped. And it was true; he wasn't with them when they died. He was in training for his mission.

She patted his forearm. "Do you have any other siblings? I have a brother, Jack. He's somewhere in England. He's a waist gunner on a B-17." She left her hand on his forearm.

"No, it's just me. We used to live in Pennsylvania, but I didn't want to go back there . . . after. I came into some money and decided to come here. I've never been to Florida before. Just needed a fresh start." That was a safe way to describe what happened, he thought.

"I'm so sorry. You must miss them terribly. Were you and your parents close?"

"We weren't as close as I'd have liked," he said. So very true. "But I definitely loved them. I'd hoped one day we would all come back here and start our relationship over." He was suddenly overrun with emotion. "That's what I wanted." Tears began welling up in his eyes. He had to stop talking.

"I'm sorry, Ben." She reached down and grabbed the bear's paw and held it up. "I don't have any tissues," she said, smiling.

Ben wiped his eyes with the bear's paw. It was silly but oddly comforting. As he did, the Ferris wheel stopped. They were at the nine o'clock spot, just a few seats away from the bottom.

"Let's don't talk about this anymore," she said.

"I think that's a good idea."

When their seat rolled into the last spot, the attendant unlatched the rail and they got off. Ben handed her the stuffed animals. She looked back at the clock tower. "We better get going."

"You're right. Follow me." He almost reached for her hand. They began walking south along the walkway, out of the amusement area. "It's only a few blocks. I'm actually looking for another place to live."

"Somewhere here?"

"Yes, definitely. Maybe one of those cottages near the ocean or a small house nearby. I just want more privacy. It's not a bad place, where I'm staying now. Just kind of noisy."

"It might be hard." She leaned over and said quietly, "With all these WACS in town." A group of four girls in uniform had just passed by.

"Yeah, I know. Every hotel is filling up. They're talking about building little tent cities at a few places in town."

"My mother said they've taken over the hospital . . . Hey, speaking of my mom, what are you doing for dinner tonight?"

"What?"

"Instead of dropping me off, do you want to stay for dinner?"

"I can't do that."

"Of course you can. I'm inviting you."

"I don't want your mom's first impression of me to be a guy who just shows up unannounced for dinner."

She stopped walking. "Ben, she's not like that. Nor is my dad."

"Your dad will be there?"

"My dad's always there for dinner. But relax . . ." They started walking again. "You'll like him. He's very nice and very easy to talk to. When we get to my house, you just stay in the driveway for a minute, let me go in and tell them."

"What if they say no?"

"They won't. I'm telling you, my mother loves company. I'm sure she'll want to meet you. She's already seen you. I don't know when." They turned left at the corner, onto Atlantic Avenue. She laughed. "She thinks you look like Gary Cooper."

"Gary Cooper?" Ben smiled but inwardly felt a moment of panic. He'd heard that name in his training. He was a famous singer, or maybe a movie star. He couldn't remember. "What do you think?"

"I see some resemblance. But he's an old guy, at least forty." As they walked, she put her arm around his. More the polite, courteous version than something romantic.

But he loved it, and he imagined one day they'd walk together in the romantic version. He tried to think thoughts like that, instead of the fearful thought of meeting her parents in the next twenty minutes over dinner.

All the questions they'd ask.

And all the new lies he'd have to tell.

Chapter Nine

Ben sat in the driveway, thrumming his fingers on the dashboard, waiting for Claire to stick her head through the front door. Hopefully, to signal it was okay to come in. Darkness had nearly pushed the sunset from the sky. But with the light that remained, Ben could easily tell the house was magnificent. Most of the houses on this part of Ridgewood Avenue were like mansions.

Ben had seen homes this size in Germany, many of them confiscated from wealthy Jews, then turned into headquarters for high-ranking Nazi officers or used for special training missions. Like the estate house his team had been assigned near Brandenburg, out in the Prussian countryside. He remembered something his Abwehr commander had said as they sipped cognac in the living room: "Can you imagine . . . a *Jew* owning something like this? It's almost obscene, an absolute waste!"

Claire's house might actually be bigger than that one. It had two stories, a third if you included the attic. It was surrounded by ancient live oaks with moss hanging down from every limb. A wide porch wrapped across the front and down the right side. At the end of the driveway stood a garage larger than most of the homes on the beachside that Ben had been looking at to rent.

Whatever Claire's father did, he did it well.

Ben thought about what he'd seen these past two months in terms of the American economy. He'd only spent time in the Daytona Beach area so far. Things could be much worse in other parts of the country. But he hadn't observed much in the way of suffering or privation. Nothing close to the propaganda he'd heard about back in Germany. War posters were everywhere, challenging everyone to conserve and do their part. The new gasoline and food rationing policies were well under way.

But from what he'd seen and heard on the radio, Americans had much more than the mere necessities of life. Much more than German civilians, now at war for three years. Even the gasoline rationing had nothing to do with a shortage of oil. There was plenty of gas in America for ships, planes, tanks, and automobiles. But since the attack on Pearl Harbor, rubber was suddenly in short supply. America had imported 90 percent of it from what were now Japanese-held countries. The gas rationing was mostly about keeping all those rubber tires off the road.

People were certainly making sacrifices in their food choices. Pretty much everything was regulated. But no one seemed to mind. Everywhere he looked he saw Americans pulling together, cooperating eagerly, full of patriotic zeal. He'd felt it too. He loved this country, loved everything about it.

America had its own propaganda machinery in motion, but it was different here. And he knew what the difference was. Americans were being told to believe in things people should believe in. True things. In Germany, it was all lies. The German people were forced to follow, forced to comply, forced even to wear the smiles on their faces as they looked the other way. Forbidden to say what they thought, to challenge anything they didn't agree with. Forbidden to even ask questions.

His parents had been lured into a trap. He'd been dragged along with them. And for this, they had paid the ultimate price.

Heil Hitler.

He would never have to say those two words again.

Tap-tap-tap. "Ben?"

He looked up, startled. Claire was right there outside his car window.

"Didn't you see me? I was waving at you on the porch."

"I'm sorry."

"Daydreaming again?"

He opened the car door. "I'm sorry. So what did your mother say?"

"She said, 'Bring him in, I'd love to meet him. Dinner's in ten minutes.' "

Claire started walking toward the house. Ben quickly caught up. He ducked suddenly at a loud noise overhead. He recognized the sound: radial-engine airplanes. On the U-boat, if you heard that, it was panic time. Everyone would scramble to get below. Bells would go off. Men would yell, "Alarm, alarm, alarm."

Claire turned around. "It's okay, Ben."

He was embarrassed. "They're so loud," he said, trying to recover quickly. He looked up as four Dauntless dive-bombers flew past in formation, heading west.

"They're probably heading to the Naval Air Base in Deland. My dad's company just got a big contract there. He said we'll be hearing a lot more of those planes from now on. Maybe he'll tell you about it over dinner. At least, what he can. Are you hungry?"

"Starving." He really was. He hadn't eaten a home-cooked meal since . . . he couldn't even remember when.

"Very nice to meet you, Ben." They stood in a large foyer, just in front of the stairs. Claire's mother took off a cooking mitt and reached out her hand. She wore a whitish apron over a floral dress.

"Great to meet you, Mrs. Richards."

"Dinner's almost ready," she said. "Maybe five more minutes. Would you like to take a seat in the dining room or wait in the living room?"

"Either one," Ben said.

"Well, here," Claire said. She took his arm gently and led him to the dining room. "You sit here, Ben. Like some iced tea? Mom, do we have any left?"

"We do."

"I'll get it," Claire said. "You sit tight." She followed her mother into the kitchen.

"So-o-o-o," her mother whispered. "What's this we have here? Bringing Gary Cooper home to dinner?"

"Shhh," Claire said. "He'll hear you."

"No he won't."

Claire opened the icebox and pulled out the glass pitcher of tea. "It's really nothing. When the concert ended, the gang had to leave early and Ben offered to take me home."

"I see." Her mother smiled as she shoveled mashed potatoes from a pot to a serving dish. "So he has a car."

"Listen, Mom, we just have a minute here." Claire walked closer. "I need to tell you something. I'll tell you more after he leaves, but I found out something you and Dad need to know about Ben." Her mother's expression changed, reflecting the concern in Claire's tone of voice. "Ben's parents were both killed in a bombing raid in London just a few months ago."

Her mother gasped. "How terrible." She looked

toward the dining room but couldn't see Ben from this angle.

"I just . . . well, I just wanted you to know, so you won't be asking too many probing questions. It's still very upsetting for him to talk about."

"Well, of course, it would be."

"I'm going to run upstairs and tell Dad."

"That's fine, dear." She sighed, then looked again toward the dining room. "The poor thing."

Claire hurried back to the table with Ben's iced tea. "You sip on that, Ben. I'm going to run upstairs and see what's keeping my father."

"Thanks." He took the tea from her hand. "I'm fine here."

As Claire made it to the top of the steps, she saw her dad coming out of the bedroom. She motioned for him to back up into the hallway.

"What's going on?" he whispered.

"Nothing, I just need to tell you something about Ben. I already told Mother."

"Ben? So have you and Jim . . . are you and Ben . . ."

"Ben is just a friend. Now, shush, you need to hear this and we just have a second." She told him about Ben's parents.

"That's so sad," he said. "You read about these things, but—"

"Well, I'm telling you so you and Mother don't ask too many questions. He told me this at the amusement park. When he did, he—"

"You went to the amusement park with him?"

"Oh no." She just realized. "I left my stuffed bear and tiger in his car."

"He got you stuffed animals? At the amusement park?"

"Dad, would you stop? It was nothing. We were just walking past the shooting gallery and—"

"Must be a good shot."

"He is, now will you listen? Ben and I are just friends. I invited him home to dinner, because he's all alone. And I felt bad for him when I found out about his parents. I knew if I didn't tell you, you'd ask him all kinds of father questions." Claire turned toward the stairs.

"I'll behave," he said. "But I don't know what I'll say to him now. Asking questions is my job." He followed her.

She stopped at the first step and spun around. "You can still do your job. Just don't ask questions about his family. You'll be fine."

Chapter Ten

Claire sat on a bench seat in front of her mirror and vanity, brushing her hair. It wasn't that late, but she was tired. She'd already put on her nightgown and turned down the bed. On the nightstand was the latest Hercule Poirot mystery by Agatha Christie, *Murder in Retrospect*.

Claire loved a good mystery. But in books, not in her life.

She glanced down to her left at the box of stationery she'd bought at Woolworth's right after Jim had shipped overseas. She'd picked it out especially for him. It had a nice pastel beach scene with a palm tree in the top right corner, to help him feel closer to home. She'd written him so often, the box was already half gone. But she decided she wasn't writing him another letter until she received one back from him.

She glanced to her right, at the last letter she'd received, over two weeks ago. Setting the brush down, she picked it up. "Why won't you write me?"

"What, dear?" Claire's mother opened her door and poked her head inside. "Did you say something?"

Claire put the letter down and started brushing her hair again. "Just thinking out loud."

Her mother stepped a little farther into the room. "I think your father really liked Ben."

"Oh?" She pretended mild interest.

"Said some nice things about him after he left."

"Really? Like what?" Claire turned to face her.

"I don't know, just things like how well he listened, how articulate he was. He even talked about his sense of humor, that it was a good thing to see, in light of all he's been through recently."

"He really is easy to be with," Claire said. So much more she wanted to say.

Her mother stepped closer, noticed Jim Burton's letter on the vanity. "Are you starting to have second thoughts about Jim?"

Claire set the brush down hard. "Oh, Mother. I don't know." She wished she could will all this tension away. "Why won't he write me more often?" She reached for his letter. "When I got this two weeks ago, I was so excited. I read it a half dozen times that day. Then I started reading it before bed every night, holding it like it was some kind of treasure."

"But now you've met Ben. A piece of paper hardly compares to a real person."

"It's not just that, Mother. It's what you said this morning on the porch. I was just making excuses for Jim, about why he doesn't write more. I really believe he could if he wanted to, like Jack does with you and Brenda."

"I wasn't trying to upset you, Claire. You know that."

"I do, but . . . why doesn't he *want* to write me more? I don't understand. If you say you love someone—"

"Has Jim said that? Have you two said you loved each other?"

Claire thought a minute. "Not exactly. We kind of talked around it. But at the train station, he kissed me like someone in love. And when he does write, he says 'Love, Jim' at the end of his letters."

"Does he say anything romantic in the letters themselves? How much he misses you, how he can't stop thinking about you? How he wished he could hold you in his arms—"

"Mother!"

"What? Those are the kinds of things a man can't help saying when he's in love. Your father talked like that with me. He still does, whenever he goes on a long business trip."

Claire sighed heavily and set the letter down. Jim's letters never mentioned things like that. Tears began to form. Her mother bent down and hugged her. "I'm sorry. I hate to see you sad. But you know we just want what's best for you. I don't want to see you get hurt."

"Is it possible Jim's just not the romantic type?"

"It's possible, I suppose." She stood back up. "He's crazy about you, you know. Ben, I mean."

"No, he's not. We're just . . . friends."

"Claire . . . you can't see the way he looks at you? Even your father noticed it. A few minutes ago he said, 'Does Claire realize how Ben feels about her?' "

"Really?"

"I think he may already be in love with you. If you're not interested in him that way, you better be careful. After what he's suffered with his parents dying, you don't want to hurt him any more."

"No, I don't." *Ben is in love with me?* The thought stirred instant excitement inside her, followed by a sense of dread. "Did it look like I was leading him on tonight? Did I seem flirty to you?"

"No, you were just being your fun, sweet self. But when a young man's in love, he doesn't need much encouragement. I'm just saying be careful."

Claire turned to face the mirror again and talked to her mother through the reflection. "I'm so confused."

"Dear, that's common at this stage of life," her mother said. "So you do have feelings for Ben? I thought so."

"No, I . . . I don't know. I'm not allowed to have feelings for Ben. I told Jim I'd wait for him. I don't want to be one of those girls—I read about them all the time in my magazines—they get lonely and impatient and fall for the first guy who shows them a little interest. Meanwhile, the guy they promised to wait for is overseas in all kinds of danger, and the only hope he has is the girl waiting for him back home. I can't do that to Jim."

"Then . . . you better be careful when you're around Ben."

It was a pleasant experience overall.

But it had left Ben exhausted. Such a range of

conflicting emotions, the tension of keeping them all in check: love for Claire, passion even, a desire to impress, fear of saying the wrong thing, fear of saying too much, fear of being asked the wrong thing.

He sat on the bed, his stomach full, for once, with good food. Roast beef, mashed potatoes, corn, fresh bread. Then Mrs. Richards brought out homemade apple pie. Ben lay back on the bed, looked up at the ceiling. Apple pie, with cinnamon.

This was the life he wanted.

To live in America, where he was born. And stay there. Meet a nice girl from a nice family. Go out on dates, fall in love. Get to know the girl's nice family, let them get to know you. The real you. A few months later, have that big nervous talk with the father, ask his permission to marry his little girl. Get down on one knee, pull out a shiny ring.

That was the life he'd wanted. But he didn't get that chance. It had been stolen.

Dad, why didn't you listen to me? You never listened.

Ben kicked his shoes to the floor. How could he possibly live a normal life from this point? Mr. and Mrs. Richards probably had a fond impression of him right now. Why wouldn't they? They'd seen a nice young man at their dinner table. Polite and respectful. He smiled a lot, took an interest in their lives, answered their questions. Some of his answers were even true.

No, most of them were. But that was only because they were clearly being careful, not asking the kind of questions he'd expected to hear. Claire must have coached them, told them about his parents dying recently. But that was okay. It showed she cared for him.

She cared for him.

That thought made him smile. It was true, she did. He thought of the scene at the clock when she'd almost taken his hand. Then the dance. How she stayed after the gang left, just to be with him. The way she looked at him on the Ferris wheel, the tenderness in her touch when he'd talked about his parents. She didn't love Jim Burton. Whatever she felt, it wasn't love. But Ben knew she wasn't free to express whatever feelings she had for him. Not now. She'd given her word to wait for Burton.

He had no idea how this could work, how they could ever be together. But he knew she cared for him. And that mattered.

Tonight, it mattered a lot.

He released a deep exhale then shifted in the bed, sliding up to rest his head on the pillow. He was too tired to even change out of his clothes. He reached up with one arm and turned off the lamp, laid back and closed his eyes.

Maybe he was too tired to think. He hoped so.

Lately, reading was the only way he'd found to shut his mind down before bed. The only thing that kept him from reliving that night on the beach.

Tonight, he was too tired to read.

Chapter Eleven

"Can you believe it? It's really happening. Tonight's the night."

Ben looked over at Jurgen holding on to the rail. He nodded, feigning the same enthusiasm. The first team of saboteurs was already in their rubber raft but hadn't pulled away. Sailors from the U-boat tried to steady themselves in the rough surf as they loaded the raft with crates and suitcases full of money, clothes, and explosives.

"Jurgen, keep your voice down," one of the men said. "Could be patrols on the beach."

"Stop calling him Jurgen," the other man said. "English names only from now on."

"Right, sorry." He looked at Jurgen. "George, shut up."

Ben looked toward the darkened beach. He could barely make out the line of sand dunes onshore. The captain had picked a moonless night and a location that was supposed to be miles away from the closest town. The temperature was warm but pleasant, as expected for an August night in Florida. A slight wind occasionally whipped salt spray into his face, but the water was surprisingly mild.

The plan was for U-boat sailors to row the two teams on separate rafts, drop them and their gear off on the beach, then row back. Quickly and quietly. As a precaution, the saboteurs dressed in Kriegsmarine fatigues, compliments of the German navy. Once on land, they'd change into street clothes and give their uniforms back to the sailors.

Earlier, Jurgen had asked the captain what difference it made if they wore the uniforms now, for such a short time. The captain had said, "If you're caught in the rafts in uniforms, you'll be treated as POWs. If you're caught in street clothes, you'll be shot as spies. But not just you, my men also. Once you're on land, you're on your own. My job is over."

"George, Ben, your turn," the captain said now from the conning tower. "Get in the raft."

Two sailors were already sitting in the front section. Ben nodded at Jurgen, letting him go first. The raft bobbed up and down. It was like trying to sit on a bucking horse. "Be careful, it's easier if you stay low," one of the sailors said.

Jurgen fell but caught one of the ropes to steady himself. He sat then looked up at Ben. "Okay, your turn."

Ben's insides were churning, more from fear

than the seas. He was finally here, in America, where he'd wanted to be since he was sixteen. Soon he'd be free of his Nazi shackles. But he knew, to really be free, before this night was over, he'd have to kill the man sitting in front of him. Jurgen was completely committed to the mission; there'd be no chance of talking him out of it once they were onshore.

In the last few months, Ben had learned a dozen effective ways to kill a man. But he'd never actually done it. He was terrified that he didn't have what it took to follow through. But there was no turning back. Jurgen's singular ambition was to kill as many Americans as he could in the coming months.

He had to die.

Ben made it onto the raft with surprisingly little trouble. A German sailor came in behind him. Together, they began receiving their load of crates and suitcases, all wrapped in watertight bags. Ben looked back. The first team had just pulled away and began rowing toward shore. Jurgen waved at the two men, gave them a "Heil Hitler" salute. One of them returned it. Ben was relieved he wouldn't have to deal with the Nazis ever again, from this moment on. Both teams had their own assignments, and once onshore, they were to split up and go their separate ways.

"Okay, men," the captain said, standing on the deck. "Time to shove off. Oberfähnrich, Schultz?"

"Yes, Captain." It was the German ensign at the front of their raft.

"Remember your training. The waves near the shore are rougher here than when we practiced, but do everything you've been told and you should be fine."

"Yes, sir, Captain. I'll have the men on the beach in no time."

"Get back quickly. I want to head out to sea in fifteen minutes. Remind the men in the other raft."

"I will, Captain."

"Good luck."

Off they went into the blackness before them, the sailors rowing in a furious rhythm. Jurgen and Ben sat in the middle, holding tightly to the guide ropes. Ben could hear the roar of the waves crashing up ahead.

The bobbing effect grew steadily worse the closer they got to shore. Now it felt like they were riding an angry horse. One wave tossed a suitcase high in the air. Ben grabbed it just before it went overboard. The only consolation for the fear of the surging waves was that it blocked the fear of what he must do to Jurgen once they landed.

"Okay, men," the ensign said. "Any minute now, a wave will catch us and we'll ride it into shore. Remember your training."

The sound of the waves now was deafening.

The seas were much rougher than what Ben had expected. He was terrified.

"I don't like this," Jurgen said.

The next moment, the raft pitched upward. "Hold on, men!" the ensign yelled. "This is the one."

The wave rolled them high in the air, too high it seemed. Ben remembered, they were supposed to lean back, shift their weight to the rear, but he—

"I can't hold on," the sailor behind Ben yelled. He went flying forward out of the raft.

Ben fell forward into Jurgen. A suitcase flew up and hit Jurgen in the head, then dropped and hit Ben in the back. He moaned and shoved it into the water. The raft shot up once more, nearly vertical, then went end over end, tossing all of them into the ocean. Ben heard men yelling, then he went under. He opened his eyes underwater, but it was pitch black. Jurgen banged into him once. He grabbed hold of Ben's arm, but the churning water pulled them apart. Ben fought to come up for air, but he couldn't surface. The swirling water shoved him farther down. He was almost out of breath.

He felt sand beneath his palms. The ocean floor. He spun around so that his feet touched bottom then pushed up with all his might. He finally broke through and sucked in his first breath of air.

Bam! Another wave hit him from behind, took him under again. And again, the turbulent water paralyzed him, keeping him from getting to the surface. He was going to drown. He remembered what just happened and deliberately swam downward till he felt the bottom again. He pushed himself up through the water and was able to catch another breath. This time, when he tried to tread water, his feet scraped the sandy bottom.

He turned to see another wave coming right at him. He dove under it and missed the full impact. The water shoved him around, but he found he had more control. He pushed off the bottom again and this time was actually able to stand, the waterline just above his shoulders. He looked around a moment but saw no one. He spent the next few minutes half-walking, half-swimming toward the shore. When he got to ankle-deep water, he collapsed from exhaustion.

He'd never been so frightened in his life.

A few minutes later, someone lifted him by the arms. "Ben, are you all right?" It was the ensign.

"Yes." The ensign and another sailor helped him to his feet. He was soaked from head to toe.

"We need your help," the ensign said. "My other man is holding the raft. But we need to gather up the crates and suitcases. They're floating in the water."

"Where's Jurgen?" Ben said. "I mean, George."

"I don't know. We need to find him. Can you walk?"

"Yes, I'm all right now."

"Then the two of you start gathering the packages. We must account for them all. You know our orders, we must leave no trace that we've ever been on this beach. I'll keep looking for your partner."

Ben nodded. He and the other sailor walked along the shoreline. Their eyes had adjusted enough to see dark shapes floating in the shallow water. Soon, they had all of the packages in a pile next to a large sand dune. Both men sat, trying to catch their breath.

A moment later, the ensign walked up and stood in front of them.

"Where's George?" Ben asked.

"He must have drowned in the surf. But we cannot wait any longer. If we're not back in five minutes, the boat will leave without us. Change into your street clothes. We need to take your uniform back with us."

"But what about George? What should I do?" Ben got up, found the suitcase with his street clothes, and started removing his wet uniform.

"I'm not your superior. But if I were you, I'd wait here until his body washes up on the beach. The current is heading straight in, so he shouldn't come in too far away."

"Right," Ben said, trying to sound more confident.

"You better hope he washes up before sunrise," the ensign said as Ben handed him the wet uniform. "And when you bury him, make sure you take off his uniform. Bury him in street clothes. Okay, men, let's get back." He looked at Ben. "Good luck."

Ben sat back on one of the crates and watched the three sailors push the raft back into the water. He didn't envy their return voyage. After his strength returned, he got up, now with a mission radically changed from the one he'd been assigned. Just two things on the list: find Jurgen's body and bury it deep in the dunes.

For the next several hours, he walked back and forth, looking, but with no luck. Just as the sky in the east began to offer the first signs of light, he saw a large misshapen lump far down the beach, rolling in shallow water. He ran all the way there.

It was definitely a body, in a German uniform, lying face down in the water. Slowly, he bent down and turned the body over. Staring back at him was the lifeless face of his partner Jurgen, staring at nothing.

It startled him. He looked away.

He turned back and looked at Jurgen's face once more. Suddenly, Jurgen's lifeless eyes blinked. Once, then twice.

Ben gasped and jumped back.

The next moment he sat straight up in his bed. He was back in his apartment on Grandview Avenue, his body drenched in sweat.

Chapter Twelve

Claire was glad it was Monday, and that she was at work. After church yesterday, she didn't have near enough to do to occupy her mind, which gave her too much time to think. She tried to pay attention to the pastor's sermon, at times even tried to apply what he said to her situation. But it just didn't seem to fit, or else she wasn't seeing things clearly.

He talked about trusting God in times of uncertainty, and gave a number of biblical examples of people who experienced times even worse than what America was facing right now. She guessed knowing that was supposed to help somehow, and he might even have said other things that would have helped her understand the connection. But her thoughts kept leaving the pew.

Ben loved her. That's what her mother had said. She could tell he liked her, but . . . *loved* her? She kept reliving moments with him, at the diner on Friday with the gang, at the concert Saturday, after the concert at the amusement park, at her house for dinner after that. The way he looked at her and talked to her when she walked him out to the car. She loved how it made her feel, but was that love? He'd been coming around for over a month, but something this weekend seemed to have changed between them. But . . . was it love?

While she sat in the pew, more tormenting thoughts had followed, about her commitment to Jim, to wait for him and write him often. Which she had. But his infrequent responses and, now, the things his letters *didn't* say really bothered her. What did she feel for Jim? What had she felt before he left that made her so quickly promise to wait for him? Was that love? If it was, what did she feel for him now? Did her feelings—should her feelings—even matter? She had made a commitment. What kind of person would she be if she abandoned that so easily?

She recalled that her mind reentered her body, sitting in that pew, just in time to hear the pastor say, "And that's why we must put our trust fully in God and not lean on our own understanding!" Everyone around her had said "Amen," so she did too. The pastor then asked everyone to bow their heads and pray. So she did. But it didn't seem to take. She sure hadn't spent the rest of her Sunday trusting God. The same troubling thoughts kept running through her mind all day.

"Miss Richards."

Claire looked around. She was standing in one of the front windows at Woolworth's, holding a poster rolled up like a tube.

"Miss Richards. I really need those rationing posters put up this morning. That's why I asked you to come in a half hour early."

She had just left Woolworth's the same way she'd left the pew yesterday at church. "I'm so sorry, Mr. Morris. Guess I started daydreaming." She stepped carefully around a display of kitchen utensils and serving dishes toward the glass window. "It won't happen again."

"When you're finished putting those up, I have some in-store ration signs I need you to put up. Got a new listing from the OPA of some point changes in the candy aisle. I'll leave the list on my desk."

"I'll get right on it," she said. She didn't know if he'd heard her. He'd already turned and started walking down the main aisle. She hated disappointing him. He'd been so nice to her.

She unraveled the poster. It was a picture of a handsome GI with a big smile, holding up a tin cup, as if saying "Thanks." Above it the caption read: "Do with less—so they'll have enough!" She quickly turned it around so she wouldn't see his face. He didn't look a lot like Jim, but he made her think of him. Jim was over there going without, so she could have it easy over here. Do with less. Sacrifice. That was her job, the job of every patriotic American.

It was time she did her part. She had to stop thinking about Ben. She flattened the poster against the bottom edge of the glass and taped one corner to hold it in place.

"There you are. Your mom said I'd find you here."

Claire taped the second corner down then looked behind her. "Barb, what are you doing here?" She looked beyond Barb, scanning the aisles, looking for Mr. Morris. "I can't really talk right now."

"When do you get off for lunch?"

Claire looked at a wall clock over the lunch counter. "In about an hour."

"Got any plans?"

"Not really."

"Good, 'cause we need to talk."

Barb's face looked pretty serious.

"About what?"

"Thought you couldn't talk now."

"I can't, you're right. Can you come back in an hour?"

"I'm free till this afternoon, so yeah."

"Meet me back here, and we'll go get something. I don't want to eat here."

"Well, I don't want to meet where we usually hang out, in case someone we know comes in."

"Sounds pretty serious."

"It is, in a way. But don't worry, it's not life or death . . . more like health and happiness."

"What's that mean?"

"Don't worry about it. I'll come back in an hour."

• • •

Claire and Barb found a seat at Ligget's Drugstore, and the waitress was there in two minutes. "I'll have a tuna fish sandwich," Claire said. "And a Coca-Cola."

"I'll have a Coca-Cola too. But make mine a hot dog, mustard and relish only."

"Got it, ladies." The waitress took their orders and headed back to the kitchen.

"So . . . what's up?" Claire said. Should she brace herself for bad news? Barb seemed upset but not distraught.

"We're good friends, right?" Barb said.

"The best, why?"

Barb looked down a moment then back up. "I don't know how to say this, so I'll just say it. Is there something happening between you and Ben?"

Oh no, Claire thought. "What do you mean?"

"You know, do you guys have . . . feelings for each other?"

Claire didn't know what to say. She and Barb were good friends. But so were Jim and Barb's boyfriend, Joe. They all knew each other in high school, even went on a number of double dates together their senior year. "I want to be honest with you, Barb."

"Please do."

Claire looked in Barb's eyes. She didn't seem mad or offended. What was going on? "If you asked me a few days ago, I would have said absolutely not. But my mom and dad were asking me the same thing after Ben came over for dinner Saturday night."

"Ben came over for dinner Saturday night? When, after the concert?"

"Not right after, but . . . soon after. I felt bad for him. He told me some difficult things he'd gone through, so I asked him over after we went on the Ferris wheel together."

"You and Ben went on the Ferris wheel together?"

Had she done something wrong? Why was Barb acting like this? "It was just a Ferris wheel, Barb. It's not like we—"

"No, I'm sorry, Claire. I'm not upset. If anything . . . I'm happy about it."

"You're happy?"

Barb sighed. "Relieved may be a better word."

"I don't understand."

"I'm sure you don't. But before I tell you what I came to say, you have to promise you won't get mad at me. And you have to promise you won't say where you heard this."

"What? What are you talking about?"

"Okay . . . you remember Sally Hamilton, right? From high school?"

Of course Claire did. Sally had been Jim Burton's girlfriend before he and Claire had started dating. Sally and Jim were together for three years, from ninth grade through the summer between their junior and senior year. "I remember Sally. Why?"

"Oh, Claire . . . if this had happened before you and Ben started—"

"Barb, Ben and I haven't started anything. We went on a Ferris wheel together."

"But I've seen the way he looks at you. Joe's seen it too. We both can tell Ben is crazy about you. Haven't you noticed?"

"I wouldn't say he's *crazy* about me."

"Well, he is. The thing is, until this weekend, I didn't see anything on your end."

"What do you think you see now?"

"I don't know, something. It's like something happened at the concert. Or maybe before. But the way you looked at him when the two of you were dancing. Right then, I thought, *Uh-oh, Claire's in trouble*. It's the way I look at Joe. But now, I'm thinking—"

"What, Barb, what are you trying to say? And what's this have to do with Sally Hamilton?"

"Jim Burton, your Jim, and Sally are back together. There, I said it."

"What?"

"Well, not back together. Jim's still overseas. But I think you should know, he's writing her letters. A lot of letters. Like boyfriend and girlfriend kind of letters."

Claire was stunned. It felt like Barb had hit her in the stomach.

"You're upset. I'm so sorry, but I had to tell you. You're my best friend. I knew this would hurt, but now with Ben in the picture—"

"Barb, Ben's not in the picture. Maybe he is. I don't know. But what are you saying? How do you know this?"

"I was walking the dog yesterday afternoon," Barb said. "You know Sally lives just five doors down from me. She was out getting the mail. Her family had gone somewhere Friday and Saturday, so she was getting it yesterday. Anyway . . . I stopped to say hi while she was flipping through her mail. She stopped at this one envelope and got this dreamy look on her face. Jim, she said, as if I wasn't there. Jim wrote you? I said. And she said, yes, like it was no big deal. She said they'd started writing each other again. I'm telling you, I wanted to smack her right there. I couldn't believe it. So I played dumb and started asking her some questions. Turns out, she and Jim are in love again. He said he was sorry for being such a fool and would she take him back. Of course, she said yes. But Claire, I'm telling you, Sally had no idea you didn't know about this. I don't know what kind of lies he's been telling in his letters, but she was under the impression Jim had written you and told you all about this."

This was terrible. Claire couldn't help it. She started to cry.

"Oh, Claire, I'm so sorry. Jim hasn't said a word

about this, has he?" She reached across the table and patted Claire's hand. "I'm so sorry, Claire. That Jim, he's a first-class heel."

Claire reached for the napkin and dabbed her eyes.

"But see, Claire, don't you see? You're free. You and Ben. You can be a couple—if you want to, that is. And with Ben's heart murmur, you don't even have to worry about him being shipped out to fight in the war."

Claire sighed. She was free.

Then why didn't she feel happy?

Chapter Thirteen

Father Aidan Flanagan, seated in the darkened confessional of St. Paul's Church for the last half hour, had heard pleas for God's mercy from the faithful, sought to give out a fair penance, granted absolution. It was Monday, now nearing the lunch hour. No one else had come in for a few minutes.

Aidan heard a noise. He looked through the mesh screening that allowed him to see out from the confessional. No one standing in line or kneeling nearby. He hoped he had done some good; he said a prayer of thanks and opened the door.

That's when he saw one young man sitting near

the back; he looked to be maybe twenty or twenty-five years old. He didn't seem Catholic—you could tell such things. Even by the way he sat in the pew, like he was resting on a park bench. Was he waiting for someone? Aidan looked around. The church was empty.

The man looked right at him, then looked away.

Aidan walked closer. "Can I help you? Are you here to make a confession? We can do that."

The man looked troubled; Aidan could see it in his eyes. "I need to talk to someone. But I'm not sure—"

"Then here, I'll go back in, and you come in when you're ready." Aidan turned to head back to the confessional.

"I don't know . . . maybe I should come back later."

Aidan stopped, his hand on the knob. "That's okay too. You could come back on Wednesday after the morning Mass. Or if you want to come in before then, you could call the rectory. Ask for me, Father Flanagan. I can meet you almost any time."

The man stood up. "I don't want to put you to any trouble. You're here now."

"Okay, son." Aidan stepped into the confessional. He waited a few moments, heard footsteps. Then the door on the other side opened and closed. He slid the little wooden door over. A screen provided visual privacy but allowed them to hear each other just fine. No one said anything for a few more moments. "Is there something you'd like to confess?"

"I don't know what to say," the young man said. "I don't . . . know how this works."

"Usually people start off with a prayer. Something like 'Bless me, Father, for I have sinned,' and then they say how long it's been since their last confession."

"I'm not actually Catholic."

"Oh."

"I'm Lutheran. Well, I was raised Lutheran, but my parents stopped taking me to church after we moved to Germany."

"You lived in Germany?"

"Up until very recently, in fact."

"I see. How recently?"

"That's the thing, Father. That's why I'm here. I . . . I needed someone to talk to. Someone in private. Now it's true, right? Anything we say in here stays private? You can't tell it to anyone else."

"Yes, that's true."

"Good, that's what I need."

"Are you here, though, to make a confession?"

"Yes, but I'm not sure if I'm confessing sins. Well, I know lying is a sin, and I've been lying nonstop. For years, it seems."

"I see."

"I don't think what I'm lying about is a sin. But if anyone knew what I've done, even who I am, I'd be arrested and probably executed."

Aidan said a quiet prayer for wisdom. This sounded quite serious. "Why would you be arrested? People are usually only arrested for committing crimes."

"What I've done is a crime, a war crime. But I don't think I've done anything wrong. Not really. If you knew the whole story, I think you'd agree. At least I hope you would. I don't see that I had any choice. No one ever gave me a choice." The young man was becoming agitated.

"Well, son, were you forced into doing . . . this thing? Is that why you don't feel you had any choice?"

"Forced? In a way I was. But you'd have to hear the whole story for any of this to make sense."

"I'm in no hurry."

"I waited till everyone else left."

"That was considerate of you. Tell me your story. I'd like to help you if I can."

"Even if I'm a Lutheran? I haven't been to church in years."

"Those things aren't important right now. What is important is that you're here, that you've come to God for help." He thought of a verse in Psalm 46: God is our refuge and strength, a very present help in trouble. This young man needed God's help, desperately, it seemed. God had been Aidan's refuge so many times; he didn't want to put any obstacles in this young man's way.

"And you really can't repeat anything I confess to you in here?"

"I really can't, nor would I."

He heard a loud sigh through the screen.

"I came to America two months ago, on a German U-boat. We came onshore in two rubber rafts, just a few miles north of here."

Aidan was stunned. He'd expected the young man to confess to being an Army deserter or something of that sort. Nothing like this. "So you're a . . . German spy?"

"No, I'm not. That's why they sent me here, but that's not why I came."

"Why did you come?"

"To get back to America. I never wanted to leave. I was born here. My parents dragged me off to Germany in 1935. That's where they were born. They came here after World War I but went back to be part of all the *wonderful* things Hitler was doing for the Fatherland." He said this last part with obvious sarcasm. "I hated Germany. I hate everything the Nazis stand for."

Aidan was relieved to hear that. "You said 'we' a moment ago. Are there others? Do they feel the same as you do about Hitler?"

"No, they are Nazis, in heart and soul. Well, two of them are. My partner is dead—but I didn't kill him, Father. He drowned in the surf the night we came onshore."

"Where is he now? Where are the other two?"

"Why do you need to know that?"

"I'm just trying to understand, trying to help you. Remember, nothing you say will be reported to the authorities." He wondered at this moment if that was the right thing to say.

"The other two-man team is heading north, pursuing their mission. My partner, I buried him in the sand dunes not far from where we came ashore."

This was hard to fathom, almost hard to believe. But the young man sounded completely sincere. "Is their mission . . . to hurt people, to kill Americans?"

"Yes. That's the main mission. And to disrupt war production any way they can."

My, my. What should he do? This was awful. "Were you planning to do this but changed your mind?"

"No, I would never have gone through with it. I only pretended to be a Nazi so I could be picked for this assignment. My goal the whole time was to get back here, to start over. The thing is, I can do that now. I'm free. I can start over. But I don't feel free inside."

No, I don't suppose you do, Aidan thought. "Why is that?"

"Because, I'm lying all the time. To everyone. You're the first person I've told any of this to. I can't talk to anyone else. They'd have to turn me in. You know what they do to Nazi spies."

Aidan remembered reading about this. They had executed six of them just a few months ago.

"But I'm not a spy. I didn't do anything wrong. I haven't hurt anyone, let alone killed anyone."

"But you're going to sit by quietly while your friends go off on their mission. Isn't their mission to kill Americans?"

"They're not my friends, Father. I don't support them or anything they're planning to do."

"But you're not doing anything to stop it, either." He instantly regretted saying this. He was pushing too hard.

"You don't understand. How could you? How could anyone?" The young man stood up. "I have to go."

"Please don't go. I didn't mean to offend you."

"I know. It's just . . . I don't know. I may come back and talk some more, if that's okay."

"Anytime, son. You can come back on Wednesday, if you like. Or just call the rectory and ask for me. I'll meet here with you anytime."

"Father Flanagan, right?"

"That's right."

"Thank you, Father. I've gotta go. You have a nice day."

Aidan heard the door open and close. He waited a few moments. He needed some time, to gather his thoughts and to pray.

This had been the strangest confession he'd ever heard in his forty years as a priest.

Chapter Fourteen

Later that day, Ben drove his Ford coupe over the Broadway Bridge toward the downtown area. After leaving the church that morning, he'd spent the first part of the afternoon looking at houses to rent. He found the right one on Vermont Avenue, just around the block from his apartment. A nice little two-bedroom bungalow. What sealed the deal was the owner saying he normally lived down here through the winter but his business was booming, and he needed to head back to Baltimore right away.

That meant he wouldn't be around to check up on the place, or on Ben. He'd given Ben the keys, so Ben went right to the hardware store and bought new locks for the doors. He bought an additional lock for each exterior door and a separate lock for the small bedroom door, where he'd put the suitcase filled with money and ration coupons.

It felt so good to get that suitcase out of his car.

Coming off the bridge, he turned right at the light. He saw the big Woolworth sign on the wall above the metal awning and started hunting for a place to park. On the seat beside him were the two stuffed animals Claire had left in his car. "I want to thank you two." He smiled at the silly grins on their faces. They'd given him the excuse to come see her today without "the gang."

He'd called Claire's mother earlier. She told him Claire got off at 4:00 today. She seemed very happy to hear from him and actually talked a few minutes before he hung up.

Overall, he was feeling pretty good. His chat with Father Flanagan had initially upset him. But he soon realized it was just all the pent-up tension he'd felt, holding all these dark things inside. And the fear of getting caught if he opened up to anyone. Thirty minutes later, it dawned on him . . . it was okay.

Father Flanagan presented no danger. He hadn't said anything that helped Ben, hadn't given him any practical advice. Ben didn't stay long enough to give him a chance. But still, talking had helped. It was as if a part of the weight he'd been carrying was lifted, just because another human being knew what he was going through.

A green Buick backed out a few parking places down from Woolworth's front door, so Ben pulled in behind it. He looked at his watch. She should be coming out any minute. He glanced through the display windows, beyond the war bond and rationing posters, hoping to catch a glimpse of her in the store. *Keep calm,* he told himself. Not the time to start pushing this too hard. Didn't want to scare her off, come off looking like Hank. But it was so hard.

There she was, coming through the glass doors.

He got out of the car. She was so beautiful, but something seemed wrong. "Claire." She turned in his direction, searching for the voice. "Over here." He walked a few steps forward, by the fender.

"Oh. Ben," she said, a big smile now on her face. "I thought I heard your voice."

"Your mom told me when you got off. I was out on some errands this afternoon with a couple of your friends here in my front seat. They kept falling on the floor every time I hit the brakes."

"What?" She walked toward him.

He walked back to the car and grabbed the stuffed tiger and bear, held them up. "You left them in the car Saturday."

"Aww," she said, hurrying over.

He handed them to her and she hugged them. "Thanks, Ben. I really need them right now."

"Are you okay? You seem . . . upset."

"Is it obvious?"

"I can see it in your eyes." She leaned against the fender. "Careful," he said, "needs washing. Don't want your skirt to get dirty."

"That's the least of my worries right now."

"Did something happen in the store?"

"No. I just got some discouraging news at lunch, from Barb."

"Is Joe okay?"

"He's fine. It's just . . . something's happened. Barb found out about it. She met me at lunch to fill me in."

He didn't know what to say. They stood there a few moments. She looked up at him, something new in her eyes. A warm feeling rushed over him.

"Thanks so much for bringing these." She hugged the stuffed animals again. "I just realized, I never thanked you for winning them for me on Saturday. I guess I was kind of shocked, the way you shot that pistol."

"Just something I learned how to do last year." He hoped she didn't ask anything else about it.

"It's a shame the Army turned you down. Seems like they could use a man who can handle a gun like that."

What should he say?

"But I'm glad they did . . . turn you down, I mean."

"You are?"

She looked in his eyes that same way again. "Yes, I am."

It seemed to Ben time slowed in that moment. As if unspoken words passed between them. He wanted to risk telling her, right then, how deeply he loved her, how much she meant to him. What he said was, "Care to talk about what's bothering you? I don't know if I can help, but sometimes just talking about problems takes the edge off.

For me, anyway." *Listen to you, as if you're some kind of expert.*

"Maybe I would," she said. "Dinner's not until 5:30."

He looked across the street. "We could take a walk in the riverfront park over there, then I could drive you home."

"I think I'd like that."

"Then let's do it. Here, let's put your two friends back in the front seat." She handed them over and Ben put them in the car. "Do you need to call your mom first, to let her know you're not coming right home?"

"No, she's used to me doing things after work. Sometimes I have shopping or I do something with Barb. As long as I'm home for dinner, she won't be worried."

"Great, then let's go."

They walked down to the intersection, waited for the traffic light to change, then crossed the street together. Ben had to fight off the impulse to reach for her hand.

But he had the strange impression that if he did try, she wouldn't pull away.

173

Chapter Fifteen

Daytona's Waterfront Park was a beautiful place. Ben had never seen anything like it. October was the last month of pleasant weather in Germany. It could still be warm, occasionally even sunny. In Pennsylvania, where he'd grown up, it would be pretty cold right now. But here, it was not only warm and sunny but the park was filled with palm trees. There were big pink flowering bushes called oleanders. Flowers lined the walkways, in bloom as if in spring.

Walking beside him was the most beautiful young woman he'd ever seen. He didn't know how it happened or what had brought it about, but somehow Jim Burton no longer seemed to be standing in his way. "Would you like to walk or sit on a bench?" he said.

"Let's walk for a little while, maybe that walkway over there, the one along the river."

Ben took the fork in the sidewalk. "So what happened? What did Barb tell you?"

Claire sighed. "It's about Jim."

"Oh?"

"Apparently, we are no longer a couple."

It was all Ben could do to contain his joy. But

he saw how this saddened her. "I'm sorry," he said.

"I am too, I guess. I'm more upset by how it happened."

"Yeah, I was about to ask why you found this out talking to Barb."

"I can't believe Jim would do this. He's such a coward."

"What did he do?"

She explained how Barb found out he'd resumed his relationship with his old girlfriend, someone named Sally. He'd started writing her again, frequently. "Here I've been writing him several times a week, making excuses for why he hardly ever wrote me back. And here he is, writing Sally all these letters he was supposed to be writing me. He doesn't even have the courage to send me one letter explaining how he felt."

"That's pretty lousy," Ben said. "You didn't deserve that."

"No, I didn't."

They stopped near the middle section of the park. Behind them stood the American Legion Memorial, its white pillars gleaming in the sun. Ben turned back toward the water. "Hey, look." He pointed to a spot halfway across the river. "Did you see them? Fins came up out of the water. Two of them, one bigger than the other."

Claire turned to see, put her hand across her forehead to shield her eyes from the sun. "I don't see them."

"You think they're sharks?" Ben said, still staring at the spot.

"Probably dolphins. Were they swimming in a straight line or rolling?"

"More like rolling. There they are again, a little farther to the right. See them?"

She looked to where he pointed. "No, I missed them again."

"Here." He stood behind her, bent over so that his chin rested on her right shoulder. "Give me your hand." They were standing as close as they had on Saturday night slow dancing. She didn't pull away. If anything she leaned in closer. With her hand in his, he lifted her arm out straight, right to where he expected the dolphins to surface again. "Keep looking, right . . . about . . . there," he said softly.

The dolphin fins surfaced again.

"I see them!" she shouted. "Right there. Oh, Ben, aren't they wonderful? I love dolphins." They went underwater again but came right back up. "See that smaller one, I'll bet it's a mother and a baby, swimming together."

"I'll bet you're right," he said. Reluctantly, he let go of her hand but remained standing behind her. He noticed she didn't move away. They stood there a few moments, until it seemed the dolphins had left the area for good. "Do you want to keep walking?"

"No, let's sit over there." About fifty yards

ahead was a bench under a cluster of palm trees, facing the river. "Maybe they'll come back."

They walked there in silence but closer together. Several times her hand brushed against his. It was all he could do not to take it. More than that, he imagined taking her in his arms, then raising her face to his lips. Then he would kiss her. Jim Burton was no longer an obstacle. Ben had felt guilty about some of the thoughts he'd been having lately, of Jim not making it home from the war, freeing Ben to have Claire all to himself. It was a terrible thing to think, and he knew it. But he couldn't imagine anything short of death that would cause someone to relinquish such a prize as Claire.

She seemed more angry than heartbroken, and that seemed like a good thing to him. It confirmed what he suspected all along: she didn't love Jim Burton.

They sat down on the bench, right next to each other.

"Do you mind if I ask what's bothering you the most about all this?"

Claire looked down a moment, then out to the water. "I just don't understand why he would treat me this way. He was the one that asked me to wait for him. It wasn't my idea. My parents were actually kind of upset with me for saying yes."

"They didn't like Jim?"

"I don't think that was it. They didn't really know him."

"Weren't you dating for a year?"

"We were, but he never seemed to want to get to know them. Now I think I know why. He wasn't over Sally, and he wasn't that serious about me." She looked at him. "Believe it or not, you spent more time with them at dinner Saturday than he did the entire year."

"Really."

She nodded.

"Did they . . . say anything about me?"

She smiled and poked him playfully in the ribs. "They liked you."

"They said that?"

"Even my dad. He said, 'Ben seems like a nice young man, very easy to talk to.' You know what that means?"

"No." But Ben liked the sound of it.

"It was my dad's way of saying he wouldn't mind if I brought you around again."

"Really."

"Yep. But he'd never say something like that. Because even though he didn't agree with it, he knew I'd promised Jim I'd wait for him. But he's probably going to be more upset with Jim than I am, when he hears what he's done."

"So you're more upset with Jim for how he treated you, than . . ."

"You mean, did he break my heart? No, I'm not

heartbroken. I know now, I didn't really love Jim. But still, it's so wrong, the way he treated me. It's deceitful and cowardly."

"I agree." What was Ben saying? That's exactly what he was doing with Claire, right here, right now. And all along. Wasn't he being deceitful and cowardly?

"And from what Barb told me, Jim also lied to Sally."

"How so?" Ben felt himself tensing up.

"Barb said Sally had no idea that I didn't know the two of them were back together. Jim must have said things in his letters to make her think that, right? He must have told her he'd written me to break it off. But I haven't heard from him in over two weeks. He's written her a bunch of letters in that time, so he certainly could have found the time to write me. I'm just glad I found this out about him now."

"Why?"

"Because you can't have a healthy relationship with someone who lies."

Ben's heart sank; the words were like a punch in the stomach.

She stood up and reached for his hand. "So, Ben Coleman, are you going to ask me out or not?"

"What?"

"Everyone I trust—my mom and dad, Barb— say you're crazy about me. They said they can't believe I didn't know. Well . . . are you?"

Ben stood up. "Claire, I'm guilty." He took her hand, instantly felt heat shoot up his arm. He squeezed it tight then took her other hand. "I've been in love with you, I think, since the first day we met."

She looked right into his eyes and said, "I don't know if I love you yet, Ben. But I know I already care more for you than I ever cared for Jim."

"You do?"

She nodded.

His sick feelings all disappeared. He had no idea how he'd ever overcome the last huge obstacle between them—telling her the truth about his past—but right now he didn't care. He loved her deeply, completely.

She rested her head on his chest. He hugged her tightly. Ben knew he'd remember this moment—when Claire's heart first turned toward him—for the rest of his life. Something deep inside him shifted right then. He could feel it; something more than the joy and release of romantic desire. He wanted to protect her, to keep her safe from all harm, no matter what it cost him. He leaned down and kissed her softly on the cheek, then reached up and turned her head toward him, caressing her cheek, finding her lips, promising everything—a lifetime—in his kiss.

She turned and faced the river, still leaning against him. He put his arms around her shoulders and pulled her close. He knew nothing in his past, nothing in his future, would ever equal the value of this precious woman he held in his arms. She was so warm but also so fragile. He knew what it meant for Claire to give herself to him now: she was placing herself in his trust. He felt the weight of that trust like a tangible thing. He could not, would not break it. Somehow, he'd find a way to become worthy of her trust; then once he had earned it, he'd do whatever he must to keep it intact.

He was holding the love of his life.

Suddenly, several seagulls nearby began cackling loudly, startling them. Claire pulled away and they both laughed.

The seagulls stood between the sidewalk and the river, looking right at them. "It looks like they approve," Claire said.

"Actually, I think they want food."

"Speaking of food," she said, "would you like to come over for dinner again tonight?"

They began walking back toward the car, holding hands. "Oh yes, I definitely would."

Chapter Sixteen

"So nice of you to join us, Ben." Claire's father took his seat at the head of the table after giving his wife a peck on the cheek. Mrs. Richards sat at the other end, Claire and Ben across from each other. They were four at a table that could comfortably seat twelve. Claire looked radiant. Her whole face seemed lit up with happiness.

Her expression matched the way Ben felt on the inside. "When Claire asked, I said yes immediately. I haven't stopped thinking about that roast beef and mashed potatoes from Saturday night." He looked at Claire's mother. "I have never eaten a tastier slice of apple pie. I'm not exaggerating."

Mrs. Richards smiled. "I'm glad you enjoyed it. There's about half a pie left."

"If you throw in a cup of coffee, you can talk me in to staying for dessert," Ben said. Her parents laughed.

"Well, let's say a blessing and dig in," her father said.

Ben looked at the food on the table. Pork chops, green beans, and roasted potatoes. Then he looked up at Claire staring back at him. She smiled. His eyes focused on her lips as he remembered their kiss from an hour ago. As her father prayed, Ben closed his eyes. He was most definitely thankful for everything and everyone around this table.

The sheer force of his present elation and joy had temporarily suppressed any of the dark, disturbing thoughts seeking to ascend the stairway of his mind. For some unexplainable reason, the God he all but neglected from his youth had opened a new door for him, and he had no intention of looking back.

Not this night anyway.

"Dig in, Ben," Mr. Richards said. "Guests first."

Ben reached for the green beans, though his eyes were firmly fixed on the pork chops. It might make a better impression on Mrs. Richards if she saw that he thought vegetables were an important part of one's diet. "Mr. Richards, Claire told me you got some big contract recently with the military."

He smiled. "Yes, we did. Actually, it's just gotten even bigger with all of these young ladies moving into town. You know, the WACS."

"Is that what they're calling them?" asked Mrs. Richards. "Doesn't sound very nice."

"That's how these things go, dear," Mr. Richards said. "Everything gets abbreviated. Who wants to keep saying Women's Auxiliary Corps?"

"They're all over town now," Claire said. "More and more come in the store every day."

"Are you allowed to say what you do, what

kind of work you do with the military?" Ben said. He figured if he asked the questions, he wouldn't have to answer so many.

"I can't talk about the details, of course, but mostly we're about fixing and overhauling airplanes. Pretty much all our work converted to supporting the military after Pearl Harbor. We have a shop at both the Daytona and Deland Airports. I work out of the one in Deland. Both airports have become naval air stations now."

"We saw four Dauntless dive-bombers fly overhead on Saturday," Ben said. "Claire thought they were heading to Deland."

"So you know your bombers?" Mr. Richards asked. "Most people can't tell the difference from one plane to another."

Ben got a little nervous. "I'm . . . airplanes really interest me," he said. "I would have liked to become a pilot."

"Really," her father said. "I've actually got my pilot's license. Haven't flown a plane in years. But I used to love it. Did you ever try to join the Army Air Force? They'll be building hundreds of planes in the next year. Sure they could use more pilots."

"Ben can't serve in the military, Dad," Claire said. "Remember?"

"Oh . . . right."

Ben released a quiet sigh. Claire to the rescue, subtly introducing his fake 4-F rating. Everyone

184

squirmed in their seats a moment, as if allowing some time for an embarrassing faux pas to clear the air. "What will your company be doing that involves the WACS?" Ben asked.

"We'll be training them mostly," Mr. Richards said. "With so many men heading off to war . . . uh, I mean . . . well, you know, there's a big shortage of men available to do jobs traditionally done by men."

Ben could tell that Mr. Richards was still struggling with Ben's supposed 4-F status, trying not to say things that might embarrass him. "It's okay, Mr. Richards. I understand what you're saying. Millions of men—a lot of them my age—have signed up. You don't know how badly I wish I could join them. I'd do anything to defeat the Nazis." Ben meant that sincerely.

Mr. Richards smiled. "Thanks, Ben. Well, because of that, we'll need thousands of young women to be trained to do these kinds of jobs. That's why the WACS are here in Daytona."

"So your company will be training some of them to fix military planes, like the Dauntless?" Ben said.

"Everything from repairing engines to putting air in the tires. Say, Ben, don't let that last pork chop go to waste."

"I'm fine, sir, thanks."

Claire stuck her fork into it and lifted it off the serving dish. "I know you want it," she said. "Put your plate here." Ben obeyed. "Did I tell you, Dad, Ben rented a house today."

"You did?" Mrs. Richards said. "Where is it?"

"On Vermont Avenue, just around the corner from where I've been staying."

"A house is much better," Mrs. Richards said.

"If you don't mind me asking, Ben, what kind of work do you do?"

"Ben doesn't have a job right now, Dad," Claire said. "After his parents—"

"But I do plan on getting one," Ben said. "I came into some money after my parents died, so I'm not in a hurry."

"That's probably a good idea," Mrs. Richards said. "You've been through a terrible thing, losing your parents like that. You take all the time you need."

"Thanks, Mrs. Richards."

"I was just asking," Mr. Richards said, "because I might be able to get you a job where I work. You seem like a sharp young man, well spoken. Do you have any college education?"

"A bachelor's degree. But it's in English literature."

"You have a college degree?" Claire asked, obviously impressed.

"Does that surprise you?" he said.

"No . . . I knew you were smart. I just didn't realize you were so old."

"Old? I'm just twenty-four."

"That's not so old, Claire," her mother said. "You're nineteen."

"I'm only kidding, Mother."

"Well, I don't care what your degree's in," Mr. Richards said. "The fact that you have it says a lot about you. It's a mark of achievement. You might make an excellent trainer. How do you feel about talking in front of people?"

"I don't know," Ben said. "I've never done it. You mean, like a teacher?"

He nodded. "We'll be doing hands-on training but also a lot of classroom lectures."

"But I don't really know that much about planes."

"Ben, we've got manuals that spell out everything from A to Z. The main thing is having someone who can communicate well."

"And someone who's not boring," Claire said. "And Ben is definitely not boring."

Ben looked at Claire. She was loving this. He was rather enjoying it himself. He liked her parents, both of them.

"Well, give it some thought, Ben, and let me know. Don't want to rush you into anything."

"No, I appreciate it, Mr. Richards. Really. I'll give it some thought."

"Wouldn't that be great?" Claire said. "If you and my dad worked together?"

Ben smiled. He wanted to do anything that made her happy. But something bothered him, an unformed thought, something someone said.

"Great," Mr. Richards said. He looked across the table at his wife. "What do you think? Can we have that apple pie now, hon? Everyone okay with that?"

"I'd take a small piece," Claire said.

"I have room," Ben said.

Mrs. Richards stood up, started clearing the table. "I'll start the coffee and put the pie in the oven to get warm."

"I'll help you," Claire said.

She walked around the table and took Ben's plate and stood right next to him. He couldn't believe it. They were together now. It had all happened so quickly. Just a few days ago, he'd felt hopeless, wouldn't have imagined ever being in this place. He didn't want to do or say anything that would jeopardize their future.

As she walked toward the kitchen, that disturbing thought suddenly became clear. It had to do with Claire's dad and his job offer.

Her dad worked with the Navy, fixing the latest military fighters and bombers.

Ben could never work for him. How could he? It would require clearance and extensive background checks. Who should he put down for references, his Abwehr commanders? What should he put down for the school he graduated from, the University of Munich? That his degree in English literature was actually part of the reason they thought he'd make an excellent spy?

"Everything okay, Ben?"

"Hmm?" Ben looked up at Claire sliding behind her mother's chair, heading back to her seat at the table.

"Something bothering you?"

"What could be bothering him?" her father asked. "He's about to eat your mom's apple pie."

Chapter Seventeen

Ben didn't sleep well last night.

He didn't dream about Jurgen; that was some relief. He was just restless, tossing and turning in his bed. He should have been flying high after the turnabout with Claire. He'd kissed her, twice. No, three times. Twice by the river, then again at the car when they'd said good night. It was that thing at the end, about the job. He would love to do something like that, and thought he'd be good at it too. He might make a great teacher. And he really did love airplanes, would have loved to become a pilot. But there was no way he'd ever fly airplanes for the Luftwaffe, against the British or Americans, so it was out of the question.

He sat in a pew at St. Paul's Church, a few rows back from the confessional, waiting for Father Flanagan. He wrestled about calling him all morning before deciding it was the right thing to do. Last night, for the first time in ages, he'd actually prayed. He couldn't remember any of the prayers he'd learned as a good Lutheran boy, so he just talked to God the way you'd talk to anyone, but with more respect. It was the last thing he did before he finally fell asleep. When he awoke, the first thought he had was to call Father Flanagan.

So here he was. He had no idea what he was going to say.

He looked around at the insides of the church. It was a beautiful place, not nearly as fancy as the exquisite cathedrals he'd seen in Germany, but close to some. It had tall, looping arches on either side, finely trimmed, set on thick stone pillars. An impressive dome rose high above the altar. Several elderly women stood near the front, lighting candles.

He heard the echo of a side door opening and closing. There was Father Flanagan, walking down the side aisle. He looked around, noticed Ben, and smiled. He bent over and set something down in a pew next to the confessional. Ben got up and hurried into the nearest side. It was dark, and he was glad it was. He heard a door open and close, then the little door separating them slid over.

"Morning, Father."

"Morning, Ben."

Ben had decided to tell the priest his name

when he'd called. It didn't seem to matter now—and it wasn't his real name anyway. "What was that thing I was supposed to say? Bless me, Father, for I have sinned. It's been . . . one day since my last confession?"

Father Flanagan laughed. "Something like that."

"Well, the FBI didn't come after me."

"Did you think they might?"

"No, well . . . I hoped not. Didn't seem like a priest would lie."

"Your secret is safe with me. See, the idea is, people need to feel like they can be honest in here. If they thought we—that is, priests—might share what people say to others, they'd never feel like they could talk freely."

"Are they?" Ben said.

"Are they what?"

"Are most people honest in here?"

"Good question." A long pause. "Some are, but I get the sense a lot of people still hold back with me. It's hard for people to talk freely with anyone. Hard for me too, I guess."

"Really, you have a hard time being honest?"

"Not when I'm sharing facts or admitting things I've said or done. But sharing how I'm doing deep down inside . . . with other people? Yes, Ben, that's hard for me."

"I never would have thought that," Ben said.

"Priests are just people. But the thing is, God sees through it all. He sees our hearts as they are, as they really are, every moment of the day. That's why we don't have to play games with him, try to pretend we're doing okay when we're really hurting inside. We can come in whatever condition we're in, knowing he loves us and knows exactly what we're thinking and feeling. I've been through something myself recently, where I've rediscovered just how true that is."

Ben didn't know what to say. "Does the Bible say that?"

"It does. I'm thinking of a psalm I've read often lately, Psalm 139. It says: 'You examine me and know me, you know when I sit, when I rise, you understand my thoughts from afar. You watch when I walk or lie down, you know every detail of my conduct. A word is not yet on my tongue before you know all about it.' "

"But God doesn't pay that kind of attention to just anyone, right? I mean, he might to someone like you."

"No, Ben, he knows you this way too, not just me. That's why you can open your heart completely to him. Not just in here, but even when you pray, wherever you are."

Ben didn't expect any of this. "I'm so tired, Father."

"I can imagine. You've been carrying a pretty heavy load."

"Do you think what I'm doing is a sin? I mean, all this lying?"

"Lying is a sin. It's one of the Ten Commandments."

"But isn't God fair? Isn't he just?"

"He is."

"Well, if he knows everything, he knows I don't have a choice. If I tell the truth to anyone except you, about who I am, how I got here, where I'm from . . . they'd arrest me on the spot. A month later, I'd be in the electric chair. How is that fair or just?"

"It's not."

"I haven't done anything wrong. If it were up to me, I'd have stayed at my high school and gone on to Penn State. I might be flying fighter planes right now for the Navy or Army Air Force. I'm of German descent, but I love this country. I hate what the Germans are doing to the world right now. Should I have to pay for that? For my parents dragging me off to Germany the way they did?"

Ben waited, for what seemed like a long time, before Father Flanagan replied. "No, Ben. I don't suppose that's right. I don't think you should have to pay for things you aren't guilty of. I don't think God expects that, either."

"You don't?"

"No, I don't. You haven't betrayed this nation, and you aren't spying for its enemies."

"I'm not, Father. And I wouldn't have harmed a single American. There was no way I'd ever have followed through with my orders. And you know

193

what I think? I think God took my partner that night on the beach. Let him drown in the surf, so he wouldn't do what he came here to do. He was going to commit murder, as many times as he could, smiling the whole time. I knew I had to stop him. But I didn't want to, kill him, I mean."

"I'm glad you didn't have to have that on your conscience, Ben."

"But why is my conscience still so unsettled? I mean, if I'm not doing anything wrong."

"It's a good question. Have any ideas?"

Claire's beautiful face flashed in his mind. Then a scene from the dinner table last night. All the lies he had to keep telling and keep afloat with her and her family. "There's a young woman I've fallen in love with, Claire. She's . . . the woman I want to marry. Have a family with some day. And her family, her mom and dad, they're really wonderful people. I hate lying to them, to all of them."

A long pause once again.

"I don't think I can help you with this one."

"What do you mean?"

"I do think lying to people is wrong. And there's one other matter, Ben. Something that keeps bothering me about all this. I think I have to mention it."

"What is it, Father?"

"I talked about it yesterday, briefly. And it clearly upset you. I imagine it might if I bring it up now."

"Tell me."

"You said a few minutes ago that you wouldn't have harmed a single American. And there was no way you'd ever have followed through with the orders your Nazi commanders gave you."

"That's right."

"But you know of two men hiding somewhere in America right now, who are completely committed to carrying out those orders. Many innocent Americans will die by their hands . . . if you do nothing. That's a serious thing."

Why did he have to mention that? "I know, Father. But there's nothing I can do." Instantly, Ben knew it wasn't true. He'd thoroughly blocked these men from his mind, as if he'd shut them away, buried along with Jurgen's body.

"Ben . . . there must be something."

"Father, the FBI is all over this, now they know what the Nazis are up to. They had over thirty agents working the last case. The Coast Guard is setting up hundreds of teams with horses and dogs patrolling the beaches. If I breathe a word of this to anyone, I'll get caught. And executed."

"You can't even send in an anonymous note?"

"I've read about these G-men. They have handwriting experts and big laboratories in Washington. They'd be able to trace it back to me. I know they would. And I'd be finished."

Ben was exhausted. He was actually sweating.

He could hear Father Flanagan breathing on the other side of the screen.

"Well, there's something I'd like you to consider, maybe pray about. It's one thing to turn yourself in to be executed for something you haven't done. It's another to risk your life to save countless innocents from being killed. The people your friends plan to kill aren't even soldiers."

"They're not my friends."

"I'm sorry. I shouldn't have said that. But you know what I mean."

Ben did. He didn't want to think about it. "I need to go, Father. Thanks for meeting with me."

"You're welcome. I'm sorry if I've said things that offended you. But you wanted help with your conscience. What did you call it . . . unsettled?"

"I guess."

"We can't run from a guilty conscience. And I think you're going to have more trouble in the days ahead, not just from this issue about the other saboteurs. What did you say her name is, the girl you love and want to marry?"

"Claire."

"Yes, Claire, and her parents. It's one thing to decide not to volunteer information to the authorities that would result in your unjust execution. But I don't think it is ever okay to lie to those we love."

"But, I can't tell her. Or her parents. They'd

never understand. It would ruin everything between us."

"Are you sure, Ben? I think *not* telling her will ruin everything. And the longer you wait to tell her, the worse it will be when she finds out. That's how these things work. It might hurt a little now, but true love should be able to weather something like this."

What do you know about true love? You're a priest.

"I can't tell her, Father." He stood up. "I just can't."

"Ben."

Ben opened the confessional door.

"Before you go, I brought you a Bible. You don't have one, do you?"

"No."

"I set it in the pew right outside. I put a list of psalms to read inside it, ones that I think will help you right now. They've really helped me. After that, you might read the Gospels."

"Thank you, Father. I can pay you for it."

"No need. I'll be praying for you."

"Thank you."

Ben walked out, picked up the Bible, and headed down the aisle toward the front doors. Father Flanagan really was a kind old man, but he didn't understand. How could Ben ever tell the truth to Claire? Something she'd said yesterday at the park ran through his mind. The thing that had upset her most about what Jim Burton had done: *You can't have a healthy relationship with someone who lies.*

If she couldn't bear the weight of Jim Burton's singular lie about returning to his old girlfriend, she'd be crushed by the avalanche of Ben's lies falling down upon her.

It would ruin everything.

13

I carefully set the manuscript down on a little table I had pulled up next to me. Didn't want the pages to tear. What time was it? *No way,* I thought as I glanced at my watch. I'd been sitting here for almost five hours.

Jenn!

I'd forgotten all about Jenn. I reached in my pocket for my cell phone. It wasn't there. *No, no, no.* I spun the chair around and searched the desk. It wasn't there. Must have left it out in the kitchen. Had she called? She must have. How could I not hear it? I ran out into the kitchen. She must be worried sick.

The whole house was dark. I flicked on the light switch. There it was, next to the microwave. My heart sank when I flipped my phone open and checked for messages. She'd called at least a half dozen times. I hit the send button.

It rang and rang, and finally I got her voice mail. "Jenn, I'm so sorry. Didn't even hear your calls. I left my phone out here in the—" My phone started beeping. I looked. It was Jenn.

"Michael? What time is it?" She sounded groggy.

"It's a little after 1:00 a.m. I'm so sorry, Jenn."

"I was so worried."

"I know, I'm sorry. I left my cell phone out here in the kitchen."

"Where've you been?"

"Nowhere. I've been here at the house the whole time."

"I called and called."

"I know, I'm sorry."

"I even called the hospitals." She was sounding more awake. "I figured, it's a modern city. If he got in an accident, the hospitals would know. Since they didn't have anything on you, I figured you were probably fine."

"Jenn, I . . . no excuse. I hate that I put you through that. Really, I'm sorry."

"Okay. You just forgot all about me, that I even exist."

"It's not that. I was just preoccupied, reading Gramps's book. I was back in his office, had the door closed."

"All this time?"

"I haven't moved from that chair since I called you last."

"Not even to go to the bathroom?"

"No. Speaking of that—"

"You better not take me into the bathroom with you. I'll be able to tell if you do."

I laughed. "I won't. But I can't talk as long."

"Then you can call me back."

"Don't you have to work in the morning?"

"Yes. I need to go back to bed."

"Well, you do that. We can talk tomorrow." I walked toward the refrigerator, poured myself a glass of iced tea.

"So, it's that good?" she said.

"Totally sucked me in." I drank a sip of tea. "It's not like any book of his I've ever read. It's almost a love story."

"Really?"

"It's got some action and suspense, but so far I'd definitely not call it a thriller."

"Do you think it will sell?"

"Jenn, it's my grandfather. They'd buy his grocery list."

"I'm glad you're safe."

"Sorry I made you worry."

"Next time you read, keep your cell phone in your pocket."

"I will, I promise."

"Don't just promise."

"Okay. Love you. Can't wait for you to read this book."

"If your grandfather wrote a love story, I definitely want to read it."

I woke up the next morning pretty groggy.

The sun was shining brightly through the

curtains. I rolled over and looked at the digital clock. It was after 9:00. I reached for my cell, thinking of Jenn. How could I have missed her call again? She left for work at 7:30. When I flipped it open, I saw that I hadn't. Jenn had let me sleep in. I was so glad she was coming back for the weekend. I got up and took a shower. Got dressed and went downstairs. After a cup of coffee and bowl of Cinnamon Life cereal, I was ready to head back to Gramps's office and pick up where I'd left off.

Before I did, I looked outside. A much better location to work. I walked out on the veranda. The temperature was cool but not cold. Very little wind. I went back in, refreshed my coffee cup, put my cell phone in my pocket, and picked up the manuscript pages I hadn't read yet.

As I walked back toward the porch, I pondered why my grandfather had decided not to turn this in to get published. It was definitely up to par with his other works. Was it the love story angle? Gramps always included a measure of romance in his novels, though no one would have ever pegged him as a romance writer. It wasn't the time period; he'd certainly written novels set in World War II. *Back to Bastogne* and *Remembering Dresden* came to mind.

So what was it?

I opened the front door. A couple of chairs at the far end of the porch were clearly purchased for comfort. I sat in one, pulled a little wicker table close to hold the loose pages after I read them. Propped my feet up and set the manuscript on my lap.

I was going to be here a while.

Chapter Eighteen

Mid-January, 1943

For the next three months, Ben followed his own advice and did his best to put most of what Father Flanagan had suggested behind him. He genuinely appreciated the priest's concern for his welfare but decided Father Flanagan just didn't fully understand Ben's situation. How could he? The clergy lived a rather sheltered life and Catholic priests didn't even marry. So how could he know what was best for Ben and Claire?

Ben did, however, receive much help from the Bible he'd been given, and made it a habit to read it every morning. He'd started with all the references Father Flanagan had written out for him on a sheet of paper. First the Psalms, then the Gospels. Most of the psalms on Father Flanagan's list spoke of God's ability to know all things, including the condition of every heart at every moment of the day. This made sense to Ben, the more he thought on it. If there was a God, then he was God almighty, the most majestic and brilliant of all beings. It made no sense to believe in a small God.

Modeling David's prayers in the Psalms, Ben

tried to make a habit to talk to God that way, telling him whatever he thought, as honestly as he could. It was wonderful not having to keep everything locked up inside anymore. He was so grateful that he felt compelled to send Father Flanagan a thank-you note with fifty dollars inside. Although, Ben felt quite sure, someone of Father Flanagan's virtue would likely give most of it to the poor.

Ben and Claire were now very much in love. Claire first said she loved Ben within a week of their first kiss. Now each spoke of their love constantly. They went out on dates two or three times a week, and Ben ate dinner at her house at least that often. The gang had somewhat dissipated after Barb and Joe's wedding just before Thanksgiving. Right after their honeymoon, Joe had shipped out to boot camp. He was now stationed somewhere in California, preparing to be sent to the Pacific theater.

They'd occasionally see Barb, and even Hank, and share a meal together at McCrory's, maybe take in a movie at the theater. That was the plan, in fact, for this afternoon. Ben was on his way to McCrory's right now. Claire had met Barb there for lunch. Hank said he'd meet them at the theater for the matinee.

Hank had finally given up on Claire. Now he mostly complained about not being able to find the right girl in this town. Ben thought that strange, seeing as there were over ten thousand WACS walking about. You'd see at least two dozen at every gas station and grocery store at any given time. Just that morning, hundreds of WACS paraded by in neat rows on the boardwalk next to the Bandshell, as they did every Saturday morn-ing, right past the spot where Ben and Claire had their first dance.

"You're just too picky, Hank," Barb would say.

That's part of it, Ben thought silently whenever she'd say it.

Ben had just one more stop to make, to drop off a story he'd written for his employer, the Daytona *News Journal*. A human interest piece about a group of WACS who drove and fixed their own fleet of military trucks around town. Ben had gotten the job to give him something to talk about at the dinner table, to offset any more conversations about him working for Claire's father. He'd started off freelancing, picked up a nice portable typewriter at Upchurch's Office Supply, and hammered the articles out at home. They liked what he'd given them so much that they offered him a steady job. He split his time now between his desk at the News Journal on Orange Avenue and his kitchen table.

He dropped off the story to his editor. Everyone at the paper was buzzing about some major winter storm blowing in from the Gulf this evening. The paper was actually running a story on the front page, warning people to brace themselves for high winds and rough seas through the weekend. Storms like this often made their way across the state then out to sea. Temperatures were expected to dip below freezing overnight, and the weatherman predicted up to eight inches of rain in the next two days.

As Ben walked out to his car, he looked at the sky toward the west. It looked dark and stormy already. He wondered if they should cancel their movie plans this afternoon. On a nice day, he would have walked the distance between the News Journal office and the diner on Beach Street; it was just around the corner a few blocks. But it looked as if the rain might start cutting loose any minute.

It took two minutes to reach the diner but almost ten minutes more to find a parking space, compliments of the WACS. As he walked past the diner's glass windows, he saw Claire and Barb sitting inside. Claire saw him, ran outside, and all but leaped into his arms. "I'm so glad you're here," she said.

Ben kissed her passionately. As their lips parted, he glanced through the store window, saw Barb rolling her eyes. He smiled at her over Claire's shoulder. He didn't mind her chiding; he loved the way Claire greeted him and didn't care how it looked.

"Oh my," Claire said. "It's getting cold out

here." She stepped out from under the awning and looked up at the sky.

"Big storm coming," he said. "One of the weathermen at the paper said it was going to be a bad one."

"Really?"

"Strong winds, almost as bad as a tropical storm. And eight inches of rain."

"When?"

"Let's get inside." He opened the door, put his arm around her, and guided her in. "The worst of it's supposed to come later tonight, but I don't know if we should go to the movies this afternoon. Hi, Barb."

She waved. "You two," she said. "Every time you meet it's like Rhett and Scarlett in *Gone with the Wind*."

Claire looked at Barb. "I love that scene you're talking about, but we're not going to end up like Rhett and Scarlett. Our story's going to have a happy ending." Turning to Ben, she said, "Can't we go to the movie? It's only two hours."

"What's playing?" he asked.

"It's an Alfred Hitchcock movie," Barb said. "Called *Shadow of a Doubt*, with Joseph Cotton and Teresa Wright. Supposed to be good, very suspenseful. Joseph Cotton plays this creepy uncle who comes into town. He seems wonderful at first, but . . . he's not who he pretends to be." She said the last part in an eerie voice.

Oh great, Ben thought, *that's all I need.* "I don't know, Claire. These weathermen don't always get the timing of these things right. By the look of that sky outside, I'd say it could break loose any minute. And look"—he pointed to her chair —"you only have a light jacket. You shouldn't be out in weather like this in that. The temperature's going to be dropping all afternoon."

"Maybe we can go tomorrow after church." Claire turned to Barb. "What do you think? Can you make it tomorrow afternoon?"

"Sure. I got no plans."

"Umm . . . this storm is supposed to last all day tomorrow and maybe even through Monday."

"Ben, you're spoiling everything," Barb said. Both women got up. Ben helped Claire put on her jacket.

"Maybe so," Ben said. "Just trying to be a voice of reason." Just then, a drizzling rain began outside. "Look, it's already starting. We better get to the car. Can I drop you home, Barb?"

"That'd be great."

As they walked through the front door of the diner, Ben looked at the storm clouds overhead, grateful for their assistance. He was for anything that kept them from having to sit through a movie about a nice guy coming into town who's "not who he pretends to be."

Chapter Nineteen

After Ben dropped Barb off at her place, Claire reminded him about Hank. Sure enough, he was standing in line at the theater for the afternoon matinee. Ben double-parked just long enough to tell him they weren't coming.

When they pulled into Claire's driveway on Ridgewood Avenue, the rain had temporarily halted, but the wind was blowing harder and now the whole sky was dark and threatening. "Let's hurry before it starts coming down again," Ben said.

Claire's mom must have seen them coming. She had the front door open as they stepped onto the porch. She closed the door behind them; the house was nice and warm. "I'm freezing," Claire said. She walked over to the radiator and stood as close as she could. Ben took his coat off and draped it around her shoulders, then rubbed her arms.

"I'm thinking, Ben, that you should put that coat right back on," Mrs. Richards said.

"Why, Mom?" Claire said.

"I just got off the phone with your father. He said this storm is going to be pretty bad. The winds are getting so strong, they have all their crews tying down the airplanes at the base. They get the latest weather reports out there. He also said the rain's going to come down in buckets off and on the next few days. Some low-lying areas on the beachside are expected to flood. He suggested Ben should head over to his house and pack a bag, maybe stay here until it passes."

"Oh, I like that idea," Claire said.

"We have a number of nice guest rooms upstairs, Ben."

Claire shot her mother a look, as if that point needed to be clarified. "You could stay in Jack's old room," she said. "Right across the hall from mine. It will be so much fun."

"I think I'll do that," Ben said. "You still cold, Claire? I can get your coat out of the closet."

"No, I think I'm warm enough now. Want me to go with you?"

"I wish you'd stay here," her mother said. "I could use some help with dinner. Your father is coming home early, as soon as the base is secure."

"I'll be fast," Ben said, putting on his coat. "I pack light." He leaned over and gave Claire a kiss. "Thanks, Mrs. Richards, for the offer to stay here. And thank your husband for me."

"You're welcome, Ben. But you can thank him yourself. You'll probably be back here before he will."

"Right, well, I'll see you both in about twenty minutes."

Claire walked him to the door. As she opened

it, they both heard a loud crack. It startled Claire. They watched as a palm frond dropped on the front lawn. Instantly, the wind whipped it down the street. "Be careful," she said.

"I will."

Ben zigzagged through the downtown area, then crossed the Broadway Bridge toward the beachside. At one point, a wind gust hit him broadside, actually caused him to swerve and hit the curb. The wheels screeched. He pulled back to the left and just barely missed a car coming head-on in the other direction.

He noticed how dark the river water had become, reflecting back the color in the angry sky. The normally calm waters seemed to be almost boiling, with hundreds of little whitecaps tossing water into the wind.

Ben had to admit, the whole thing was pretty exciting. He especially looked forward to getting to spend so much time with Claire. As he turned down Vermont Avenue, he wondered whether the area could actually be called low-lying, and whether there was any real danger of flooding. It didn't matter, he had to take precautions just in case. His thoughts immediately went to the suitcase filled with cash and ration coupons locked in the second bedroom.

Sure didn't want that thing floating down the street.

He pulled into the driveway and hurried to the

front door as heavy drops of rain began to fall. Once inside, he double-checked all the windows to make sure they were closed tight, then pulled out his keys and unlocked the bedroom. He pulled the suitcase from under the bed and set it on top.

The drapes were closed, as usual. He walked over and turned on the lamp. After opening the top dresser drawer, he slid out the watertight bag he'd originally wrapped the suitcase in, back on the U-boat.

He hadn't used it since that night. Really, this bag and the suitcase on the bed were the last remnants of his old life. It was a good feeling.

Well, there was the pistol, which he hadn't used since the night he'd dug the suitcase out of the sand. To be safe, he bent down and pulled out the bottom dresser drawer. There it was. He tossed the gun and the bag on the bed, intending to wrap it up inside the watertight bag with the suitcase. He peeked outside; the rain had stopped again. Maybe he should pack a bag first, get it out in the car before the rain started up again.

He walked across the hall to the larger bedroom where he slept. As he did, he heard the wind whistling through the kitchen. There was a large window in there, facing the backyard, next to his dinette table. It provided great lighting when he typed his articles for the paper, but it obviously had some leaks. If air could get in, so could a hard rain. He didn't want his typewriter ruined. Better take that with him too.

Where was the case? he wondered. The typewriter worked wonderfully, but the portable case that came with it was a piece of junk. It was cracked across the bottom, and two of the corners had to be taped together. There it was, on top of the icebox. He quickly put the typewriter in the case, tried in vain to get the latch to close, then held it in both arms and hurried out the front door. He'd have to come back for the ream of paper, maybe put it in the suitcase he brought to Claire's.

With the typewriter in the backseat, he went back inside to pack his bag. After he'd put it in the car, he went back to secure the bigger, more important suitcase. A series of even darker, more ominous clouds were moving in from the west. He'd better hurry.

He opened the suitcase and thought through how much cash and ration coupons he needed for the week ahead, and for that purchase he planned to make at his last stop before heading back to Claire's. He wedged the gun in a side pocket, zippered it shut, then closed the lid and slid the watertight bag over it.

He stood back and looked at the dresser. Hard to judge how deep the water might get if the street did flood. A picture of the dresser flipping on its side and floating down the street, the suitcase drifting right beside it flashed in his mind.

No . . . that wouldn't do.

Then he saw the perfect spot. He picked the suitcase up, turned it on its side, and lifted it onto the closet shelf. It was at least six feet off the ground and bolted to the wall. He closed the closet door, locked the bedroom door, took one last look around the house, then went outside and locked that door too. As he did, the rain started pouring down. He was nearly soaked by the time he got in the car.

Just one more stop to make, downtown. This time he'd have an umbrella. The Duval Jewelry Store on Beach Street. He'd had his eye on a particular item for weeks.

A diamond ring for Claire.

Chapter Twenty

When Ben arrived at Claire's house, Mr. Richards's car was already in the driveway. The rain came in squalls, pouring down heavily for several minutes then easing to a drizzle. The wind caused it to come in almost sideways. Ben waited in the car until the most recent torrent subsided.

He reached in his coat pocket, pushed the box containing Claire's ring as far down as he could, then got out and flipped open his umbrella. The wind instantly turned it inside out. It was useless.

He opened the back door and pulled his suitcase out first. He didn't dare lift the typewriter case by the handle; it would fall apart. He'd have to make two trips.

"Hurry, Ben, before it starts up again."

He turned around to see Claire on the porch, holding the front door open. "Coming." He shut the door and made a run for it. "I'll just set this down here. Got to go back for my typewriter."

"Do you have to work?"

"Probably not," he said. "But my editor may call. If so, I can work from here, not have to go back out in the weather."

"I'll bring this inside," she said, reaching for the suitcase.

"But don't carry it up the stairs. Let me do that." He ran back for the typewriter. She held the door open for him. He walked through, cradling the typewriter in his arms. As he entered the foyer, Mr. Richards was coming down the stairs.

"Ben, glad you made it. It's getting pretty mean out there."

"Hi, Mr. Richards. I—"

A loud crash. The typewriter fell to the floor, leaving Ben standing there holding the case, now in two pieces. Ben looked down. Apparently, the crack in the bottom had broken through. "Oh no."

"Ben, are you okay?" Claire rushed over.

"I'm fine. Not sure my typewriter is." He bent

down to survey the damage. She bent down beside him and picked up a few of the pieces of the case that had splintered off.

"It looks okay," she said.

"It does." He lifted it up. "I wish I could say the same for the floor." They looked down at a nice gouge carved into the wood floor where the corner impacted first. "Missed the throw rug by two inches."

"Don't worry about it."

Ben looked over his shoulder to see Mr. Richards bending over behind them, surveying the scene.

"Nice thing about wood floors. We'll rub in a little stain, a little polish, and it'll be fine, just a little more rustic."

"Will you still be able to use it?" Claire asked, looking at the typewriter.

"We'll see." He walked over to the dining room and set it on a place mat on the table. "Okay if I put it here?"

"For a little while," Mr. Richards said. "We'll have to find a more suitable place if you need to work."

"No, I just want to test it out."

"Here." Claire handed him a piece of paper. "It's not typewriter paper, but will this work?"

"It should be fine." He rolled it in and started typing. After a few moments, he announced, "Looks like no permanent damage."

"Glad to hear it," Mr. Richards said. "I'll just be in the den until dinner." He got up and left the room.

"You type fast," Claire said.

"Twice as fast as when I started."

"What did you write?" She rested her hands on his shoulders and leaned over to see.

> I love Claire;
> Claire loves me.
> Because of this, I'm so happy.
> q-x-y-z!

"Aww." She kissed him on the cheek then whispered in his ear, "It's pretty corny, but I love you too. What's q-x-y-z?"

"Just trying to make sure all the keys work. Where should I put this?"

"There's a desk in Jack's old room, the room you're staying in."

"Great. I'll put this and my bag up there, hang a few things in the closet so they don't wrinkle, and be right back."

"I'll finish helping my mother. Dinner's almost ready."

"How much time?"

"Maybe ten minutes."

Ben carefully climbed the stairs and walked down the wide hallway. He paused briefly and glanced in Claire's room. Centered on her bed were the stuffed animals he'd won for her back in October. Still wearing their same silly grins.

The dinner was delicious. Ben was amazed at Mrs. Richards's cooking. He could just imagine what she'd put on the table if she had no rationing restrictions. When he had come downstairs wearing a tweed jacket, Claire had asked if he was cold. He'd said he was just trying to rid himself of the chill he got from loading and unloading the car.

That was true, but the greater reason was the coat had better pockets to hold her ring box. If he put it in his pants pocket, she'd instantly know what it was.

"I'm going to light a fire in the den, Ben," Mr. Richards said. "Want to help me?"

"Sure."

"You two make it all nice and warm in there," Mrs. Richards said. "I'll clear the dishes and Claire will make us some coffee." The wind howled outside so strong it rattled the windows.

"I hope this storm doesn't mess up our radio reception," Claire said as she headed toward the kitchen. "Some of my favorite shows are on tonight."

Ben walked across the foyer, through the living room, and into the den, which occupied the far left corner of the downstairs. A big leather sofa and three comfy chairs surrounded a Zenith console radio. A finely finished brick fireplace occupied half the back wall. The other two walls were lined with dark, mahogany bookshelves. Mr. Richards was already bent over the fireplace, building a small teepee with twigs.

"Can you hand me a few sheets of newspaper there, Ben?"

"You're not going to burn one of my stories, are you?"

Mr. Richards laughed. "Only if that's what you hand me."

Ben pulled out a few sheets from the classified section, tore them up into little pieces. Once the twigs lit, Ben handed him some pieces of kindling. "While we're alone I wonder if I could talk to you about something."

"Sure." The kindling wood began to catch fire. "We'll let that burn a bit." He turned toward Ben. "So . . . let's talk." He eased into one of the leather chairs.

Ben took a seat in the adjacent one. "I think you know by now how much I care about Claire. Well, I love her. I'm *in* love with her."

"I get the picture, Ben."

"I'd like to ask her to marry me . . . with your permission, of course. I've tried to wait a respectable amount of time before bringing this up, but I knew she was the only one for me the day I met her." Ben felt the little finger on his right hand twitch for some reason. He had to calm down.

Mr. Richards looked at the fire's progress, then leaned back in his chair.

"I had a feeling we'd be having this conversation soon."

"You did?"

"I felt the exact same way about Claire's mom." He didn't seem upset, or even on edge. Ben began to relax. "And I've watched how you've treated Claire these past months. I've liked what I've seen, and I know how she feels about you."

"You do?"

"I'm her dad. She's my little girl. I make everything that concerns her my business." He said this, still, without any tension in his voice. "Because of that, I hope you don't mind, but I telephoned your editor earlier this week." Ben was surprised. "Since I figured this conversation might be coming up, I wanted to know how you were doing over there at the paper, what kind of future you might have."

"What did he say?"

"He likes you too. Thinks highly of you, in fact. He told me he felt you've become quite the reporter and that you have a bright future ahead of you at the News Journal."

Ben liked the sound of that. He reached into his coat pocket. "I'd like to show you something." He got up, walked over to the doorway. He could still hear the ladies chatting in the kitchen. "Here," he said, opening the lid to the ring box.

221

Mr. Richards got a big smile on his face. "She's going to love that." After a few moments Ben closed the lid. "When you going to give it to her?"

"I thought sometime this weekend, since we'll be shut up here in the house with this storm."

"No, you don't want to do that."

"I don't?"

"No. You want to make it special. Do something memorable, something she'll want to brag about to her friends. Not just about the ring but the way you gave it to her. Women love to tell stories like that. Have you ever heard Mrs. Richards tell our story?"

Ben shook his head no.

"And you never will. I botched it up."

"So what should I do?"

"You're a smart guy, Ben. Think about it. Something will come to you."

Ben appreciated the advice, but he was a little disappointed as he put the ring back in his pocket. He'd set his heart on giving it to her tomorrow, or the day after. But he hadn't given it much thought, other than getting down on one knee.

Mr. Richards got up and carefully set a small log on the fire. "But there's something I'd like to give you."

"What's that?"

"It's right over here." He walked across the room to one of the bookshelves. "Something I think you'll get more use out of than I ever have." He reached up and pulled a large wooden box down from the top shelf. He blew off the dust then turned and held it out as he walked toward Ben.

As he got closer, Ben knew this was no ordinary box. It was exquisitely hand-carved, on every side and on top, very ornate. Among the shapes carved into the surface was a large tobacco leaf in the center.

Mr. Richards set it down on the coffee table. "The moment I saw that typewriter case fall apart, I thought you could use this. Looks just about the right size. It's a humidor, made of solid rosewood, hand-carved in Cuba. See the tobacco leaf etched in the top? My father bought it in 1898. Did I ever tell you about him?"

"I don't think you did."

"He fought with Teddy Roosevelt and the Rough Riders up San Juan Hill. He picked this up in Havana before they shipped him back home. Dad was quite a fellow, smoked Cuban cigars all his life. Stored them all right in here. Before he died, he gave it to me. But I don't smoke cigars."

"What about Jack?"

"Jack doesn't smoke them, either. I figure you could use it for that typewriter. All you'd need is to screw a nice handle on the side."

"Mr. Richards. I couldn't take this. It's a family heirloom."

"I guess it is. But you're going to be part of the family soon."

"I . . . I don't know—"

"Go on up and get that typewriter. Let's see how it fits."

"You sure?"

"Ben . . . I want you to have it." He looked Ben right in the eyes and said, "I'm a pretty good judge of character. You're one of the finest young men I've ever met. I know for a fact Claire's going to say yes the moment you pop the question. And I'd be honored to have you marry my daughter."

Ben felt a rush of emotion come over him. He got up before it came to tears. "I'll be right back." He rushed out of the den, almost knocking Claire over. She was carrying a tray of coffee cups. "I'm sorry."

"Ben, what's wrong?" she asked. "Are you okay?"

"I'm more than okay. I love you, Claire." He leaned over and kissed her. "I'll be right back."

As he climbed the stairs, he heard Claire say, "What was all that about?"

"Nothing," her father said. "We just found Ben a nice carrying case for that typewriter of his."

14

Legare Street, Charleston
10:30 a.m.

I had a feeling about this before it became a thought. A string of feelings, in fact, stirring beneath the surface, growing stronger as I read.

That humidor.

I flipped back to the page.

As he got closer, Ben knew this was no ordinary box. It was exquisitely hand-carved, on every side and on top, very ornate. Among the shapes carved into the surface was a large tobacco leaf in the center.

I dropped the page. As I reached for it, I almost knocked the rest of the manuscript to the ground. I lifted it back up on my lap but set the rest of the pages on the wicker table. I leaned forward and read something Claire's father had said:

It's a humidor, made of solid rosewood, hand-carved in Cuba. My father bought it in 1898.

And then:

I figure you could use it for that typewriter. All you'd need is to screw a nice handle on the side.

It had to be the same. I shot up, dropped the page in my chair, and hurried across the porch to the front door. A moment later I stood in the office doorway staring down at one thing—the typewriter case. Specifically, at the top. At the large leaf that had been carved in the center. And I could tell now, it *was* a tobacco leaf. I'd never paid any attention to the case before. It had always just been Gramps's typewriter case. But now I could see it for what it really was: a rosewood cigar humidor.

Had it really been hand-carved in Cuba? Brought home by one of Teddy Roosevelt's Rough Riders in 1898? Did Gramps make that part up? I stepped closer. The case had dramatically increased in value. I unhooked the latch. Slowly lifted the lid, bent over, and inhaled the pleasing aroma.

Just wood, though, no trace of cigar smell.

I knew my grandfather loved this typewriter, and the case. But why write about it? As a writer, I knew what it was to incorporate real-life elements into your story, even things from your life. To spice up a scene or add some interesting details. Is that what he was doing here?

I closed the lid and glanced at my watch. It was

too early for lunch but not for a snack. I poured a glass of Coke, grabbed a tube of Pringles, and headed back out to the porch. Reading about Gramps's typewriter case was the first thing in the book that had drawn me out of the story and reminded me my own grandfather wrote it.

I knew as I finished the book I'd keep an eye out for more of Gramps's little secrets.

Chapter Twenty-One

Justice Department Building
Washington DC
January, 1943

Gene Conway, Assistant Director of the FBI, stepped into the wood-paneled office of J. Edgar Hoover. Two American flags stood like sentries behind the director's desk on either side. Conway glanced up at the blue and white FBI seal hanging over Hoover's head on the back wall then down at Hoover, who hadn't looked up yet. He was signing papers. Both men were impeccably dressed in dark suits, pressed white shirts, and modest ties. What had become, unofficially, the G-man's uniform.

"What is it, Gene? You said it was important."

"It's happened again, Mr. Hoover. Nazis have landed more saboteurs, probably from U-boats again. Off the beach in Florida, maybe somewhere else."

Hoover looked up with angry eyes. "*Maybe* somewhere else?"

"We only know about Florida for certain at this point. I'm judging by what they did last time, sir. Multiple teams in two different states."

"When did this happen?"

"We don't have an exact date. They may have come onshore several months ago."

"Months ago? How is it that we're just finding this out now?"

"The report is still preliminary, but—"

"What do we know, Gene? Give me the facts."

"The nor'easter pounding New England right now started in Florida a few days ago. The wind and seas tore up the beaches pretty good down there."

Hoover shot him a look that said "get to the bottom line."

"We found a body, sir. In the sand dunes."

"Bodies have been washing up on the beach off and on for the last year," Hoover said. "Merchantmen from those ships sunk by U-boats."

"This body didn't wash up on the beach, Mr. Hoover. The storm eroded the sand dunes, which exposed where the body was buried."

"It was buried?"

"That's how we know the saboteurs have been here for several months. By the condition of the body."

"We need something more specific than several months."

"We should know more after the autopsy."

"Just the one body?" Hoover asked, leaning forward on the desk.

"We've got crews digging in the area nearby.

But looks that way so far. Don't know how the man died yet, but I've been told there were no gunshot wounds. None of the bones were broken."

"Might've drowned," Hoover said. "But the Nazis never send in just one man."

"That's our thinking, sir. Based on what we learned from the last bunch, they always work in teams. Last time it was two teams of four. And the four-man teams operated, really, in teams of two."

"Anyone talk to Dasch and Burger?" Hoover was referring to George Dasch and Ernst Burger, the two Nazi saboteurs from the team caught last summer. The two who were still alive. They had turned in the other six, who had been executed. Dasch and Burger were reluctantly spared because of their cooperation and were given long prison sentences.

"Got a team heading to the prison now for an interview," Conway said. "But Dasch and Burger already told us there were only eight men in their squad, and only eight, even back in Germany. All present and accounted for."

"Doesn't mean the Germans didn't train other teams in other locations," Hoover said. "And kept them in the dark about each other."

"Need to know, you mean?" Conway said.

"Right." Hoover leaned back in his chair. "If these new teams have been here for months, I'm surprised we haven't had any incidents. There haven't been any, right?"

Conway shook his head. "You'd be the first to know, sir. But we have tightened up security at all the targets Dasch and Burger told us about."

"Doesn't mean anything," Hoover said. "Plenty of new targets to pick from."

"Maybe we haven't heard anything because they chickened out, like Dasch and Burger did."

"Maybe. Bunch of Keystone Cops, that crew. But we can't count on it. We need to find out what these other teams are up to."

"Everyone from last time is already on it, Mr. Hoover. The Florida and New York teams."

"Well, double it!" Hoover said. "Triple it, if you have to. We need to round these men up, wherever they are."

"Right, sir."

Hoover stared down at a spot on his desk. "The president thought making public examples of the first saboteurs—and their swift executions—would deter the Germans from sending in any more teams. I didn't think it would. They're a devious lot." He sighed. "And those imbeciles at the Coast Guard. Told them last time this was going to happen again and keep on happening if they didn't start beefing up the beach patrols. They've got huge gaps all up and down the coast."

"It seems like they did respond to at least some of the things we mentioned," Conway said.

"A horse patrol found the body in the dunes."

"But they know this is our case," Hoover said. "From top to bottom."

"The Coast Guard knows, sir," Conway said. "I made it clear. They didn't even put up a fight."

"What about the locals? I don't want any trouble from them."

"I don't expect any, sir. But how do you want to handle the press?"

"No press. None. Even after we catch these guys. I'll confirm with the president, but I'm sure he'll concur. The public thinks we got the last spies rounded up, either in jail or executed. We want to keep it that way." Hoover looked up at Conway and smiled. "I want Americans to keep vigilant, but I don't want them thinking the Germans are really here."

"But sir, we'll have dozens of agents in the area trying to hunt these guys down, asking lots of questions. The press will get wind of that. Supposedly word's already leaked out about finding this body in the dunes."

"That's okay. Is the scene blocked off?"

"Completely, and no reporters have shown up yet," Conway said.

"Then we control the story. When we're ready, we'll tell them it's just another body washed up on the beach. No ID. For all they know, could be a sailor from one of these freighters that blew up. That's all they need to know."

"Right, sir."

"Who's in charge in Florida?"

"Special Agent Victor Hammond."

"A good man. Tell him everything I said, right away."

"I will."

"You didn't mention, Mr. Conway, how we know this dead body's from a U-boat. Was he wearing a German uniform?"

"No, he was dressed in street clothes. All bought in the US, at some point. But whoever put those clothes on him must've been in a hurry. Left his German dog tags on."

"We need to find that man," Hoover said.

"We will, sir. We will."

Chapter Twenty-Two

Special Agent Victor Hammond surveyed the scene. The coroner had just driven away with the body of a Nazi spy. Two teams explored the sand dunes for a half mile in either direction, looking to find anything else the Germans might have buried that night, things the storm may have recently exposed. Other teams were poking and digging holes in the immediate vicinity. Hammond had picked the same men who'd found the last cache of weapons, explosives, and cash buried back in June by Dasch and Burger's men.

The storm was long gone, but its effects were still present. It was low tide now, but the waves were still huge. From what the local sheriff had said, at high tide the water still came much farther up the beach than normal. Where Hammond stood would be under a foot of water later that day. The wind blew so hard, he'd given up holding onto his hat and left it in the car.

He saw his partner, Nate Winters, walking through the soft sand, heading his way. "How many more hours before the tide changes, Nate?"

"Four or five. But I don't think there's anything more we can do here, Vic. They'll call us if they find anything."

"Here," Hammond said, handing him a sheet of paper. "Give this to that huddle of reporters up by the road."

Nate looked at it, read a few paragraphs, nodded his head. "Body washed up on the beach. Hinting at it being one of our guys, from one of the Liberty ships?"

"That's the way the boss wants it," Hammond said. "They might be suspicious, want to know why we have so many agents out here for something like that. But they'll cooperate. Where are the rest of the men?"

"Waiting in a little restaurant on Atlantic Avenue, between here and Ormond Beach. That's the closest town. I told them to shut it down, tell the owner we need his place for a briefing. He was fine when I said we'd all be buying lunch."

"Well, go give this to the press. I'll get the car and pick you up." Hammond walked through the beach sand, then the sand dunes, up to his car. He'd parked it just off Atlantic Avenue along a lonely stretch, with nothing but more sand and sand dunes as far as the eye could see.

As soon as he turned the car on, a call came in on the radio about an explosion in a shipbuilding plant near Savannah, Georgia. He wrote down everything he'd been told. Details were sketchy. More to come in another report an hour from now. But he was to send a team up there right away.

On the way to the Seaside Cafe, Hammond had briefed Nate about the explosion near Savannah. They parked among a dozen identical cars in the small restaurant parking lot. Inside, twenty field agents sat in a handful of booths and tables, sipping coffee, drinking soda, and eating sandwiches. As soon as they saw Hammond, the conversations stopped. Everyone gave him their full attention. Hammond looked to the left, saw the cook standing behind a counter with a woman in a waitress outfit.

"Hi," the woman said, walking up with a menu. "I'm Matty. This is my husband, Bill." She gestured to the cook.

"I don't need a menu, ma'am," Hammond said.

He noticed what two agents at the nearest table were eating. "My partner and I will have that."

She pulled out her pad. "Two BLTs. Want that on white or rye?"

"Rye is fine." He looked at Nate.

"I'll have the same."

Hammond leaned toward her. "Matty, can you get those out in less than five minutes?"

"I think we can do that."

"Then I'm going to need you and your husband to leave for about fifteen minutes."

"You mean . . . leave the restaurant?"

"Yes. I need to speak to my men in private. National security matter."

"Oh . . . sure. We can do that." She leaned over and whispered, "This about that body they found in the dunes up the way?"

"Can't say."

"You men want anything to drink?"

"Coffee is fine."

Nate nodded, indicating the same. Hammond turned away from her, toward his men, to send her a message. "Eat up, boys. I'll brief you in about ten minutes." He sat at an empty table close to the front door. Nate sat beside him.

In a few minutes, Matty and her husband brought out the sandwiches, chips, and coffee, then hurried out the back door. Hammond wolfed down his BLT, took a few sips of coffee, then stood up. "Men, all of you were involved when we caught the last bunch of spies last summer, so you know what this investigation will look like. Not saying it will be identical. As far as we can tell, this new team had no involvement with the last group. Dasch and Burger didn't know anything about them."

"Do we believe them?" someone asked.

"Yeah, we do," he said. "As far as they knew, their two teams were the whole program. So be ready for some surprises."

"Do we even know for certain there are other Nazi spies in the country now?" another man asked. "Don't we just have the one body? No other evidence?"

"We haven't found any other suitcases or crates, correct?" said the agent right in front of him. "Like we did last summer."

"If you're asking me," Hammond said, "if I might be sending you out on a wild goose chase, with no good leads, and probably nothing to show for all your hard work and long hours in the end"—Hammond paused a moment—"the answer is yes." The men laughed. "We could be looking at a lone German soldier buried in the sand dunes, but then you have to ask yourself why. Why would a German U-boat come onshore, risking capture, to bury one man? Why would they change him into American clothes? It doesn't add up." He looked down at Nate. "You drinking that water?"

Nate handed the glass to Hammond. "From

what we've learned in our interviews with Dasch and Burger, this dead guy had a partner. They always work in pairs. And there was probably at least another team of two Germans that came onshore that night from the same U-boat. Could even be more. Back in June there were eight. Four in Florida, four on Long Island. We don't know if this dead guy's partner set out on his own or joined up with the others."

"So we've got a lot less to go on this time than before," a voice in the back said.

"We do. But I just received word of a small explosion in a shipyard just east of Savannah. Could be nothing or it could be the work of this new team of saboteurs. The timing is very suspicious." As voices rose, Hammond called the men back to attention. "Listen up. Remember what broke the case wide open last time? It wasn't because we found a needle in a haystack. It happened because Dasch and Burger got cold feet and turned the others in. We don't need to find all these guys. Just one. We're working on the assumption that this new team paid attention to what happened to the last team and learned from their mistakes."

"So we're not wasting time checking out all the military targets the last team went after," Nate said.

"That's right," Hammond said. "They would know how much tighter security would be at those locations. Narrows our search down a little." He picked up a thin stack of papers. "I'm holding your assignments here. All the military bases and defense plants in a two hundred mile radius. We don't have an exact date this new team came onshore. But judging by the body, it was likely sometime in August or September."

"Then they can be anywhere by now," one of the men said. "Look how far the Florida team traveled back in June. In less than two weeks they were in Chicago and Cincinnati."

"Your job will be to head to your assigned targets and start looking for anything that doesn't add up. Start with strangers who've moved into the area in the last few months. Men without families. They'll probably have lots of cash. Most of their possessions will be new. Most of the guys on the last team spoke English pretty well, but some of them had German accents. If there's a German section of town, start there. You get the idea."

Hammond took one last gulp of coffee. "I'll start around here, the towns nearby, working on the assumption that the partner of this dead guy set out on his own. I don't think they'd have made a threesome. That would draw too much attention."

"But we can't rule that out, either," one of the men said.

"No, can't rule anything out at this point," Hammond said, putting on his fedora. "As for the

Savannah team, your assignment just changed. Nate here will be heading that up. You guys leave immediately and go right to that shipyard, just outside of town. You'll be getting an update on the radio. The rest of you—keep this in mind—we just need to get one of these guys. Just one. He'll already know we put six of his buddies in the electric chair last August and that fate awaits him if he doesn't cooperate. Get any leads back to me or Nate."

He lifted his coat off the chair. "We'll find these guys, gentlemen. It's just a matter of time."

Chapter Twenty-Three

Claire put on her sweater and stepped outside. She wanted to finish her coffee on the porch. The sun was shining again. The temperature had warmed up to a pleasant sixty-two degrees. Standing at the wood rail, she gazed up and down the street. She loved the way things looked after a big storm. Tree limbs and palm fronds meshed together in dark piles beside every driveway. But everything else looked bright and green and alive. Especially the palms. She remembered something her father had said when she was a little girl and frightened by the thunder. "You know how Daddy prunes the hedges? Well, storms are God's way of pruning the trees."

Something else excited her this morning. Ben had just called her from the News Journal, asking if he could see her after she got off work this afternoon. He sounded excited, saying he had something "very important to talk about." She was pretty sure she knew what it was.

"Mind if I join you?"

Claire turned to see her mom come through the screened door. "Not at all. I was just admiring the scene."

"That was quite a storm," her mother said. "But not as bad as they expected, I guess. I read in the paper there was a little flooding in Holly Hill, but nothing major."

"Ben called me last night when he got home. No problems on his street or any of the streets nearby."

"Did his house leak?"

"Nope, everything was fine."

"You seem pretty chipper." Her mother sat in a rocking chair.

"Ben called me again this morning," she said, suppressing a smile.

"What? Is something going on?"

Claire told her about the call, about meeting him after work and her suspicions. She was almost giggling.

Her mother smiled. "From what your father said the other night before bed . . . you might be right."

"Really?"

She nodded. "That's why I wanted to talk with you, find out what you're thinking."

"You mean if he asked me to marry him, would I say yes?"

"That's pretty much it."

"Of course I would!" Her hand knocked her coffee cup over. It spilled all over the porch. "I'm so sorry."

Her mother laughed. "I guess you're a little excited."

"I'll get something to clean it up." She ran into the house and came back with a wet washcloth. As she rubbed it back and forth, she stopped and looked up. "Mom, I love Ben, more than anything else in the world. I've been so happy these past few months."

"No lingering thoughts about Jim Burton?"

"Not a single one. I don't know what I felt for Jim, but it was nothing like this."

"Has Ben said anything to you, maybe hinted at wanting to be married yet?"

"He tells me he loves me every time we see each other. He's talked about wanting to spend the rest of our lives together, even talked about wanting to grow old together."

"That's pretty strong marriage language."

"And you'll love this," Claire said. "I asked him where he'd like to live. If he ever wanted to go back to Pennsylvania where he grew up, or move someplace else."

"And . . . ?"

"He said he loves it here. He'd like to stay right here and raise a family someday."

"With you?"

"He was looking right at me and smiling when he said it."

"So you've been thinking about marrying him for a little while, then."

"Lately, it's all I think about."

Father Flanagan hurried, as quietly as he could, down the side aisle of St. Paul's Church, hoping not to disturb the handful of women praying in the first few rows. Ben wasn't anywhere near the confessional. Aidan was running a little late; maybe Ben had already gone inside. He looked up and saw the little red light was on above one of the penitent's doors.

Someone was in there.

He slipped into the center compartment and said a little prayer. It sounded like someone was crying on the other side. Clearly, a man. He slid the little door over. The crying stopped.

"Ben, is that you?"

"Father Flanagan, my life is over."

It was Ben. When he'd called an hour ago, he sounded very upset, but he didn't want to explain anything over the telephone. "What do you mean? What's happened?"

"Things were going so good, wonderful even.

I thought God had finally made a way for me to start over. I was just about to ask Claire to marry me. She loves me. I know she does. But now . . . it's over. It's hopeless." He began to cry again.

"It's never hopeless, son. Tell me what's wrong. What's happened?"

"The storm, Father. And now the explosion, near Savannah. It's all falling apart."

"Slow down, Ben. Catch your breath. What about the storm? The one that just passed?"

"Yes, some reporters were talking about it at the News Journal. They said the FBI is involved, just north of town. And then there's this story, just came in over the wire, about an explosion in a shipyard just outside Savannah."

"What do they have to do with each other? With you, Ben? I don't understand." He heard Ben inhale and exhale slowly.

"I'm sorry, Father. My head is spinning. I don't know what to do. I'm sure the FBI is going to come here, maybe today. Certainly by tomorrow. It's Jurgen's body. They've found it."

"Jurgen?"

"My partner, remember? The German agent I was with the night I came ashore. The one who drowned in the surf."

He remembered. "They found his body?"

"The storm eroded the sand dunes where I'd buried him. Someone from the Coast Guard Beach Patrol found his body."

"Oh my." This was terrible. "What makes you think the FBI is involved? It's a terrible thing, but bodies from ships have washed up on the beach—"

"That's what they told our reporters," Ben said. "But nobody's buying it. I mean, that's what they'll report in the paper, but they know this body couldn't be a sailor. They found him half buried in a sand dune. And the reporters said there were five times as many FBI agents crawling around the scene, compared to other times when a sailor's body did wash up on the beach."

"I see."

"That means I have to leave. Now. I can't stay here. It's just a matter of time before they come here and start asking a lot of questions. If I get caught, they'll kill me. And they might even come after Claire and her parents."

"Where will you go?"

"I don't know. Oh no . . . Claire." He began crying again. "I can't just leave her without saying anything."

The poor lad. Aidan didn't know what to say. "What about this explosion? How does that fit in?"

"It's the other team, Graf and Kittel, I'm sure of it. They've started executing their mission."

That was what Aidan had been afraid of. He'd hoped the men might have given up or been caught by now. So many months had gone by. "Was anyone hurt or killed?"

"I don't know. It's too early to say. We'll

probably know more by the evening edition. But . . . how can there not be casualties? That's the whole point of their mission. Kill Americans. Strike fear into the hearts of the enemy. That's what we were told, over and over again."

"Do you know for certain it was them?"

"No, but I know the shipyard in Savannah was one of their targets, and another shipyard south of there . . . in Brunswick."

"Then you have to report this. You can't let anything else happen."

"I can't report it, Father. They'll trace it back to me. I know they will, somehow."

"But Ben—"

"I'm not going to let them hurt anyone else, Father." He said this with a new tone of voice. Strong, as if he'd found a switch and turned off the tears. "I should have done something, long before this."

"The authorities, Ben. Let them handle this. I can report it for you, if you'd like."

"No, Father. Thank you, but no."

He heard Ben stand up.

"I know what I must do now. It's crystal clear."

"Ben, don't leave, not yet."

"Pray for me, Father. I will stop them or die trying. But first . . . I need to talk to Claire."

"Ben . . . wait."

"Pray for me, Father."

He opened the door and walked out.

Chapter Twenty-Four

As soon as Claire saw Ben walking toward her on the sidewalk, she knew he hadn't come to have the conversation she'd been daydreaming about all day. Something was terribly wrong. It looked as if he'd been crying. She had just clocked out at Woolworth's and met him at the front door.

"Ben, what's wrong?"

"We have to talk." He embraced her but pulled away before she could kiss him.

"Are you okay? What's happened?"

He looked over his shoulder. "Let's take a walk, in the park."

Claire wrapped her arm around his. He wore a gray raincoat and black fedora. They stood there waiting at the curb for the traffic light to change. She looked up at him, but he looked straight ahead. This was totally unlike him. It made her tense up.

They stepped over a puddle and hurried across the street. "What is it, Ben? What's going on?" He looked down at her and seemed like he was about to speak but then shook his head and stared straight ahead. Tears were forming in his eyes. They walked toward the river, turned right where the sidewalk curved, and kept walking. Up ahead was the bench where they first kissed.

"I love you, Claire," she heard him say as they walked. "Please remember that."

It frightened more than comforted her.

When they reached the bench, he sat down. She sat beside him. Then he stood up and paced in front of her, a few steps forward then back.

"Ben, come sit beside me. Please, calm down. Just tell me what's wrong. I love you too. Whatever it is, we'll get through it together."

He looked into her eyes for the first time. "I wish that were true. So much."

She sighed. What could have gone so wrong in such a short amount of time? He stood there looking at her. She could see in his eyes that he was rehearsing what to say next.

"Ben, it's me."

"I know, it's you, Claire. But see . . . it's not me, Ben."

"What?"

He walked over and sat next to her, took her hand in his. "Before I say anything else, I want you to know. All the feelings I have for you, everything I have ever said to you about my love for you, my hopes and plans for our future . . . it's all true. Every last word."

"Okay . . ."

"Claire, I haven't been totally honest with you about who I am."

• • •

The look on her face was so hard to read. Ben didn't know if he should start from the beginning and ease into the hard part or just start off with it.

"Who you are, Ben? I don't understand. You're not . . . who you are?"

"I am, Claire. I mean, mostly. But there are some things I haven't told you. Some big things. Not because I didn't want to but because I couldn't."

"Ben, what are you saying?" Her expression was now alarmed. "What could keep someone from telling the truth to someone they love?"

Those were almost the exact words Father Flanagan had said to Ben. He had been right. But whether Ben had told her the truth then or now, what difference did it make? He was about to lose her. That was the truth.

"Ben, I need you to start talking plainly to me. What are you trying to say? What big things about you aren't true?"

"Claire, I am going to tell you everything—the whole truth—in this conversation. But I'm afraid if I start with the hardest part, you'll just get up and run away from me as fast as you can." *That didn't come out right.*

"Why, Ben? Have you done something horrible? What's going on?"

He had frightened her. He put his hand gently

on her shoulder. "Claire, I'm going to share some facts about who I am. When you hear them, you'll immediately know why I didn't tell them to you up front. But you need to know . . . I am *your* Ben. The man you've fallen in love with is who I am. These facts—the ones I'm going to tell you —they don't change that. Okay?"

"Just tell me, Ben. This is killing me."

"I will, but promise me, you'll let me tell you everything before you react."

Claire sighed.

"If you love me, Claire, promise me you'll hear me out."

"Okay, I will."

He looked out at the river then deep into her eyes. "Remember when I told you my parents died in a bombing raid?" She nodded. "Well, they did. But they weren't in London. You said that, and I didn't correct you."

"Where did they die?"

"In Cologne. A city in Germany."

"Germany."

"Yes, Claire. My parents are—I am—German."

"I don't understand. How did they get to Germany? We're at war."

"They went there before the war, in 1935. I was born in Pennsylvania, that is true. But they weren't. They came over here from Germany after World War I. I was born here, went to school here, *loved* it here. But they were always homesick and never felt like they fit in. Then in 1933, Hitler came to power in Germany and started turning everything around. Of course, all they knew were the reports they heard about how everything in Germany was wonderful now. Hitler started making appeals to all good Germans to return to the Fatherland."

"The Fatherland."

Ben shook his head. "That's how they think. It's all this nationalism. It's crazy."

"Is it like patriotism?"

"Not really. There's no freedom. It's like . . . picture FDR gets elected, and he takes over the military, secretly starts killing off all the Republicans and anyone else who doesn't agree with him. Then he takes over the press, the newspapers, and the radio. People only hear what he wants them to hear. From now on. He takes over the schools and children are brainwashed to think only one way. All for the glory of the Fatherland and the Fuhrer. The Fatherland, the Fuhrer. Everywhere you look, red banners and swastikas. I hated it there."

"So how did you escape?"

He could see it in her eyes. So far, she was sympathetic to his tale. "Now we come to the hard part. I didn't escape."

"Then how did you get away, how did you get back here?"

"I was sent here. I came in a U-boat."

"What!" She stood up, looked all around, as if someone might hear them.

"Claire, please, sit down. Let me explain."

"You came here . . ." She sat down, whispered loudly, "On a U-boat?"

"Yes, back in August."

"We only met in September."

"I know, and I loved you from the first moment I laid eyes on you."

"Ben . . . are you saying . . . you're a German spy?"

"No . . . well, not in my heart."

"What does that mean?"

"I came here for only one reason, to get away from the horror my parents put me through in Germany. After they died, I had no reason to stay. When the Nazis offered to train me as a spy, to send me here to the US, I knew it was my chance to get away. To come back to the land I love and start over."

Tears formed in her eyes, fell down her cheeks. "I'm so frightened. I don't know what to say."

"Say . . . you love me."

She was trembling. "Ben, I do love you, but I don't know. This is so much . . . too much, I think."

"What does that mean?"

"Ben, how can we just go on from here? I read about what they did to those German spies they caught over the summer. They killed them."

"I know, that's why I've had to create a new identity for myself. So I could start over. But I've been doing it. It's been working just fine. The only hard part has been lying to you, keeping all this from you and your parents."

"My goodness, Ben. My parents!"

"I know . . . I . . . I don't know what to do about them. What we should tell them."

"You said you had to create a new identity. Does that mean . . . your name isn't really Ben?"

He shook his head.

"Your name isn't Ben Coleman?"

"No."

She burst into tears. She buried her face in her hands. All he could hear muffled through her sobs was, "I don't even know your name."

"But I am Ben, Claire."

"No, you're not." She still hadn't lifted her head.

"I am. My name doesn't matter. I'm the same person on the inside. I haven't lied to you about that."

He waited there for several moments, rubbing her back gently as she cried. Finally, she looked up. He handed her a handkerchief. "What is your real name?"

But it was her eyes. Ben could see; it was as if the light had gone out of them. "It's Gerhard Kuhlmann. Well, in Pennsylvania, it was Gerard Kuhlmann."

"Oh my gosh." She looked at him as if he was suddenly a total stranger.

He felt sick inside.

"Well, tell me . . . *Gerhard Kuhlmann,* what else? I want to know everything you haven't told me. No more lies."

"Claire, I haven't been lying to you."

"No? What do you call it, then?"

"I haven't . . . I haven't volunteered things about me, things about my past, but I've worked very hard to be as honest with you as I can, especially about my heart, my feelings for you, my hopes for our future together. I even bought a diamond ring. Right over there at Duvall's Jewelry Store." Ben pointed toward Beach Street.

"It's not supposed to be hard, Ben. You're not supposed to have to work hard at being honest with someone you love."

"Claire, when could I have told you this? What would have been a better time? Can you imagine this ever being something that would be easy to hear?"

She looked away, toward the river. "I don't know. But I do know I need to hear everything else. I don't want any more lies."

Ben sighed. Then he told her. About the night he came ashore. About Jurgen drowning in the surf. About how he'd buried his body in the dunes. About the suitcase full of money and ration coupons.

With each new piece of information, her face grew more alarmed, her eyes more distant from him. "So what made you decide to tell me the truth now? Why now?"

Ben told her about Jurgen's body being discovered because of the storm. About the FBI agents who were probably on their way here now. About the other two German agents, Graf and Kittel. About their plans to kill Americans. About his fears that they may have already begun to do just that, about the explosion in the shipyard near Savannah.

Her expression changed. It now included fear.

He stood up.

"Where are you going?"

"It's obvious. I knew this would happen. In telling you the truth, I've lost you forever. I wanted a new life. That's all I wanted. A new life, an American life, with you. With your family. Here. But I can't have that anymore, can I?"

"What are you going to do?"

"The only thing I can do. I have to try and stop Graf and Kittel, before they hurt anyone else."

"But Ben, you'll be killed."

"If I stay here, the FBI will catch me, and then the American government will kill me. But they won't just kill me, they'll destroy you and your family. They'll humiliate you all. I won't let that happen."

He started to walk away.

"Ben, don't go."

He heard a tenderness in her voice.

"I do love you."

He turned and ran to her, stroked her cheek with his finger. "I'll probably never see you again. But I want you to have this." He pulled the ring box out of his pocket and opened it. The diamond sparkled in the sun. "This ring, and all that it stands for, are true. I love you with all my heart, and I'll love you till my last breath." He handed it to her, leaned over, and kissed her forehead.

"Good-bye, Claire."

He walked away.

"Ben, wait! Don't go."

He picked up his pace and dared not look back. Tears falling down his face.

15

Legare Street, Charleston
Noon

I felt so bad for Ben . . . and for Claire. What a terrible situation. It bothered me to see them go through this. Then I laughed, reminded myself it was only fiction. Gramps just made all this up.

On the emotion-meter, my story with Jenn flatlined compared to theirs.

I reached for my iced tea. All that was left was a little bit of water from the melted ice. My back was getting stiff, so I shifted my position on the chair. Probably not the best thing to sit there like this all day, but I didn't want to stop reading.

In this last conversation between Ben and Claire, I felt pretty sure I'd just found another example of Gramps drawing from his real life. Like the typewriter case.

I also realized a habit I had slipped into, without trying. I suppose every reader does this: creates images of the characters in your head, then for the rest of the book you see them like the lead actors in a movie. I had done this long ago for Ben and Claire.

I didn't really remember what Gary Cooper

looked like, if I ever knew, so when that description of Ben came up early on in the book, it didn't do anything for me. I found myself thinking back to the earliest pictures of Gramps and Nan, ones I had recently seen again in the photo albums in the pirate chest upstairs. Ben had morphed into a young Gerard Warner and Claire had become a young Mary.

Then here in the most recent scene, Gramps gives Ben his own first name—Gerard—when he revealed his real identity to Claire.

Gerard Kuhlmann.

Sounded German enough. Even more when you change out Gerard with Gerhard.

I wished I had known when Gramps had written this. It was so different from his other novels. Made me wonder if he'd ever been to the Daytona Beach area before. Jenn and I had gone to the beach there a few times. It was just an hour's drive from where we lived in Orlando. But I'd never spent any time in the areas Gramps described in the book. Next time we went to Orlando, I decided I wanted to go to Daytona, see if any of these places were still around.

It also made me wonder about this whole Nazi sabotage thing with the U-boats. I'd never heard about any of this before and wondered what parts were fact or fiction. Gramps always liked to mix it up. He did impeccable research, so you'd have to look things up in order to tell.

I set the manuscript down then was startled by my cell phone. Picked it up and smiled when I saw Jenn's name on the screen. "Hey, hon. On your lunch break?"

"Yes. So good to hear your voice. I can't talk too long, some of the girls are taking me out, kind of a farewell lunch. I'm in the car, heading to Gerardo's. Can you believe it? Remember that Italian place with—"

"Gramps's first name?" I finished the sentence for her.

"Made me kind of sad, though," Jenn said. "I didn't know him like you did, but ever since they asked me about going to lunch there a few hours ago . . . I keep thinking about him."

"I feel like I've been with him and Nan all morning, and last night."

"You mean reading the book?"

"Yeah."

"I understand why you'd feel more connected to your grandfather, since he wrote it, but why Nan?"

I told her how I kept seeing a younger version of Gramps and Nan as Ben and Claire, and about how he'd used his own first name in the last scene I'd read. Hard part was not telling her too much, since I knew she wanted to read the book.

"That's kind of odd," she said.

"What is?"

"Of all the names to pick from, he used his own name?"

"He's written a ton of books. I imagine it must get tricky coming up with names you've never used." Then it dawned on me—since the manuscript pages had yellowed with age, most of Gramps's books were probably written *after* he'd written this.

"I guess," she said. "But using your own name?"

"Well, that's not the biggest thing. Wait till you hear this."

"Be quick, Michael, I've really got to go."

"I will." I told her about the typewriter case, how Gramps used it in the book. Where it originally came from . . . in the book, that is. When I finished, she didn't say anything for a few moments. "Jenn . . . you there? Did I lose you?"

"I'm here. It's just . . . well, never mind. There's the parking lot for Gerardo's up ahead. I better go. I love you, miss you so much."

"I love you too."

"You going to read the rest of the day?" she asked.

"I don't have a choice. I'm totally sucked in. Call me when you get off work?"

"I will. Talk to you soon."

After I hung up, I gathered the manuscript together and brought it into the house. Talking about Gerardo's put me in the mood for some nice Italian. Figured I'd take a quick drive over to

Bocci's on Church Street. Get a nice dish of veal marsala or maybe some chicken picatta.

Then I'd head back home, try to put a big dent in what was left of the manuscript. I looked at it sitting on the kitchen counter.

I might even be able to finish it before dinner.

Chapter Twenty-Five

Special Agent Victor Hammond drove south into Ormond Beach, along Atlantic Avenue. Once in town, the ocean, which had been constantly visible out his left window, was blocked by a handful of beachfront cottages for rent by the week or month and the occasional Victorian-style hotel. In between these buildings were dozens of sand dunes.

It was an attractive little town, but Hammond imagined it must be a miserable place in the summer, probably for most of the year. Hot and humid, with no chance of relief. Mosquitoes and gnats flying all around. An agent friend who'd come down this way chasing a mob fugitive had told him to watch out for the cockroaches and spiders. Said they were the biggest he'd ever seen. This guy had been in machine gun battles with mobsters. Said he was more afraid sleeping in that hotel room at night than he'd ever been on the streets of Chicago.

Hammond saw the little sign informing him that he'd now entered Daytona Beach. A few miles south, he came to Broadway Avenue, saw signs pointing right, to a bridge and the downtown area.

That's where he was headed.

From FBI reports and the interviews with George Dasch he'd read, Hammond knew these guys mostly ate in diners and restaurants. Hammond had made a name for himself in the Bureau because he followed his instincts. Most of the men went by the book, methodically uncovering the facts and following wherever they led. He did that too, but he also believed you had to think like the criminal. Put yourself in their place. What would you do if you were in their shoes?

It wasn't hard. Few of them were geniuses. He found most to be of subpar intelligence. That was certainly the case with that last batch of Germans. He marveled that German High Command had approved them to be sent over here to do anything requiring wisdom and cunning. They didn't seem to possess even a modicum of common sense. He smiled as he drove up to the bridge separating the beachside from the mainland. With enemies like these, the Allies were certain to win this war.

Coming down the far side of the bridge, Hammond observed several blocks of shops and businesses that ran parallel to the river. Most were two stories, occasionally three. There was a nice park on the river side of the road filled with flowers, ponds, and palm trees. Except for the palm trees, the downtown area could pass for any number of small towns he'd seen up north and throughout the Midwest.

He immediately saw a few names that piqued his interest, places a man might go for a quick bite to eat. He'd stop first at McCrory's and Woolworth's. Those stores usually ran a small diner on the side. It took a few minutes to find a parking place. He decided to park in between the two stores and walk. It was a nice day.

As he got out of his car, a number of passersby on the sidewalk stared at him. He recognized the look. He liked the look.

Victor Hammond was a G-man.

He didn't approve of everything the Boss— J. Edgar Hoover—did at the Bureau. In fact, he struggled with several things he'd seen and heard. Most recently, the way Hoover had lied to the press about how the first group of saboteurs were rounded up and captured. Hoover's version made it sound like the Bureau had done it all by themselves, through their own cleverness and sophisticated police work. Hammond knew the truth. Better than 90 percent of their leads had come straight from the mouth of Dasch, one of the German saboteurs, who'd decided he wanted nothing to do with the Nazis anymore. There was no mention of that to the press.

Of course, Hammond wasn't stupid. Kept thoughts like these to himself.

But he did like the way the Boss increased the

public's sense of awe and reverence for the G-man. He was a master manipulator, especially with publicity and the press. And he expected FBI agents to look and act the part, to strengthen this public persona every chance they got. Hammond nodded to various people as he made his way through the front door of McCrory's. He didn't smile. Some nodded back, some looked away.

Once inside the store, he walked over to the diner section, saw a waitress taking an order for three women in uniform at the end of the counter. Must be WACS. That's right, he'd read something about them being based in this town. The diner was mostly empty. Saw a few college-age youths sitting in a table near the jukebox. He walked midway down the counter and stood, eyeing the waitress.

She looked up then looked him over, noticed he didn't sit down, got the message.

"Something tells me you didn't come in here for lunch."

Hammond looked at the name on her blouse pocket. "Miss Jane, you guessed right." He took out his ID.

"FBI." She said it loudly. The others looked.

Hammond didn't mind.

"What's the FBI doing in Daytona Beach?"

"Not at liberty to say. Just have a few questions, if you don't mind."

"Don't see how I can be any help, but fire

away. You want some coffee? On the house."

"Sure, that would be nice."

Miss Jane went to fetch the coffeepot. Hammond took a seat on one of the red swivel stools.

"Let me just check on those kids over there, and I'll be right back."

"Is that a real G-man?" he heard one of them say. Hammond looked over his shoulder at a homely guy with curly blond hair and thick glasses. Miss Jane nodded and told him to pipe down. Then she walked back over.

"I'm all yours," she said. "But only for a couple minutes."

"That's all I need. Looking for a man, young man, maybe in his mid-twenties to mid-thirties, probably came in here a lot to eat, possibly back in September or October."

"Are you kidding me? I'm supposed to remember who ate here several months ago?"

"It would help if you'd try."

"He's not in the military?"

"No, he'd be dressed like a civilian."

"But he wasn't a civilian."

"Can't say."

"What's he done?"

"Again, can't say. Does that mean you have someone in mind?"

"No, just curious. Got a lot of locals that age come in here from time to time. Not just back in the fall, though."

266

"Not looking for a local. This guy would have come in from out of town. Probably had plenty of cash, maybe a better-than-average tipper. Might have had an accent."

"Don't recall anyone like that, not anyone with an accent anyway. You mean like a New York or Boston accent? What kind you mean?"

"I'm thinking more like a foreign accent." Hammond thought about the earlier batch of saboteurs. They'd been picked because they supposedly spoke English well, but all of them had German accents.

She shook her head. "Not ringing any bells."

"How about if we drop the accent?"

She thought a moment. "Still not ringing any bells."

"Are you sure? No one at all? Might have just stayed in town a few days or a week."

"Mister . . ." she said.

"Hammond."

"Mister Hammond, this is a tourist town. We get all kinds of people come in here for a few days or a week. I can't remember them all. Really wish I could help you. But I need to get back to work."

"That's fine, Miss Jane." He stood up, took out his card. "If anything comes to you, anything at all, just call that number. They know how to get hold of me."

"I will. Want a refill on that coffee before you go?"

Hammond put on his fedora. "No, I've got a few more stops to make before the stores close. Thanks." He walked toward the front door, heard a chair scrape the floor behind him.

"Excuse me." A young man's voice.

Hammond turned. It was the homely kid with the curly hair coming his way.

"I overheard some of the questions you asked Miss Jane."

Hammond took his hand off the door and backed up toward the front of the counter.

"I think I know someone who matches your description," he said. "Only, he doesn't have an accent. And he didn't stay for a few days or a week. He's still here."

"Really," Hammond said. He took out his memo pad and pen. "And your name is . . ."

"Hank. Hank Nelson."

Chapter Twenty-Six

Hammond learned a lot from his chat with Hank Nelson. The kid seemed a little too eager to tell what he knew about a young man named Ben Coleman. Hammond discerned something brewing there, some kind of resentment Hank harbored against Coleman. Nothing in his words, but it was there. He'd mentioned a girl's name several times—Claire Richards. Hammond figured jealousy might have fueled Hank's cooperation more than civic duty.

About halfway through, Hank had asked if there was any reward money involved, seemed almost reluctant to share when he found there was not. Hammond had to lean on him a little, threaten him with the old "obstruction of justice" angle. It worked. He had three pages of notes from the interview.

But he wasn't sure any of it mattered.

The subject, Ben Coleman, did line up with several points on his checklist, enough to warrant more examination. But there were some missing ingredients. Coleman seemed far too . . . American. Not only was the German accent missing, but Coleman seemed to love this country and showed the same level of patriotic zeal most red-blooded American men had for the war effort.

In fact, at one point in the interview, Miss Jane walked over to interject her two cents, said Hank was wasting Hammond's time talking about Ben Coleman that way. Whatever kind of dark character Hammond was looking for, Ben Coleman was anything but. "One of the nicest and most considerate young men I've ever served in this place," Miss Jane had said. Hammond noticed the disgusted look that came over Hank's face.

Presently, Hammond was on his way back

across the bridge to an apartment house on Grandview Avenue. Hank didn't know where Coleman lived now but remembered where he'd lived his first few months in town. Hank thought his old landlady might know where he stayed now. Hammond had asked him about this girl Claire, where she lived. Seemed like she was the romantic interest and would know exactly where to find this guy Coleman. He might even be with her now.

But Hank wouldn't talk about Claire, no matter how hard Hammond had pressed. Not a problem. He could find out where she lived in the telephone book.

He pulled into a parking space by the curb next to the apartment house. A little breezier over here, but a nice area surrounded by several blocks of small bungalows and beach houses. Stepping out of the car, he heard waves breaking off in the distance. He might like to come back to this area sometime with his wife, Angie. She'd love a place like this. But he'd need a few more pay raises before he could afford vacations in Florida. He walked around the car and up the steps.

A little note said the manager lived in apartment 101. She opened the door immediately after he knocked, then stepped back, startled by his presence. "I'm sorry," she said. "I was expecting Alfred, the plumber."

"Special Agent Victor Hammond, ma'am." He held out his ID.

"FBI? Oh my."

"I need to ask you a few questions about a young man who lived here a few months ago."

"You want to come in?"

"Sure. This will only take a few minutes."

"I'm Mrs. Arthur, by the way. Evelyn Arthur. Sorry, it's such a mess. I wasn't expecting proper company."

Hammond tried not to notice, but it was a mess. Newspapers strewn about, dishes stacked in the sink. Laundry on the coffee table.

"So who you looking for?"

"Do you remember a young man named Ben Coleman?"

"Ben? Sure I remember Ben. Nice fella."

"You remember when he came, the date? And how long he stayed?"

"Can't say I remember the actual date, but it was in August, the middle of August, I think."

"Any chance you could look that up?"

Mrs. Arthur shook her head. "He paid by cash, said he didn't need a receipt, so I never wrote one up. Is Ben in some kind of trouble?"

Paid by cash, Hammond thought. That fits. Didn't want to leave a record of his stay in writing. "Probably not, but I can't really say. Anything about Ben strike you as odd or unusual?"

"You mean the way he looked?"

"No, I'm thinking more about his conduct, things he might have said or done that seemed out of the ordinary."

She thought a moment. "He was a very nice young man. I was sad to see him go. I guess one thing was, he seemed to have plenty of money but didn't have a job. I found that odd. He might have got one since he moved out, but he didn't have one then." A look came over her face. "But you know, he did mention one time that his parents had died a few months ago. I figured maybe they had left him some money. Wished someone would die and leave me some."

Hammond jotted down a few lines. "Anything else?"

She looked up at the ceiling for a moment. "He left kind of suddenly. He paid me for a full week but moved out two days into it. When I asked him if he wanted a refund—not that he had it coming, but he was just so nice—he said, No, you keep it, Mrs. Arthur. Then he thanked me for being such a nice landlady."

"When he left, did he seem nervous or panicky?"

"No, wouldn't say that. And he just moved around the corner from here on Vermont Avenue. I've seen him drive by a few times. Always waves."

"Do you know the address?"

"I'm not sure which house it is. He drives a

Ford coupe, two-door kind, I think. It's black. Can't be but a few of those on the street."

"Thanks, that's helpful." He waited a moment. "Can you think of anything else? Anything at all? Was there ever a time he seemed upset?"

"No . . . well, wait. There was one time. Come to think of it, this was a little out of the ordinary."

"What's that?"

"I was heading off to confession, at St. Paul's across the river. He was asking me all kinds of questions about it."

"What kind of questions . . . if you don't mind me asking?"

"The oddest one was, he wanted to know if priests had to keep your secrets. You know, if you could tell them things in confession, knowing they'd never tell anyone."

Guilty conscience, Hammond thought as he wrote. "Did he tell you what he wanted to see the priest for?"

"No, but if I recall, he said he was Lutheran. We don't have a Lutheran church in this town, and I don't even know if they do confessions in that church. Do you know if they do?"

"No, ma'am. I'm Baptist."

"I think he might have gone over there, anyway, because he asked for directions."

"He did? Do you know which priest he met with?"

"No. We only had the one conversation. He

seemed a little edgy so I didn't ask him anything more about it. Religion's kind of a personal thing. To me, anyway."

Hammond handed her his card. "You've been very helpful, Mrs. Arthur. You think of anything else, just call this number."

"I will, sir."

He turned and walked toward her front door.

Mrs. Arthur added, "But I gotta say, I can't see Ben being your man, no matter what he's supposed to have done. Not Ben. I'm a good judge of character. Lord knows, this place is full of 'em. But Ben . . . not a mean bone in his body. I can't see him committing any kind of a crime."

"Well, thanks again, Mrs. Arthur."

Hammond walked out to his car, jotted down a few more details in his pad. He drove around till he found Vermont Avenue, then rode up and down the street a few times. Didn't see any black Ford coupes. He looked at his watch. He might have enough time to interview one of the priests at the church.

Guess I'm heading back over the bridge, he thought. He wasn't looking forward to this. Priests were notorious for clamming up when questioned, especially about something they heard in a confession. But Hammond knew, you ask the right questions the right way, and it's amazing how much you can get them to say.

Chapter Twenty-Seven

At least his hair looked nice.

Father Flanagan smiled at his reflection in the mirror as he stood in the foyer of the rectory. He'd just taken off his hat and coat. He didn't really even need the coat, it was such a nice day. He'd just come from a walk to the barbershop downtown, about a half mile away.

His soul had been troubled the whole way home.

It wasn't the conversation at the barbershop—for the most part, anyway. Chatting with Joe and the customers was a pleasant experience. He'd been going there once a month since he'd come to Florida, and went out of his way to disarm the tension that always accompanied his black attire and white collar. Now they greeted him cheerfully when he came in, and except for the considerable effort expended to restrain their profanity, the conversations were mostly light and cheery.

What had troubled him was the content in a *Life* magazine he'd read while awaiting his turn in the barber chair. It was a two-page article in the July issue. The banner headline read: THE EIGHT SABOTEURS SHOULD BE PUT TO DEATH. It talked about how the FBI had captured the "eight

Nazi terrorists." The whole tone of the article centered on the outrage people felt toward these evil men the Nazis had sent to our shores. The last sentence said something about how much these men deserved to die, and that nothing short of death would satisfy patriotic Americans.

Joe and some of the men at the shop had seen what he'd been reading, and a conversation started about it. It was clear and unanimous: everyone at Joe's Barber Shop felt the same way.

One of the men pointed out that a military tribunal had convened a month after the article was written. All eight men were found guilty, but only six were executed. The men at the shop expressed outrage that two of the "stinking Nazis—pardon the expression, Father" had been spared. They'd been given long prison sentences instead.

The point was . . . Ben had been right, and Aidan had been wrong.

He had urged Ben to turn himself in to the authorities, to tell them what he knew about the other saboteurs and let them handle it. Ben had said they wouldn't listen. They'd arrest him and probably execute him. Now he had to agree; Ben was right.

As he stood there in the foyer, one of his favorite psalms floated through his mind, a comforting verse in Psalm 131: "O Lord, my heart is not lifted up, my eyes are not raised too high; I do not occupy myself with things too great and too marvelous for me."

Lord, he prayed, *this situation with Ben is much too great for me. Help him, Lord. And help me know how I might help him . . . if there is anything I—*

The doorbell interrupted his prayer.

Hammond waited a few moments, then a few moments more. He was just about to ring the rectory doorbell again when it opened. He already had his FBI badge in hand.

A priest answered. "Good afternoon, how can I—" The priest took one look at Hammond and froze.

"Hello, Father, I'm Victor Hammond, special agent with the FBI." He held out his ID. "I wonder if we could talk. Are you the parish priest or the one in charge?" Hammond had a hard time discerning the look on the priest's face. Almost seemed like fear. But that didn't make any sense.

"Why, no . . . do you need to speak with Father Murphy?"

"Possibly, but maybe you can help me. I've been told by one of your parishioners that a young man may have come here for . . . some advice." Why mention the word *confession* so soon? he thought.

"Do you know the young man's name? Oh, pardon me, where are my manners. Would you like to come in?"

"I could, but this will only take a few minutes."

"As you wish."

"The man's name? It's Coleman, Ben Coleman." There was that look again in the priest's eyes. A strong reaction to Coleman's name.

"I . . . I remember that name. I've talked with him. But it wasn't for advice exactly. I spoke with him in the confessional."

"I see. But from what I understand, Coleman is a Lutheran, correct?"

"I think he may have said that."

"Isn't that somewhat . . . irregular?"

"Yes, I suppose it is. But we don't have a Lutheran church in town, so I suppose that's why he came here. But I'm sure you know, Agent Hammond, what a parishioner shares in the confessional is privileged information."

"But he's not really a parishioner, Father. You've just said it. He's not even a Catholic."

"That doesn't matter."

"I think it might."

"I suppose we'll have to disagree on that point."

"I mean no offense, Father, but we're concerned about this young man and need to know his whereabouts, and his plans. Can you at least tell me if you've spoken to him recently?"

"Yes, I guess I can answer that. I spoke with him earlier today."

"Today? Do you know where he is now?"

"No, I don't. May I ask what this is about?"

"Well, guess we have the same problem, Father. I can't share that with you . . . privileged information."

"You can't tell me anything?"

"I really can't. It's a national security matter. I can say that much but nothing more." Hammond waited a moment. It wasn't what the Father said next that intrigued him, but what he didn't say.

"I see."

He knows something. He definitely knows something. Both Miss Jane and Mrs. Arthur had instantly risen to Coleman's defense when Hammond even hinted that he might be in some kind of trouble. But all the Father said was "I see"? "Father, if you know something about Coleman, you need to tell me."

"But I can't tell you, sir. You know that I can't."

"Father, lives could be in danger. We just had an explosion in a shipyard this morning near Savannah. If we don't find Ben Coleman soon, more—"

"Are you implying Ben had anything to do with that?"

"No, I'm not. But we don't know that for certain, do we?"

"Yes, we do. I've just told you, I saw Ben today. Ben wasn't anywhere near Savannah this morning. It takes the better part of the day just to drive—"

"I'm not saying Ben had anything to do with the explosion personally, but he may know the men who did. He may be in cahoots with the men who did." He regretted saying that. He was supposed to be getting this priest to spill the beans, and here he was saying way too much himself. But then . . . Father Flanagan's silence just now seemed to be speaking volumes. Hammond waited a moment more, allowed an uneasy tension to build.

There, there was that reaction again in the priest's eyes.

"I believe there's nothing more to be said, Agent Hammond."

Hammond was certain now: Ben Coleman was his man. He was the partner to that Nazi corpse they had just uncovered at the beach. Coleman was a Nazi saboteur. And here Hammond was, on the verge of breaking the entire case open, all by himself. This was just the thing needed to solidify the Bureau's confidence, after giving him his promotion. "I suppose we're done for now, Father. Again, I had no intention of upsetting you. But when lives are at stake . . ."

The priest began closing the door, then stopped. "I will tell you this, sir. Ben Coleman is no threat to this country. He loves it here. I believe he is prepared to give his life for it."

"What are you saying, Father? Is he planning to do something? You must tell me."

"I'm sorry, Agent Hammond. I don't know Ben's plans, not anything specific. I'm just telling you, he is one of the finest young men I've ever met. I may not be able to tell you anything Ben confessed to me, but Ben is not the way you're making him out to be, not in the least. He would never harm a citizen of this country."

This wasn't going anywhere else. Hammond had gotten all he was going to get from this conversation. But he'd gotten plenty. "Here's my card, Father. If you think of anything else."

The priest took the card. "I can't believe I'm saying this," he said. "I hope you don't find Ben. But if you do find him, remember what I said. Please . . ." Hammond saw moisture in the old priest's eyes. "Please don't hurt him. He's not our enemy."

He closed the door.

As Hammond walked away, he thought, *I'm sorry, Father. I beg to differ*.

Chapter Twenty-Eight

Claire had cried so hard and for so long, she was near exhaustion.

First at the riverfront park, after Ben left. Then on the way home. Then at home, she'd cried for another thirty minutes. She was glad her mother wasn't there. If asked to explain herself, she wouldn't have been able to put two sentences together. She lifted her head off the pillow when she heard the back door open and close downstairs.

"Claire? Claire, are you home? Are you all right, dear?"

She heard her mother's voice through the closed bedroom door. Then footsteps up the stairs. How could she know Claire was upset?

A knock on the door. "Claire, are you in there? Can I come in?"

Slowly, Claire pulled herself up from the bed. "I'm in here."

The door opened. "I found your sweater on the living room floor. What's the matter? Is anything wrong?"

Claire burst into tears. "Oh, Mother. Everything is wrong." She fell back on the bed, facedown.

"Oh, my."

She felt the other side of the bed drop slightly as her mother sat down and began gently rubbing her back. "What is it, honey? Did you and Ben have a fight?"

Claire didn't know what to say.

"Your father and I had this big fight once, before we were married. It doesn't mean it's the end, sweetheart. What's this?"

Claire waited, her face still turned toward the wall.

"Is this a ring, Claire?"

Claire looked up. She'd forgotten; she'd put the

ring Ben had given her—still in the box—on the bed beside her. She heard her mother lift the lid.

"Claire, it's beautiful. And it looks so expensive. Did Ben propose?"

"Oh, Mother . . . yes . . . no . . . I don't know."

"Come here," her mother said, holding out her arms. "I don't understand, but you don't have to explain right now." Claire slid forward into her arms and cried into her shoulder.

She sat there a few minutes. Then felt a slight calmness come over her. "Ben met me after work," she said.

"To propose?"

"No." Claire sighed deeply and pulled back enough to see her mother's face. "I don't know how to tell you what happened." Her mother's face showed equal parts care and confusion. "When will Dad get home?"

"It won't be long. I had a planning meeting with some of the women at church and we went a little long. I called him at work, and he said not to worry. When he gets home, he's going to take us out to dinner."

"I can't go out."

"No?" she said gently.

"I can't even think about food. I can't even think."

"What's the matter, Claire? Let me see if I can help."

Claire looked at her. Her mother wouldn't understand. This wasn't something she could fix. "I know I need to tell you, but I think I want to wait till Dad gets home. I don't think I can bear to explain it twice."

Forty minutes later, Claire sat across from her parents in the den. Her mother had made meatloaf sandwiches from leftovers. Claire felt bad that her mother didn't get to go out for dinner. She always worked so hard.

Her father spoke first, leaning forward in his chair. "Are you up to talking about this now . . . whatever it is?" His face reflected a seriousness that fit the situation, but there was a tenderness in his eyes.

"I think so," Claire said. There was a long pause. "I don't know where to begin."

"Would it help if I asked questions?"

"No. I mean, you can. But I think I just need to try and say it. It's about Ben." She felt a wave of emotion rising. She had to make it stop.

"Did you two have a fight?"

"It's so much bigger than that. I wish we had a fight. That would be easy compared to this." Both of them looked thoroughly confused. "Okay, I'll just start talking. Ben came here, to this country, I mean, in a . . ." She sighed involuntarily. "I can't even believe I'm saying this. Ben came to this country back in August on a U-boat."

"A what?"

"A U-boat, Dad. This is not a joke."

"I can tell it's not."

"Ben's a German. He was trained as a Nazi spy, trained to come here and—"

The look on their faces. Both of them were shaking their heads, unable to process her words.

"Ben?" her mother said. "*Our* Ben?"

In the next fifteen minutes, Claire did her best to tell them everything Ben had said that afternoon. As each phrase left her mouth, it sounded absurd, like she couldn't possibly be explaining something real. She couldn't be talking about Ben. She still hadn't mentioned that Ben wasn't even his real name.

The look on her mother's face seemed a mixture of concern and fear. But the look on her father's face began to frighten her.

She stopped talking.

"Claire, did he say the FBI was coming here, to this house?"

"No, he meant to this town, I think. Why, Dad, what's wrong?"

Her father looked at her mother, then back at Claire. "This is very serious. I read about the spies that came here last summer. Most of them were executed."

"That's what Ben said."

"And people who helped them were arrested," he said.

"Oh, Hugh," her mother said. "What are we going to do?"

"Lord, help us." He looked down at the floor.

Claire felt her stomach turn. She'd counted on her dad to make some sense of this. He always knew what to do.

"We have to go to the authorities," he said. "Tell them everything. Before they come to us."

"But Dad," Claire said. "They'll kill Ben if they catch him."

"I know, Claire. But we have no choice." He stood up. "What am I saying?" He paced in front of the fireplace.

"Oh my," her mother said. "This is terrible."

Claire felt panic beginning to set in. Their reaction confirmed her worst fears: it really was as bad as it seemed. She had to calm down, get control of herself. "Dad, how can we be in trouble? We didn't know anything, not until today."

"And it's not as if we helped Ben do anything," her mother said. "We were just his friends."

"But they don't know that," her father said. "I've heard things about the FBI, things they do to . . . always get their man."

"Like what, Hugh?"

"I don't know. Not exactly. Let's just say, they don't always play fair. If they think we've done anything to aide and abet a fugitive, especially a spy, they might haul us all off to prison."

"But how can that be right, Dad? You're talking as if we helped him do something wrong. Ben hasn't even done anything wrong. The only thing he's guilty of is being born German, to parents who dragged him back there a few years ago. Now they're dead, because of Hitler. All Ben did was use whatever means he had to get away and come back here to this country."

As Claire said these words, it suddenly dawned on her . . . she believed them. It was as if one part of her was talking to another part of her.

Truth talking to fear.

She loved Ben. She didn't care about anything else. *God,* she prayed silently, *save Ben. Don't let anything happen to him.*

"Claire," her father said, "I know what you're trying to say, sweetheart. But that's not how the world works. Not now, anyway, not when we're at war with the Nazis."

"But Hugh," her mother said, "even if they did think we were guilty of something at first, when they looked into what we're saying, they'd have to know we're telling the truth. We didn't know anything about Ben till today, till an hour ago. And if they ask around, they'd see Ben hasn't done anything sinister the whole time he's been here."

Claire took a deep breath. "Dad, you've even talked about some of the articles he's written for the paper. Most of them have been very patriotic, supporting the war effort completely. We could show them that. They'd have to see Ben's not trying to sabotage anything."

Her father walked back to his chair and sat down. "Helen, Claire . . . I hear what you're saying, but I don't think you understand. Let's say they arrested us, then after an investigation they let us go. We'd still be ruined. Completely ruined. I'd lose every military contract our company has—they'd cut us off completely. And right now, until this war's over . . . that's about 95 percent of our business." He dropped his face in his hands, then looked up and massaged his temples with his fingers.

The doorbell rang.

"Who could that be?" Claire's mother said.

"Maybe it's Ben," Claire said. "I'll get it." She ran to the door and opened it.

Standing there was a man in a dark suit, white shirt, dark tie. A grim look on his face. "Hello, I'm Special Agent Victor Hammond with the FBI."

Chapter Twenty-Nine

Ben knew he had to calm down.

He was young and in great physical shape, but his insides were wound up, like a coil about to spring. He wouldn't be surprised if he dropped dead of a heart attack. He checked his rearview mirror again. As he had every few seconds over the last two hours. He couldn't help it.

By now, the FBI must surely know about him.

He was driving through Jacksonville on US1, on his way to the shipyard in Savannah. He was certain the explosion that morning was the work of the other two-man sabotage team. This was the month he and Jurgen would have started their attacks, so the other team was right on time. And Ben knew the shipyards in Brunswick and Savannah were on their target list because of the Liberty ships being built there.

The goal was to terrorize the merchant ship industry on land and sea. These Liberty ships were largely responsible for supplying the Allies overseas with everything they needed to fight this war. The U-boats had been doing their part, sinking these ships in large numbers the past year, in the Gulf and along the East Coast. The saboteurs were supposed to join the fight by killing and maiming as many shipyard workers as possible. The German high command reasoned this two-pronged attack would slow down, if not stop, the production of these Liberty ships altogether.

An image flashed in Ben's mind of his commander standing in front of a chalkboard: "Make them afraid to come to work each day. So afraid they refuse to work. *That* is your mission."

Ben looked at his rearview mirror again. Still clear. He'd driven most of the way along A1A, the ocean out his right window all the while. He wondered as he turned inland at Saint Augustine if he'd ever see the ocean again. It took forever driving at this speed, but he couldn't afford to get stopped by the police. He didn't dare drive a single mile over the 35 mph wartime limit.

Before leaving Daytona Beach, he'd stopped by his rental house for the last time to pick up his things. Only a few mattered: his gun, the suitcase full of money and ration coupons, his typewriter and case . . . and the one picture he owned of him and Claire, taken by her father outside their home. Everything but the picture was locked in the trunk. The photograph, in a plain black frame, lay flat on the seat beside him. He glanced down at Claire's beautiful face.

He'd wrestled about what to do with it. He couldn't leave it at the house. The FBI would certainly find it. They'd use it as proof that Claire and her family were involved. But then he worried about bringing it along. What if they caught him on the road? They'd find it in the car. But he couldn't bring himself to throw it out; it was the only picture he had of them together.

Claire. Tears instantly began to form.

He'd never see Claire again.

No. No tears. He couldn't think about her now. He had a job to do.

Reaching over, he turned the picture facedown. It made him weak. He needed to be strong now.

Strong enough to stop two saboteurs.

A few moments later, the tension returned.

Up ahead on the right, Ben saw a used car dealership. It gave him an idea. Since arriving in Jacksonville, he'd been thinking he had to get rid of this car. The FBI would know by now he was driving a black, two-door Ford coupe. Everyone in Daytona knew that.

He pulled into the car lot and found a parking space. Before he'd turned the car off, he already had his eye on a replacement. A portly salesman dressed in a cheap gray suit headed his way. Ben got out and walked over to the car, another Ford coupe. This one had four doors and was painted a pale shade of green.

"Afternoon, young man, fine day this one's turned out to be. You in the market for a car?" He walked around Ben's coupe. "This your trade-in?"

Ben nodded, looked inside the green car. It was in pretty good shape. He eyed the tires; plenty of tread left. "How many miles on this one?" He didn't care but wanted to seem ordinary, ask all the typical customer questions.

"That one? Twenty-two thousand, I believe. Runs like a top. Yours looks pretty good here. I think they're the same year. How many miles she have?"

"Eighteen thousand," Ben said.

"Hmmm," the man said. A slight look of concern.

"There's nothing wrong with it," Ben said. "That's not why I'm selling it. I'm just looking for something with four doors. Taking a trip up north . . . with some relatives." What else? He had to come up with something quick.

"I see," the salesman said. "Older relatives, I'm guessing."

Ben nodded; he'd go with that.

"Some of us older folks have a hard time getting in and out the back seat in those two-door models, especially on long trips. Where you headed?"

"Virginia."

The man walked once more around Ben's car, same concerned look on his face. "Only thing, young fellow . . ." He looked up, toward the far side of the lot. "Got two other Ford coupes over there, both two-door models like yours."

"That's not too much of a problem," Ben said. "I'd be willing to pay a little more to get a four-door." He looked in the backseat. "Just can't see my grandparents getting in and out of my car, all the way up to Virginia and back. Especially my grandmother. She's got a bad back." What was he saying? "How much would you need to trade, to make it worth your while?"

The salesman thought a moment. "I'd take seventy-five dollars."

"Make it sixty-five and you got a deal."

The man smiled. "You drive a hard bargain, young man. Sold!" He reached out his hand and Ben shook it.

"Mind if I take it for a test drive, just to be

sure?" Ben really didn't want to stay here that long, but he cared more about looking like a normal customer.

"Feel free," the man said. "I've got nothing to hide. Like I said, runs like a top. I'll go fetch the keys." He came back moments later.

Ben got in, invited the man to join him.

"That's okay. I trust you. You got a nice face. Besides, got your car here as collateral."

"I'll be right back." Ben drove out of the lot, headed north a few blocks, then pulled over. The car rode fine. He sat there a few moments, thinking he'd stay out long enough for an average test drive. Then he remembered. *You idiot.* He'd left his keys in his car. What if the salesman found them? What if he wanted to check out Ben's car?

His gun and all that money were just sitting there in the trunk.

Chapter Thirty

One thing for sure, these people were guilty as sin. You get a sense of these things when you've been working cases as long as he had. It was in the eyes, the nervous jitters, the trying too hard. Hammond stood in the spacious foyer of the Richardses' home. They had invited him in, probably just because it was the polite thing to do. Seemed pretty obvious that they wished he'd turn right around and head back out the door.

"Can I get you something to drink, Inspector Hammond?" Mrs. Richards asked. "Some iced tea, perhaps? I could make hot tea if you'd like."

"No, thanks. Could we continue this conversation in there?" he said, pointing to a parlor. "Probably best if we sit down. I think you all know why I'm here." He was playing a hunch, seeing what he could stir up.

"Now listen, Inspector," Mr. Richards said. "I'm sure we don't know what you mean." He said it sternly, the great protector, but Hammond could tell it was fake bravado. Richards led them into the parlor. Everyone took a seat.

"I'm talking about Ben Coleman," Hammond said, then looked at everyone's eyes, especially young Claire's. She seemed ready to burst into tears. This was going to be a great conversation.

"Ben? What about Ben?" said Mrs. Richards. Very bad acting.

"Okay, let's stop pretending. I'm going to tell you what I already know about Ben. How you respond will tell me how I'm supposed to treat you once I walk out that door." Everyone's expressions changed. *Good. Now we're getting somewhere.*

"Inspector Hammond, I—"

"Please, Mr. Richards. Me first, then you talk. I

know Ben came to this town, probably back in August, aboard a German U-boat." He looked at their faces. Oh yeah, that did it. "I know he had a partner, another German spy, who probably died the night Ben came onshore. Ben buried him in the sand dunes."

"But Ben didn't kill him," Claire blurted out.

"Claire," her father said.

"But he needs to know that, Dad. His partner drowned in the surf."

My, my. Hammond looked at her father, who looked down at the throw rug, shaking his head. "I didn't say Ben killed him, Miss Richards. Point is, Ben's a German spy. He didn't come to this country on the *Queen Mary*. He came in a Nazi sub, at night. And he came with orders to blow up things and kill people. That's the point."

"But, sir," Claire said. "Those may have been his orders, but that's not why Ben came here. He'd never hurt anyone." She started to cry. "In fact, I'm probably never going to see him again because of that. He left today saying he had to try and stop those men from hurting anyone else."

"What?" Hammond said, sitting up. "You know where Ben is, where he's going? If you do, you need to tell me, Miss Richards. Right now."

"Wait, Claire. Mr. Hammond, listen. There's some things you need to know first."

"Beg your pardon, Mr. Richards, but you are walking on thin ice, sir. We're talking national security here . . . treason. You follow me?"

Mr. Richards sighed. "Don't you think I know that?" he said. "We've been scared to death these last few hours, ever since we found out about this."

Few hours, Hammond thought. Could that be true? Is it possible these people just found out about this guy?

"Mr. Hammond," Claire said, dabbing her eyes with a tissue her mother handed her. "Ben loves this country. He was born here. His parents dragged him off to Germany when he was in high school. He hated it there, hated everything he saw going on over there. He especially hates the Nazis."

"He told you this?"

"Yes."

"When?"

"This afternoon."

"How long have you known him?"

"Since early September."

"They've been dating the last few months," Mrs. Richards added politely. "They were really in love. Ben was going to ask her to marry him."

It was like she didn't get it. Hammond glanced at her husband, could see he loved his wife but wished she'd shut up. Hammond's instincts told him these people weren't involved in anything sinister. But that didn't matter. Not now, anyway. "So you're saying," Hammond continued, directing his words to Claire, "you had no idea who Ben was until today. That's your story."

She burst into tears.

Guess that's my answer, he thought. His wife did that sometimes, cry like that. One thing he knew, when she did, they were talking about gut-level things. True things. Sometimes things so true, only tears could describe them. Mrs. Richards handed Claire the tissue box.

"When did you find out about Mr. Coleman?" he asked Claire's father.

"Just a little while ago," he said, all the strength gone from his voice. "I came home from work to this."

"I came home a little while before that," Mrs. Richards said, "and found Claire like this. I thought they had broken up."

"It's worse than that, Mother," Claire said through her sobs. "I may never see Ben again. He may be dead in a day or two."

"Agent Hammond, I don't know what you're getting from all this," Mr. Richards said, "but if I'm any judge of character, any judge at all, Ben is no spy. Excepting my son, he may be the finest young man I've ever known. I gave him permission to ask for my daughter's hand. Even knowing what I've found out now, I just can't . . . I can't bring myself to hate him. Or think of him as an enemy of this country. You should see the way Ben lights up at patriotic things. Songs on the radio, conversations we've had, the stories he's written in our paper about the war. That was no act. Ben's a true American. I'd stake my life on that."

This was starting to get to Hammond, this constant drumbeat of Ben Coleman fans. The waitress at the restaurant, the landlady, the priest, and now this. "All right, Mr. Richards, I'm willing to concede there may be more to Ben Coleman than meets the eye. But the fact remains, we had an explosion in a shipyard near Savannah this morning. If Ben knows anything about it, or anything about the people who did it, I've got to know. You said yourself, Miss Richards, Ben could be dead in a day or two. That's no exaggeration. He's not equipped to go after people like this by himself."

"I told him that," Claire said. "But he wouldn't listen. He left anyway."

"Do you know why?"

"Isn't it obvious?" she said. "Look how you treated us when you came in here. My poor dad, who's only ever loved and served this country —my own brother is overseas fighting right now—he's afraid of you. He's terrified you're going to arrest us and ruin our lives, just because we know Ben. Just to boost your own career, get some feather in your cap."

"Listen, Miss Richards—"

"Go ahead and deny it," Claire said, a fierce

expression in her eyes. "Tell me you don't see this as a chance to make a big arrest, get your name in all the papers. Tell me you haven't thought about what this might do for your career at the FBI."

Hammond was hating this. It was like he was under the hot light.

"I'm not the bad guy here, Miss Richards."

"No? Well, guess what . . . neither is Ben! You know what his crime is? He was born German, to parents who got fooled by Hitler. Just like millions of other people in Europe did. They made poor Ben follow them over there, and you know what it got them? Killed in a bombing raid last year. Ben had to live a lie, first over there and then here, just because he wanted to be an American again. Wanted to fall in love here, have his kids here . . ." She was falling apart.

Her words ended in another flow of tears.

"Okay, listen, maybe I got this all wrong," Hammond said. The crazy part was, he meant it. "But I need your help to find Ben. If what you're saying is true, he's in a world of danger right now. The FBI is a lot better equipped to nab these Nazi spies than Ben is. You have information I need to know . . . to help Ben."

"Really, sir?" Mr. Richards asked. "To help Ben? Is that what you really meant to say?" He looked Hammond straight in the eye.

"It is," Hammond said. "If Ben's everything you and everyone else say he is, I'm willing to consider it. But that's not the big fish right now. We've gotta catch these guys. We—the FBI. Not Ben."

"But what about your associates?" Mr. Richards asked. "What will they do if they find Ben? What will J. Edgar Hoover do?"

Hammond tried not to let it show on his face, but what Richards said was a serious problem. Hammond had no idea how he was going to handle this case now. Because he knew exactly what his associates would do, and what Hoover would do, if they got ahold of Ben.

Chapter Thirty-One

Ben set the keys of his green four-door coupe on the dresser. The suitcase, gun inside, sat on the bed along with his typewriter. It was dark outside. He was exhausted. The only lamp in this dumpy little motor lodge provided just enough light to see the only thing he cared to see in the room.

The picture of him and Claire. He stood there staring at it. Really, just at Claire.

She was leaning back against him as he leaned against the curved fender of his car, his arms around her. She was looking at the camera. He at her. Then and now, he couldn't stop looking at her. In the background on the left was the wraparound porch at her parents' house. Just visible above the wooden railing were the tops of the two rockers they'd sat in so many evenings over the past few months.

Sadness overwhelmed him. The more he looked at the picture, the deeper it grew. But he didn't care. He didn't want to look away. "You were worth it," he said aloud. He'd do it again, all of it, to have experienced her love. It had been the happiest months of his life. When he reached the point he could barely breathe, he gently laid the picture facedown on the dresser.

He looked around the room. A lumpy double bed with a frayed bedspread, no headboard. Two plain dinette chairs and an equally plain round table, in a corner by the bathroom door. The curtains made him sneeze when he closed them. No telephone. No radio. The owners called it E-Z Breeze Motor Lodge. No breeze outside, either.

It sat just off Highway 17, between Brunswick and Savannah. Beggars can't be choosers, his mother used to say. When he'd decided to turn in for the night, he'd passed four or five similar motels that were closed down. With the gas rationing, not many people toured the country these days.

He looked at his watch. It was just after 9:00. Sliding the suitcase to the far side of the bed, he lay down and stretched out. He should have brought something to read, something to help him get his thoughts off Claire. The Bible Father Flanagan had given him came to mind, though it hardly seemed right putting it in the same suitcase with a gun. But reading it had become part of his morning routine. He actually felt like he was beginning to understand God a little bit. A very little bit.

Hardly seemed the thing to read now.

Would God approve of this, the plans in his heart right now? He looked down at the suitcase, the Bible sitting inside. For a while he'd entertained a silly thought, that somehow God wouldn't see what he was doing if he ignored him.

What choice do I have, Lord?

He thought about David, the passages he'd read where David said some pretty harsh things about his enemies. Wishing they were dead, that God would strike them down and break their teeth. Not the kind of words he remembered hearing in church as a kid. He'd meant to ask Father Flanagan about verses like that, and how they squared away with things Jesus said, like love your enemies.

He'd heard a preacher on the radio one Sunday morning talk about this. The preacher had said it wasn't a contradiction in the Bible or a case of the New Testament being nicer than the Old. It was a case of one passage speaking to individuals and another to the role God had given authorities. The preacher had then read a passage in Romans that said God's appointed authorities "do not bear the sword in vain," said they are his servants "executing his wrath on evildoers."

That's all this is, he thought. *That's all I'm doing.* It was why he was on his way to Savannah, to stop Graf and Kittel, the other two German agents. They were exactly the kind of men David spoke about in the Psalms—wicked men, evildoers.

They would keep pursuing their mission, maiming and killing innocent Americans, until somebody stopped them. Father Flanagan was right when he said Ben had to get involved. But he was wrong to imagine Ben could let the American authorities take care of it. They'd throw Ben right in with Graf and Kittel, wouldn't see a shred of difference between them. Why should he be electrocuted as an evildoer? If he was going to die, he'd rather die trying to stop men like them, not as some infamous traitor, hated by everyone.

He lay there awhile longer, trying to remember his Abwehr training, hoping to get back in touch with the *mörderinstinkt*—the killer instinct—his commander had grilled into them. They'd watched films about killing, read articles about it, fired live rounds into targets day after day until killing became *ebenso natürlich wie atmen . . .* as natural as breathing. Something one does on command, as part of one's duty.

Ben sat up. It was just no use.

It hadn't become natural to him then, didn't feel natural now. He wasn't a killer. All his acquired skills in shooting, bomb making, and espionage were a pretense to get back to America. To be normal again. To talk normal and think normal. To laugh at Abbott and Costello movies, to watch Ted Williams play baseball, to hear Glenn Miller songs on the radio. He had to find some other motivation to go through with this mission.

He stood up and walked back to the dresser. Thinking about Glenn Miller quickly connected to "Moonlight Serenade," which quickly connected to a memory . . . his first dance with Claire at the Bandshell. The song began to play in his head. He closed his eyes. He could see all the couples swirling around him. Feel the ocean breeze. Claire's eyes, then her smile. Claire saying yes. He reached out, she held his hand. He could feel it now, not just her hand but how it felt to hold it. He gently spun her around. She drew near and they danced. Time slowed by half. Before the dance was over, he knew she would be his for all time.

He stopped.

It wasn't for all time. Couldn't be. It was just an illusion.

How could he have imagined he'd ever escape his past? The Nazi scourge had raised its ugly head, beyond his parents' grave, across three thousand miles of open sea, beyond all his efforts to bury it. It would never leave him . . . unless he destroyed it.

That was his motivation.

Graf and Kittel were Nazis. True believers. They represented everything he despised. The single remaining part of his past that connected him to a world he wanted to sever ties with forever.

But . . . when it came right to it, could he really do whatever it took to stop them?

Lord, he prayed, *if you're even willing to listen to me at a time like this . . . you took Jurgen, so I didn't have to. Could you—*

No. He forced himself to stop praying. It was weakness. He needed to be strong. He needed to remember . . . the Nazis had taken Claire away.

He lifted the picture from the dresser and stared at her lovely face.

Claire.

16

Legare Street, Charleston
4:30 p.m.

Claire.

I read the name a few times, seeing in my mind poor Ben standing by this dresser staring at her picture. I set the remaining manuscript pages beside me on the couch. Looked like less than fifty pages to go. Much of what I'd read since lunchtime felt more like my grandfather's normal writing, more action and page-turning suspense. But here again, in this chapter, there was this almost haunting torment going on for Ben.

I had no idea where my grandfather was going next. Does he kill off Ben as he goes after the other spies? Does Ben save the day? Does he let Ben live but get arrested? Does he ever let Ben get back with Claire? Gramps often worked a love interest into his novels, even some occasional romance, but rarely spent this much time portraying this side of his characters' lives.

I knew Rick Samson, my grandfather's agent, would love this book, even if it were a little different. He'd love anything my grandfather wrote and anything I might write about my grandfather. Just as long as I wrote about *him,* the right Warner. Gerard, not Michael.

I got up and stretched, deciding to fix a cup of coffee, when an image of my grandfather as a young man flashed into my head. I could see him bending over slightly in front of the dresser, staring at the only picture he had of him and Claire together, heartbroken. Wait, not my *grand-father.* I meant I saw *Ben.* I was doing it again, morphing one into the other.

I thought about some of the pictures of Gramps at that age, ones I'd seen upstairs in that old pirate chest full of photo albums in the guest room. My mind zeroed in on one picture in particular. There was something familiar about it. I could almost see it in my head.

Wait.

The picture on the motel dresser, the one Ben had just been staring at. It was the same picture. Had to be. Had I just found another of Gramps's real-life connections? Like the typewriter case? In my head, the picture upstairs seemed like the same photograph.

I was sure of it.

I picked up a handful of manuscript pages, the last ten or so, looking for the part where Ben described the picture in detail.

He stood there staring at it. Really, just at Claire. She was leaning back against him as he leaned against the curved fender of his car, his arms around her. She was looking at the camera. He at her. Then and now, he couldn't stop looking at her. In the background on the left was the wraparound porch at her parents' house. Just visible above the wooden railing were the tops of the two rockers they'd sat in so many evenings over the past few months.

It had to be the same photo.

I grabbed this page, ran upstairs to the guest bedroom, and opened the chest. I didn't remember which album I'd seen the picture in but quickly separated the three that had any old black and white photos. After spreading them out across the bed, I reached back and flicked on the lamp. In a few minutes, I was able to figure out which contained the oldest pictures.

I scanned the pages carefully, making sure not to tear anything. As I did, I remembered a conversation with my sister, Marilyn. One of her big "sticking points." Before my grandfather died, she had pressed him about why they had no wedding pictures. How was that possible? It had become pretty normal to take wedding pictures by that time. All her friends' grandparents had them.

Gramps's answer did not satisfy her. He simply said they hadn't taken any. It was a long story and parts of it were quite painful. He didn't want to get into it. Out of respect, she didn't bring it up again. We had, of course, assumed that meant all the pictures in these albums were taken after they were married.

I turned several more thin black pages until I finally saw it. The top right corner of the third page. There they were, Gramps and Nan in their twenties. All the pictures in the surrounding pages were of them, one or both, in a variety of poses.

But this one . . . it was exactly as Gramps described it in his book. *Claire. She was leaning back against him as he leaned against the curved fender of his car, his arms around her. She was looking at the camera. He at her.* And sure enough, just to the left, in the background I saw . . . *The wraparound porch. The wooden railing. The tops of the two rockers they'd sat in so many evenings.*

Gramps had chosen this picture to be the picture Ben had carried with him as he'd fled, the one that tormented him as he stared at it by the dresser.

I wondered why.

Was this Gramps's favorite picture of him and Nan when they were young? I knew Gramps had been crazy about her his whole life. You could see it in this picture. I looked at all the ones with them together. I had never noticed it before; he was looking at her, not at the camera.

I remembered a conversation I had with him, the weekend before I proposed to Jenn. I'd driven up here to get his advice. "Did you ever have any doubts, Gramps, about Nan?"

"No, never," he'd said. "From the moment I met her."

"I'm serious, Gramps. I know you loved her. And she was my grandmother and all. But I'm talking man-to-man. Not as your grandson. You've never had any doubts, never had any regrets?"

We were sitting right out there in the courtyard in the Adirondack chairs. It was dark. He turned toward me. I could see his face clearly in the light beaming down from his home office. "Michael, look at me. Look in my eyes, tell me if you see the slightest hint that I'm not being straight with you or holding anything back."

"Okay." I obeyed.

"From the first moment I met your grandmother, through all the difficulties we had before we got married, through all the ups and downs in the fifty-seven years after that, I knew she was the only woman I would ever love. I never once doubted that. Never had a single regret. If God gives you that kind of woman, you know it deep inside. Almost at once. Like you know your own soul. A love like that is a gift, Michael. A gift you can never earn or ever repay." He'd sat up just then, tears welling up in his eyes. Then he looked back at me. "I knew I'd found in her a woman that would make everything in my life better, and she did. The hard parts more bearable, the happy parts more fun. My," he said, looking away, "she was *so* much fun." He wiped some tears away with his finger. "I had it good with her. Really good."

It was like he was in the room with me right now, saying these words aloud. I wiped the tears that had formed in my eyes, just like he had. I realized . . . I felt the exact same way about Jenn.

During that conversation, and now.

I missed her so much. I looked at my watch. Couldn't call her; she wasn't off work yet. But I could text her. She might get that. I took a few moments to send her a love note then set my phone down on the bedspread.

Looking back at the photograph in the album, with the yellowed manuscript page beside it, I felt so close to Gramps just then. There he was in the photo as a young man in love, and here he was as an old man, thinking back to this moment and writing about it in his novel.

Obviously, I'd found a third real-life connection. The typewriter case, giving Ben his first name, and now this. I wondered what it was about this photograph that caused Gramps to single it out. A couple of pictures had become loose over the years and were gathered together in the middle of the album. I remembered looking at these before; I especially enjoyed the little notes my grandmother had written on the back.

It dawned on me. Back then, people wrote

things on the back to help them remember details about the picture later on. Like the captions we write now beneath our digital photos. And often people didn't paste the pictures into albums right away. Sometimes it might be years later. That meant all the pictures still pasted on these pages probably had little notes on the back. My sister Marilyn would kill me for doing this, especially if I ripped the photo, but I couldn't help it. I had to see what Nan had written on the back. I peeled it from the black paper, ever so carefully, and turned it over.

No.

No way.

I couldn't believe what I saw.

Ben and Claire—1943.

Not "Gerard and Mary" but "Ben and Claire." How was that possible? I quickly looked at the other loose photos, checked the handwriting on the back. I knew the other notes had been written by Nan. She'd told me so once.

It wasn't the same handwriting.

My grandfather had written the note on this picture. I just knew it. I read it again, aloud. "Ben and Claire—1943." That was all it said. But when had Gramps written this? It was difficult to say. The writing looked almost as old as the photograph itself. But that was impossible.

I had to find out what was written on the back of the other pictures. One by one, I peeled them off and read the backs. Every single one was written in my grandmother's hand, and none referred to them as "Ben and Claire." Always "Gerard and Mary."

I noticed something else. In comparing the Ben and Claire photograph to all the others, I noticed that Nan wore a slightly different hairdo. And in the Ben and Claire photo, they actually looked younger, maybe by several years. I don't know why I hadn't seen it before, but it was crystal clear to me right then. In fact, I suddenly felt stupid for not seeing it sooner. As the realization sunk in, my hands started trembling.

The typewriter case. The real first name. This picture.

I had not spent the last two days reading my grandfather's last, unpublished novel. I had been reading his memoir.

This was his story.

The story of how they met. The story the family had never heard. The answers to all the questions Marilyn had been asking.

Then I remembered my grandfather's journal. Something he'd written on the last page. It didn't make any sense then. Maybe it would now. I left everything spread out on the bed, took the photo and manuscript page, and ran down the steps, through the kitchen, and into his office.

I flipped open to the last journal page, skipped till I found the paragraph.

I'm writing these last few pages for my family. More precisely, for my grandson Michael to find. I trust he'll know what to do with it, and with the package I've left in my wooden box (which has its own story, and he'll find out about that too).

Tears slid down my cheeks.

I had found it, what Gramps had wanted me to find. Even the wonderful story about the wooden typewriter case. Where it came from. I looked down at it. Oh man. I just realized. This wooden box had actually been made in Havana in 1898, during the Spanish-American War. My grandfather—Ben—had gotten it from his future father-in-law—Mr. Richards, my great-grandfather—who'd gotten it from his father—my great-great-grandfather—who'd fought with Teddy Roosevelt and the Rough Riders. He'd actually fought in the battle of San Juan Hill.

My great-great-grandfather was an American war hero.

Everything I had been reading over the past two days . . . it was all true.

I had to call Jenn. She had to know. What time was it? Shoot, she didn't get off till 6:00. This couldn't wait. What were they going to do, fire her? I dialed her number and let the phone ring. *Pick up, Jenn. Please pick up.*

Her voice mail. I listened to her message,

waited for the beep. "Jenn, call me as soon as you get this. You're not going to believe it. This manuscript, it's not a novel, it's my grandfather's story. It's all true. I can't wait to talk with you, love you."

And I hung up.

Then another thought, this one more disturbing. Not only was my great-great-grandfather a war hero—if this story was all true—my grandfather had once been a German spy. And our family name—my name—wasn't Warner, because Gramps's real name wasn't Gerard Warner. And it wasn't Ben Coleman, either. It was Gerhard Kuhlmann.

Was that my real last name? Our family's real name? Kuhlmann?

What would Jenn think about all this . . . or Marilyn? *Marilyn will go crazy when she hears this.* What about my family? What about Rick Samson, my grandfather's agent? What about my grandfather's fans?

What about the FBI?

I couldn't think any more about this. I had to get back to the couch and see how my grandfather's story ended.

Chapter Thirty-Two

"Nate, you somewhere you can write this down?"

"I am, but let me get my pen and pad out. I'm gonna set the phone down a sec."

Hammond had checked into a fairly nice hotel a few blocks north of downtown Jacksonville. No reason to stay in the Daytona Beach area any longer. He had his man. Ben Coleman—or the man going by that name—was most certainly the second half of the dead German's two-man spy team. Hammond was talking with his partner, Nate Winters, who was already in Savannah.

"Okay, Vic, fire away. What'd you find out down there?"

"How about the ID of our spy suspect? Who he is, what he looks like—"

"Really. So how's that work? You send the rest of us all over creation beating the bushes for leads, and you wrap the whole thing up by yourself a few miles away from where we started?"

"Oh, we're far from wrapping this up. Actually, the guy's heading your way."

"He is? So who is he?"

"Goes by the name Ben Coleman, mid-twenties, light brown hair, about six feet tall."

"Not his real name."

"Hardly," Hammond said. Claire had told him Ben's real name. Once he'd convinced the Richardses he believed them, she'd told him everything she knew. Turns out, wasn't all that much. "Like we thought, looks like there's another two-man team of saboteurs involved, probably still up there in Savannah. I'm just a few hours south of you, and I plan to hit the road at sunrise. Find out anything on the explosion?"

"Still checking things out, but it looks fishy. We're telling the press it was just an accident. Hoover's orders."

"Let me guess," Hammond said. "It's an accident, no matter what we find out."

"You got it. Plenty of flammable things in this shipyard to blame. But the folks closest to the scene feel like it's sabotage. They got all kinds of safety measures in place, several layers thick. All of them were being followed, but the explosion still happened. Witnesses here are saying there's no chance this was an accident."

"When we prove them right, I'm sure you'll come up with something to get them to cooperate."

"Yeah, well . . . So, Vic, how'd you find this guy?"

"I'll tell you more tomorrow morning. But already I can tell, this isn't looking anything like the case last summer. You somewhere you can talk . . . off the record?"

A brief pause. "Sure, Vic. Just you and me talking on pay phones. Whatta ya got?"

"Remember how that last bunch of spies spent their time once they came onshore? Except for Dasch and Burger, they all started meeting up with old German friends and Nazi sympathizers."

"I recall something like that."

"This fellow Coleman hasn't done that, hasn't even tried. And he's been here six months. In fact, everybody I talked to gives him high marks. Patriotic, upstanding citizen. All that. No one knew he was even German."

"No accent?"

"None. The kid was born here, somewhere in Pennsylvania. Sounds like his partner drowned in the surf. He went to the nearest town, got a job, made some friends, fell in love. Even the girl he wanted to marry had no idea who he was until today."

"I'm guessing that was painful. But Vic, c'mon. He's still a Kraut."

"That's the thing, Nate. I'm not so sure. She says he told her—just today—he knew who the other two saboteurs were and left to go after them."

"You mean to join them?"

"To try and stop them. She's all broken up, thinks he's going to get himself killed."

"You believe her? You know these guys will say anything, especially to women."

"I know, Nate, but didn't you tell me about your

buddy in the Washington office saying something about how Dasch got railroaded by Hoover?"

"Man, I hate talking about this over the phone, Vic."

"C'mon, Nate. You said you were at a pay phone."

"Still."

"No way Hoover has these lines bugged."

A long pause. "I guess you're right. Okay, yeah, that's what my buddy said. Apparently this other German, Dasch, the leader of the first group—"

"Dasch didn't get the chair, right?"

"No, he got thirty years hard labor. But my friend said the whole case opened up because of him. And only because of him. He turned everyone else in, gave us every major lead we got in the case. All the time he's talking, the Boss is playing him like a fiddle. Told him he was a hero, said he's going to let him off when it's all over. Even let him think we'd let him help us fight the Nazis. Then Hoover sticks him in solitary where he can't talk, plays this whole thing in the papers like we busted the spy ring all by ourselves."

Actually, Hammond recalled Hoover had made it sound like he'd wrapped up the whole case by himself. It was the part of being a G-man Hammond had come to hate. The manipulation and cover-ups going on behind the scenes, starting with Hoover. Hammond knew exactly how Hoover would treat someone like Ben. "Nate, between you and me, I think this guy might be the real deal. My gut's telling me Coleman is heading your way, and it really is to stop these other two Germans who came ashore that night."

"What do you want me to do? You know, Vic, we slip up here, our necks are hanging way out there."

"I don't know, Nate. Haven't got this figured out. But you're somebody I thought could give me a hand. Somebody I could trust if we need to toss the book out the window."

"You know I love adventure."

"I know. It's just . . ." Hammond sighed. "We gotta be real careful with this or it could blow up in our faces."

"You just make a joke, Vic?"

Hammond smiled. It was good having Nate around. "Not on purpose. I don't have much else to tell you. Coleman didn't want to get his girl or her family any more involved than they already were. So, he didn't tell her much."

"Well, we know a whole lot more than we knew this morning. You did good, Vic."

"Thanks. But this thing . . . It could go wrong a thousand different ways."

"I got your back, Vic. Like you always got mine. Before you hang up, you want to reel the rest of the team in, since we know where the bad guys are at?"

"See, that's the thing. We do that, we might

scare these two Nazis off. They see that many G-men all over the shipyard, they'll just go somewhere else, and we're back to square one."

"Hoping to set a trap?"

"Something like that. Don't have it worked out yet. I'm thinking it's all going to depend on this guy Coleman. We've got to find him. Tell you what, go ahead and call five or six guys in, but that's all for now. Keep everything how it's been. We'll keep this new information between you and me, till we see how things play out. I'd like you freed up to be with me once I get on-site."

"You said about mid-morning?"

"That's the plan." He took a deep breath. "Let's see if we can do some good here."

"And keep ourselves from getting blown up."

Hammond thought a moment. "That was a pun, wasn't it?"

"You're hopeless, Vic. See you tomorrow."

Chapter Thirty-Three

Hours had gone by. At least it felt like hours.

When Helen Richards had turned out the light, their bedroom became completely dark, as it had every night since she'd first shared a bed with Hugh. She needed it to be totally dark to fall asleep. Funny how much of the room she could see now that her eyes had adjusted to the dark. She traced the complete outline of the ceiling, then focused on the flowery light fixture above their bed. She couldn't see the floral pattern, of course. But she could see the distinct shape clearly.

She lifted her head slightly. There was Hugh's dresser on the left, his side of the room. She could almost make out the big glass ashtray where he kept his wallet and keys. On the right, she saw her chest of drawers beside the closet. She could even trace the outline of the mirror.

"Can't sleep, hon?" Hugh said, his voice just above a whisper.

"Did I wake you?" she said.

"No. I haven't slept a wink."

"Me neither." She rolled on her side facing him. "I shouldn't be surprised. This still doesn't feel real to me."

"That's not my problem," he said, still on his back looking up. "Feels very real to me."

"Are you still worried . . . I mean, as much as before?" They had prayed a good while before turning out the lights, more than the normal polite nighttime prayers.

"No—I feel that same peace that came over me when we stopped praying," he said.

Helen had felt it too; it made her think of that passage in Philippians that spoke of a "peace that surpasses understanding." It was the only thing that could explain the calm they had both felt, considering their whole lives had just been turned upside down. "What are you thinking about?" She heard him breathe in and out slowly.

"Something I don't want to be thinking about, but it won't leave me alone. I feel as though I've been wrestling for the past hour or so, but I'm not sure if it's with God or the devil."

She didn't like the sound of that.

"The thing that bothers me the most," he said, "is that I'm pretty sure it's God."

Helen sat up. "May I turn on the light?"

"Might as well." He sat up too.

When Hugh's face came into focus, Helen saw tears in his eyes. "What's the matter, Hugh?" she said softly. She reached her hand up and stroked his face. She knew a hundred different things were the matter but not which one was affecting him this way.

"I keep hearing God telling me to let go, but I don't want to let go, not now, not this way." The tears rolled down his face.

She reached over and hugged him and felt the weight of his head fully on her shoulder. He let go and just cried. She wasn't sure just what he was grieving for. Not wanting to rush him, she let him rest there until it seemed he was through.

He lifted his head and looked at her.

"What do you think God wants you to let go of, Hugh?"

"It's Claire." The tears began to flow again, but

this time he fought through them. "I think I'm supposed to let go of Claire—*we're* supposed to let go of her."

"What do you mean?" She didn't like the sound of this.

"These last few months, since she and Ben got together, I've been so happy. For her, I mean. As her dad. My concern for years now—what I've prayed for more times than I can count—is that she'd find the right man. Someone who'd make her truly happy, who'd take care of her the rest of her life, treat her the way I have all these years."

"The way you've treated me," Helen said. He didn't seem to hear.

"I really thought that man was Ben. From that first night, and every moment I've spent with him since. It wasn't just how happy Claire's been. I felt like he was the man I'd been praying for all those years. Because of who he is, what he's like."

Helen knew exactly what he meant. "I did too, but now I'm not sure." She didn't know why, but she felt herself tensing up. "So, what are you saying?"

"I'm saying, I still feel the same way, that Ben is right for Claire. He's the man I've been waiting for her to meet."

"Even with all this?" She reached for his hand.

He nodded. "I don't want to think it. I've been trying to block all this out, shut it down. Claire needs to face it: it's over. We need to face it. What we feel doesn't matter. Ben's a German spy, a fugitive. That's what matters. We've got to stay a thousand miles away from him. I need to use my fatherly influence, every ounce I have left, to help her—to make her see if necessary—she has to let him go."

He said it so forcefully, Helen was a little confused. "But you don't think so now?"

"No. I feel like God is telling me to let go . . . of Claire. That Ben is not a mistake. That he's the man I've been hoping for, the one who will truly make her happy."

"But you know what that means," she said.

She looked into his eyes. He did.

The tears began falling down his cheeks again.

Chapter Thirty-Four

Ben didn't sleep well last night. No surprise there. He'd gotten up for good around 4:30 a.m., decided he might as well get an early start on closing the gap to Savannah. He'd made better time than he thought and came to the edge of town about twenty minutes ago. He was driving down Bay Street now, riding along the river as the sun began to rise.

Nice town. He remembered something about it from high school history, how it played some kind of role in the Civil War. Couldn't recall any details now. Didn't want to, either. He was not here to sightsee. But it was hard not to notice the charming old storefronts and hotels, the little park squares and huge mossy oaks. Claire would love this place.

No.

He sighed. No more thoughts of Claire. It made him weak.

He knew the shipyard was just east of town, between the river and President Street. They had studied it in Germany, along with a number of other coastal locations building these Liberty ships. He tried to recover some of the details of the mission. He had put them out of his mind once he and Jurgen had been assigned other targets. But he needed to remember them now if he had any hope of catching Graf and Kittel.

If they were responsible for yesterday's explosion, it meant that one of them had succeeded in getting hired at the Southeastern Shipbuilding Corporation. Once he was employed, his real job would be to learn everything he could about the operation, especially their security measures. So that months later, working as a team, they could come in at night and begin to set off a succession of explosions initially made to look like accidents. But as more and more explosions occurred, each more severe than the one before, they'd create a panic among the employees.

Ben remembered his Abwehr commander smiling as he talked about the fat, lazy Americans imagining themselves as so patriotic, doing their part for the war effort building these ships. The average American knew nothing, he'd said, of the realities of war, of real battles where people fight and die. "Let's see how quickly they turn and run," he'd said, "when their co-workers start dying or losing limbs in these explosions." Everyone else in the room laughed out loud. "We will shut these shipyards down," he said, "one by one."

Ben had found a way to shut his emotions down, long before then. So lunatic remarks such as these didn't eat him up inside. He'd become something of an actor, always living in character. That was how he'd endured not just the physical but the psychological effects of his training. Outwardly, he appeared the fine young Nazi, zealous for the Fuhrer and the Fatherland. No one ever suspected how he'd truly felt. He'd never yielded a single clue.

As he turned off Bay toward President Street, he realized he'd only begun to feel normal these past six months. Since he'd met Claire. He'd still had to play the actor, but at least he got to tell the truth about some things, about the man he was inside. The man she'd come to love.

He banged the steering wheel. "What are you doing?" He was torturing himself.

Up ahead the lights from the shipyard glowed

above the rooftops at the edge of town. He lifted his watch toward the windshield, trying to catch the time. Good. He'd made it. It wasn't much of a plan, but he decided to start near the gate. He knew thousands of workers would be clocking in around 7:00 a.m. He'd already grabbed his binoculars, one of the few spy tools he hadn't buried in the sand dunes that night.

He planned to find a secluded spot where he could watch the workers as they filed in through the gate, hoping to catch a glimpse of either Graf or Kittel.

Hoping he hadn't come all this way, and given up so much, for nothing.

Claire sat out on the wraparound porch in the same rocker she had sat in so many evenings these past few months. These past few wonderful months. She looked to her left at the empty rocker. Ben's rocker.

She didn't feel wonderful now.

It was probably mid-morning, although Claire had no idea what time it was. Her father had gone off to work. She'd never seen him so distraught. At breakfast he went through all the motions and routines he did every morning, but it was like he wasn't there. He drank his coffee, ate his toast, and stared at the newspaper. He never turned a single page. He looked at her once then quickly turned away. When it was time to leave, he'd gotten up without saying a word and kissed her and her mother on the cheek. His face smiled, but his eyes did not. He said he'd be home around 6:00 p.m., as usual.

A blue heron swooped down from somewhere between the trees and stood in her front yard. It didn't move for several moments, except its head, slowly back and forth, as if on guard. She loved looking at them. Normally they stood near water, in the reeds around ponds or by the river's edge. Why had it come here just now? Beautiful birds, she thought, but so lonely. Even when in the company of other herons, they seemed to stand by themselves.

The screen door creaked open, then slapped shut. "Claire, you okay? I brought you a cup of coffee."

How did her mother do it? She always found some small reserve of strength to stay positive, no matter what the challenge. Claire looked up. "Thanks." Coffee wasn't nearly as satisfying these days, since the best beans were no longer available because of the war. But she welcomed it, more for the love behind it.

Her mother sat in the rocker where Ben always sat. "Your father and I talked a little before he left. We both had a rough night. We talked a lot last night—I suppose you didn't get any sleep either."

"No, actually, I did," Claire said. "Exhaustion, I

guess. But it didn't do me any good. I woke up just as tired."

"We're all pretty weary," her mother said. "Guess that's to be expected."

"So what did Dad say?"

"Well, one of the last things he said was he felt that FBI agent . . ." It seemed she'd forgotten his name.

"Hammond," Claire said.

"Right, well, he felt Agent Hammond sounded pretty sincere there at the end yesterday. I thought so too."

Claire wondered if Hammond had just been manipulating them to get more information.

"But I can tell your father's worried sick. It's just all so big and so sudden."

Claire sipped her coffee. She hadn't even thought about what all this was doing to them. "I'm sorry, Mother. For getting you both mixed up in this."

"It's not your fault, Claire. You had no way of knowing Ben's past. Who would have ever guessed such a thing? And we came to love Ben too, both of us. I liked him from the start. Your dad was excited when he asked about marrying you. You should have heard him go on about Ben that night. It's one of the big things parents hope for . . . or dread, the person their child picks to marry."

The implication seemed pretty clear: Ben was

the wrong person, as wrong as a person could be. "I still love him, Mother." Tears welled up in her eyes.

Her mother reached over, put her hand on top of Claire's. "I know you do, sweetheart."

Claire braced for the gentle lecture she knew was coming. How she had to be sensible, to let him go. There was no way she and Ben could be together now.

"The thing is," her mother said, "we still love Ben too."

Claire looked up. A tear slid down her mother's cheek. "We don't want to lose him. But we don't have a choice."

Okay, here it comes, Claire thought.

"Your dad followed the trial of those other German spies, the ones who got caught last June. He knows we didn't get the whole story, you never do in wartime. But one thing was very clear . . . Americans were outraged. He said everyone wanted the spies dead. He'd heard rumors that the two they didn't execute were kind of like Ben. They weren't Nazis and cooperated with the investigation. That's why they didn't get the death sentence. But they both got very long prison terms. They're in prison now."

Claire didn't know what her mother was trying to say, but what she was saying wasn't helping.

"Your father thinks Agent Hammond believes us, and you, that we really didn't know anything about Ben until yesterday. But it might not matter. He said if he decides to drag us into this, we still . . . we still could go to jail. He thinks we'd be exonerated if that happened, at a trial. My goodness, I can't believe I'm saying this."

Claire sighed.

"You know, all the people who know us, and know Ben, they'd all say nothing bad was going on, that we weren't doing anything against our country. The thing is—and this is what made us both so sad—whether we get arrested or not, we don't see any way we can still be around Ben . . . ever again." She pulled a hanky from her apron pocket and wiped her eyes. "If he gets caught, even if he escapes. We don't see how we can ever see him again." She was crying now. "And that breaks my heart."

"Oh, Mom," Claire said. She buried her face in her hands and cried. She felt her mother's hand resting on her shoulder.

"But Claire . . . we don't feel it's right to ask that of you."

Claire wondered if she'd heard correctly. She tried to get hold of her emotions. "What?"

"Look at me, sweetheart."

She did.

Her mother wiped the tears from her eyes. "We love Ben. We don't feel he's done anything wrong, not before God, anyway. We don't think he should have to pay for crimes he didn't commit. And we know how much you love each other. Your father broke down last night when he said this, but he can tell Ben loves you the same way he loves me. A once-in-a-lifetime kind of love, he said. It was so sweet. We can't take that away from them, he said. Meaning you and Ben. We talked about it, prayed about it, and we don't think God wants us to."

"What are you saying?"

"Your dad remembered a verse in the Bible, in 1 Corinthians 13. Real love, it says, doesn't think about itself. That's how we love you, Claire. We don't want to lose you, or Ben. And we don't know why all this has happened. But we've decided we have to let you go."

"I don't understand." Claire was trembling.

"If Ben comes back, if he . . . if he doesn't get caught by the FBI . . ." Her mother started crying again. "You can go with him, if that's what you want. It has to be your decision. We'll miss you . . . both of you, so much. But we'll make it. If God's in this, and we think he is, he'll give us the strength neither one of us have right now."

Claire burst into tears and held her mother close. They just sat there and cried for several minutes.

When Claire looked up, she noticed the blue heron was gone.

Chapter Thirty-Five

That first morning in Savannah, two days ago, Ben had hidden in some bushes by the security entrance to the shipyard, far enough back to stay out of sight, keeping his binoculars focused on the front gate. So many workers had come through, hundreds of cars, and hundreds more came in by bus. Maybe thousands.

He hadn't seen Graf or Kittel among them.

He was pretty sure, though, that he'd seen a half dozen or more FBI agents come through the gate. Black cars, black suits, white shirts, dark ties and hats. He saw these same men walking around the different buildings, stopping people, writing down things they'd said. Their presence would make it more difficult to stop Graf and Kittel. Of course, there was always the chance the FBI might catch them first, freeing him from his duty.

So far, he'd seen no evidence of that, no signs of anything out of the ordinary.

It was now close to 3:30 p.m., quitting time. After two days of this, he was beginning to wonder if Graf and Kittel were not responsible for the explosion. If they worked here, if even one of them did, why hadn't he spotted them yet? He'd come back to this spot over the last two days on both shifts: at 7:00 a.m. and 3:30 p.m. when the shifts started, and even at midnight when the second shift clocked out.

He wondered if the FBI had scared the men off. Maybe they'd already gone to their next target, the shipyards in Brunswick a few hours south of here. If so, he'd have to start his surveillance all over again there.

A loud horn sounded in the shipyard, indicating the shift had ended. Men and women poured out of every building toward the front gate. Ben reset the binoculars. He panned past a row of three city buses and people lining up to get in. Wait, was that . . .

Among a group of men who had just stepped in line for the middle bus, a certain face. A large man had stepped in front of the man he was trying to see. "Move!" Ben muttered. "Get out of the way." The man dropped his hard hat, bent over to get it. It gave Ben a clear view of the man behind him. It looked like Kittel.

He followed the man a few moments, trying to get a better look. The man was turned around now, talking to a co-worker behind him. Ben noticed a lunch box in one hand, a hard hat in the other. He wore blue dungarees and a plaid red shirt. A few moments later, he turned back around and faced Ben, laughing at something the co-worker behind him said.

It *was* Kittel! There was no doubt in Ben's mind.

Ben watched a few seconds more, then shifted his focus to the bus. He needed to read the bus number in case he lost it in town. He scooted down a brief incline and ran a few feet farther south to get a better angle. There it was on the back, Bus #113. Only a handful of people stood in front of Kittel. Ben had to get to his car before the bus took off.

He'd parked on a deserted dirt road about fifty yards away. He got in and headed north, keeping the bus in sight out the right window. He had to catch it before it pulled out of the shipyard and drove downtown.

Bus #113 was still in sight, three or four cars ahead of him in traffic. It had weaved its way through downtown Savannah, and Ben had pulled over at every stop it made. Still no sign of Kittel. It had just pulled over again, after turning on Jefferson Street, not far from Tellfair Square. He followed the sidewalk up ahead toward a row of two-story apartments.

Graf!

Ben slid the car in a parking space behind a large Buick and ducked. Standing not fifty feet in front of him was Graf, Kittel's partner, leaning on an iron railing in front of the nearest apartment building, smoking a cigarette. Ben reached up and lowered the sun visor, then lifted his eyes just enough to see over the dashboard.

An old man with a cane got off the bus. Kittel stepped down behind him. He nodded at Graf, who tossed the cigarette in the street. Kittel walked toward him, around the old man, as the bus pulled out and drove away. When he reached Graf, Kittel said something that caused Graf to smile. Graf showed him a piece of paper. Kittel looked at it, got instantly serious, then both men walked up the few steps and through the front door.

Ben's heart was beating fast. That was it, then. He'd found them. *God give me the strength to do this,* he prayed, unsure if God would help him or even listen to such a prayer.

When the door closed behind the two men, Ben pulled out into the street, enough to read the address above the door frame. He wrote it down then drove off quickly, heading toward the little apartment he'd rented for the week off East Oglethorpe Avenue. He decided to get something to eat and wait until dark. Then he'd come back on foot. He didn't have a plan worked out yet but knew it would be easier to get away on foot. No witnesses could identify his car. The dark, narrow streets of downtown Savannah would provide plenty of cover.

When he got within half a block of his apartment, he was startled to see a black car double-parked in front. It looked just like the cars he'd seen the FBI agents using at the shipyard. He pulled into an open space by the curb. A man in a dark suit walked out the front door. Then another, dressed the same. They talked on the sidewalk, put on their hats, then walked to the car. One got in right away, the other walked around the car, opened the driver-side door, then stopped. He looked up and down the street.

Ben instantly slid down the car seat, out of sight. He felt his heartbeat in his temples. When he heard the car drive off, going the opposite way, he sat up. The coast was clear. But his plans were anything but clear.

They had to be FBI agents. What should he do? He couldn't head back to his apartment. Not now. What if they'd left another agent sitting in a car nearby, awaiting his return? He'd have to come back after dark, take his chances then. He couldn't just abandon the place. Not yet. He'd left his suitcase in the trunk of his car, but his gun was upstairs in his apartment.

So was his picture of Claire.

Chapter Thirty-Six

"That's kind of risky, Vic, don't you think?" Nate Winters said as he and Hammond drove down Price Street toward the river. "Shouldn't we at least stake the place out, leave someone watching the door? What if he gets spooked when he reads your note and takes off?"

Hammond looked at his partner. They'd been through a lot these past two years. He trusted Nate's instincts second only to his own. "It's just a hunch, Nate. But I think it's solid. You'd feel better about this if you'd been with me on all those interviews. This guy's not a killer. He's not going to want to take these two guys out if there's another way. But he's not going to turn himself in. Doesn't trust us, knows what'll happen if he does. He's here because he thinks it's the right thing to do, the only thing he can do. We gotta show him there's another way."

"But Vic, you just said it, he doesn't trust us. What makes you think he'll call? We're the authorities."

"I'm banking on two things. His Abwehr training, and that he's the kind of guy everyone says he is. He'll know we're on to him and that we've even figured out where he's staying. He'll wonder why we didn't just arrest him the moment he got back to the apartment. He'll look around outside, expecting to find us keeping him under surveillance. He'll see we're not, like I promised in the note, and that we've left the door wide open for him to run."

"You think he'll come running to us."

"Exactly." He looked at Nate, not sure if he was buying this. "Okay, it's a risk. I could have this all wrong, and . . . we lose him."

"So what," Nate said, "we just go back to the hotel and wait?"

"Got no other choice. I left the hotel phone number and our room number. Figured that way he can reach us without us getting others in the Bureau involved."

Hammond knew this whole thing could sour on him quick. But he also knew that all his promotions at the Bureau came from cases just like this, where he played his instincts. He'd still be out there beating the bushes, working the lowest rung if he'd played it by the book. He respected those guys, the ones that did, and knew they had their place. In fact, these same guys turned up this lead. Good old-fashioned police work, by the book. He should say something. "The guys did good turning up this address for us."

"They just did what you said." Nate referred to what most of the guys in town had been doing the last two days. Hammond had given them Coleman's description and told them to check every place in the south end of Savannah that rented apartments by the week. Get a list of names of anyone who'd rented a place in the last two days.

"But that was a lot of leg work, running down all those names."

"I'll tell them you said that," Nate said.

"Well, not yet," Hammond said. "We gotta keep a lid on this, see how it plays out. I'll buy 'em all a round of drinks when we wrap this up."

"You mean, if it doesn't blow up in our faces."

It took Hammond a minute. "That joke's getting old, Nate."

Ben was thankful it was a moonless night. The roads still had streetlights, but everything was dimmed due to blackout regulations. Plenty of shadows. After grabbing a bite to eat, he walked around the neighborhood until it became completely dark, then closed in on his apartment building. He checked and double-checked but didn't see anyone watching the place.

It didn't make sense.

He started to wonder if he was just being paranoid, thinking those two men were FBI agents. He walked to the front door and paused before going up the steps, half expecting to be rushed by federal agents. But no one came. He breathed a sigh of relief and made his way up the stairs, unlocked his door, and clicked on the light. He could see both rooms from the front door. No one inside.

But something was out of place. What was it?

He stepped inside and locked the door behind him. Panning the room, he finally saw it. Claire's picture. It was now on the end table, sitting under the lamp he'd just turned on. Underneath it, a note.

He began to tremble. Someone had definitely been here. He tensed and ran to the bed, reached for his gun under the pillow. It was still there. He hurried over to the door, turned off the lamp, then walked to the window and slid the curtains over an inch. He looked at the street below from every angle. No movement. No signs of anyone looking this way.

Ben was confused. He set the gun down on the bed and flicked the lamp on again. He slid the note out from under Claire's picture, sat on a nearby upholstered chair, and opened it.

Ben,
I'm Victor Hammond with the FBI. You're probably wondering why I haven't arrested you. If you've checked, you've seen I'm not even having you watched. I've talked with Claire's family and know the whole story. I'm willing to take a chance on you, Ben. I don't think you're a Nazi. But you've got to trust me and let me help you. You can't take on these 2 men by yourself. I think I know a way to get the job done and keep you out of it. Call me at the Marshall House Hotel. The number's on the back of this note. I'm in Room 312. If you don't get me, ask for my partner Nate. Speak to no one else.

Vic Hammond

Chapter Thirty-Seven

Ben grabbed the picture, the note, and a few other things he had in the apartment, put them all in a pillowcase, and turned off the light. He put his gun in the back of his waistband and walked to the back window, the one farthest from the road. Before picking this place, he'd checked to make sure he could exit safely out the upstairs window without being seen.

It was pitch black out there. He slid the window up and stepped out, tapping his foot on the ledge. Below him, a slanted roof covered a back apartment that was only one floor. He slid quietly down the roof, dropped the pillowcase in some bushes, and hung over the edge. He dropped and rolled in a small patch of gravel, barely making a sound. Still, he stood a moment to make sure.

He grabbed the pillowcase and walked through the shadows out to the nearest sidewalk. He saw no one in either direction. His car was just a few streets away, and he made it there without any trouble. As he slid in the front door, he tossed the pillowcase beside him.

Then he started breathing again.

This was crazy. What had just happened? Who was this guy Hammond? Was it some kind of trap? But that didn't make any sense. Hammond could have arrested him the moment he got back. So why didn't they arrest him? And if they were hoping that Ben would lead them to Graf and Kittel before arresting him, then why would Agent Hammond have written that note?

Hammond said he was willing to take a chance, said he believed what Claire's family had said about him. Could that even be possible?

Claire.

Would she have really said things to help him, and her parents too? He was sure she despised him now for all his lies. Then a worse thought. *They have Claire. They have Claire and her parents.* Of course they did—they were the FBI. Ben had been told that the FBI functioned with pretty much the same authority as the Gestapo. Did whatever they wanted, whenever they wanted. Unlimited power. This wasn't America, land of the free, home of the brave, but America at war. He'd been so stupid. He knew the FBI had arrested anyone who'd helped the spies they caught back in June. They had Claire and her family, probably under arrest right now.

Even if Claire had any remaining feelings for him, Mr. Richards would have told the FBI anything that might help his family at a time like this. Why should they be punished for opening their hearts and taking him in all this time? All Ben had done was tell one lie after the other.

His head slumped on the steering wheel. He'd messed this up so badly. *God,* he prayed, *please spare the Richardses. Don't let them pay for what I've done.*

Thirty minutes later, Ben had checked into a hotel on the far side of town under a different name. He sat by the desk in his room holding the note from Victor Hammond, staring at the picture of him and Claire.

Hammond had seen this picture. He knew what Ben looked like. And running away hadn't kept Claire and her family from getting dragged into all this. He'd been foolish to think it would. He thought about running again, this time for good. He could just take off and keep driving. Go out West somewhere, some no-name town, start over.

But he couldn't do that to the Richardses, or to Claire. The FBI had to know they had nothing to do with this, with any of it. A verse he'd read in his Bible ran through his mind; it was one he'd tried to memorize, something Jesus said: "Greater love has no man than this, that he lay his life down for his friends."

Ben had to turn himself in. He might be executed. Maybe they'd treat him like Dasch and Burger, spare his life and give him thirty years. But he had no choice now. He picked up the phone, gave the hotel operator the number to the Marshall House Hotel. When that hotel operator answered the phone, he said, "Room 312, please."

Someone picked up. "Hello, this is FBI Special Agent Nate Winters."

Ben didn't answer.

"Hello? Who's calling?"

Ben heard someone say in the background, "Is that him?"

"Uh . . . this is Ben Coleman, I'd like to—"

"It's him, Vic. Here."

"Hello? Ben?"

"Yeah."

"I'm glad you called, Ben."

Ben sighed. "Got your note. Don't see that I had a choice anymore."

"You could've taken off. I'm sure you checked, I left the door wide open."

"I know. What I don't know is why."

"Well, I'm inclined to believe you're not a Nazi saboteur."

"I'm not, Mr. Hammond."

"Call me Vic."

"You've gotta know . . . Vic. Claire's got nothing to do with this. Her parents either. I've been lying to them all along. Until—"

"I know, Ben."

"Are they under arrest?"

"Arrest? No. Far as I know they're sitting in their house in Daytona Beach. They're heart-broken. But I'm sure you knew that."

Ben felt a lump in his throat hearing that. But

also relief. "I don't understand, what's going on here? Why . . . why haven't you arrested me? You obviously know who I am, where I was staying."

"*Was* staying? You're not on Price Street anymore?"

"I moved to . . . another place across town. I didn't feel safe there anymore."

"Listen, Ben, that doesn't matter. What matters is, you're the only one who knows who these other two saboteurs are, what they look like. Maybe what they're planning next. We still don't even know if they're responsible for the explosion at the shipyard yet."

"It was them."

"How do you know?"

"I saw one of them, Kittel, clocking out this afternoon."

"Kittel?"

"That's his name. The other one's name is Graf."

"Kittel and Graf. Hold on. Write this down, Nate. Two saboteurs, Kittel and Graf."

"He wouldn't be using that name," Ben said. "We got cover names to use, and the papers to back them up. I forget what their names are, but I know what they look like . . . and where they're staying in town."

"You do? That's perfect. Ben, I know you don't trust me, why would you? But right now, I'm all you got. Nate here, he's my partner. Nate and I, we're the only ones who know about you at the moment."

"What?"

"We haven't reported this . . . *development* yet."

"But why?"

"Because I've talked to a number of people back in Daytona, besides the Richardses. Even that priest over at . . . what church was it?"

"St. Paul's? You talked with Father Flanagan?" Ben couldn't believe it. Father Flanagan had promised Ben that everything they'd talked about would remain confidential.

"He didn't rat you out. Father Flanagan wouldn't say a thing to me about what you told him. But he did say I was wrong if I thought you'd ever do a thing to hurt this country."

"I never would," Ben said. He was choking up again. *Thank you, God, for Father Flanagan.*

"Mr. Richards said the same thing."

Ben couldn't believe it.

"So me and Nate here are going way out on a limb for you. We could both lose our jobs over this."

"Or worse," Ben heard Nate say in the background.

"But we're thinking if you help us nab Kittel and Graf, well, that's what we're after here. To stop these guys before they hurt anyone else."

It was hard to believe, but Hammond sounded sincere. "They are most definitely going to do this again," Ben said. "Each bomb is supposed to be worse than the one before. I wouldn't be surprised if they're going to try again tonight. I was counting on it. Planning on stopping them myself."

"Then let's do that," Hammond said. "Where are you staying? We'll drive right over and pick you up."

Chapter Thirty-Eight

Ben sat in the front seat next to Victor Hammond; his partner Nate volunteered to take the back. But Nate leaned forward between them. It was still so hard for Ben to believe this was happening. When they'd met him in the lobby, he half-expected them to put him in handcuffs. "It's that building right up there on the left, right under the street-light," Ben said. "The one with the black iron railing."

Hammond pulled the car over. "You know the kind of explosives they're using?"

Ben nodded.

"Are we endangering the people who live in this building if we go in there?"

"Maybe," Ben said. "Obviously, we were taught how to make our bombs safe, not to go off until we're ready for them. But, they are explosives."

"How big a boom are we talking?" Nate said from the back. "I saw what the first one did down at the shipyard. Should I be calling my wife and kids to say good-bye?"

"I don't think so," Ben said. "The idea is to make a fairly small charge that you set next to something that will blow much bigger."

"A secondary explosion," Hammond said.

"Right."

"So," Nate said. "We might not get blown to bits here, just lose some arms and legs."

Ben smiled. "That's one way to put it."

Hammond opened the car door. As he got out, he drew his gun. Nate got out from the back, on the sidewalk side. He drew his gun too. Without thinking, Ben pulled his out from his waistband.

"Now, wait a minute," Nate said. "Vic, you okay with this?"

"I'm sorry, Ben. But—"

"Guys, I can shoot," Ben said.

"I'm sure you can," said Hammond. "But if these guys go down, the bullets need to be from our guns."

"I'm okay with that," Ben said. "But you might need a third gun. Believe me, Graf and Kittel can shoot too. We're not cut from the same cloth as the guys you rounded up back in June. Compared to the training we got, they were clowns."

"I get your point," Hammond said. "But . . . keep your finger off the trigger. You serve as backup only. And I mean, only if this thing gets away from us."

"Fine," Ben said.

They walked slowly to the door, Ben last, Nate and Hammond in front. Ben had already given them a detailed description of Graf and Kittel. They walked up the handful of brick steps and opened the door into a dark hallway. From the light let in by the streetlamp they could see two doors and a set of stairs on the left. One door right up front, one at the end of the hallway.

"You know which one?" Hammond whispered.

Ben shook his head no.

"I'm going to knock on this door. If either one answers, Nate, you and me come in fast. Ben, you hold back." He looked at Nate, then at Ben. Both men nodded.

"Hope this doesn't blow up in our face," Nate whispered.

Hammond looked at him, a slight grin on his face. He shook his head, as if to say "you idiot." He knocked on the door gently. Heard some movement inside. Footsteps coming toward the door.

"Yes? Who is it?" It was a woman's voice, an elderly woman with a strong Southern accent. The door opened a few inches, stopped by a brass chain.

Hammond and Nate lowered their guns. "Hello, ma'am," Hammond said, almost in a whisper.

"We're from out of town, got some friends we're trying to look up. They gave us this address. Two fellas, about our age."

She closed the door, unhooked the latch, then opened it. "Let me get a look at you." She was short, less than five feet tall, silver hair in curls, thick glasses. "Has to be Mr. Garner and Mr. Keller y'all are looking fer, if they gave you this address. Mr. Hemming lives down the hall, but he's older than me."

Hammond looked at Ben, mouthed the words "Garner and Keller." Ben nodded. He remembered their fake names.

"That's them, ma'am. So they're upstairs?"

"Usually they are. In the apartment right above this one, but y'all just missed them. They went out not fifteen minutes ago."

"Really. That's too bad. They say where they were going?"

"I didn't talk with them, but I think young Mr. Keller there might have been called back to work the night shift. He works down at the shipyard."

"Why's that?"

"He was carrying his hard hat and lunch box."

"Does that happen very often?" Nate asked, sounding more like an FBI agent than an old friend.

"Why, no, I don't suppose it does. You want to leave a message? You could write your names down and I'll tell them you stopped by."

"That won't be necessary," Hammond said. "We're just heading down to Florida, thought we'd stop by, see if we could catch them. But you've been very kind. Have a good night."

She closed the door, set the latch. The three men walked back outside.

"It's tonight," Ben said.

"The lunch box?" Hammond asked.

Ben nodded.

"Then we better get out to the shipyard," Hammond said. The men ran to the car, hopped in, and sped off.

A few moments later, Nate pointed at Ben with his head. "What are we going to tell the guards at the gate about him?"

Ben interrupted before Hammond could answer. "I don't think we want to come in by the front gate. I have a better idea."

Chapter Thirty-Nine

The three men drove the dark car through the even darker streets on the east end of town. Always before them, like a small sunrise, the shipyard lights glowed, creating a golden dome. Once again, Ben was struck by the absurdity and inconsistency of the blackout regulations. He knew the Germans had no means of flying planes across the Atlantic to bomb the US; the town of Savannah could have left all its lights on, all night long if it wanted, every night of the week.

If the Germans had possessed such a weapon, they'd leave the darkened town alone and bomb the shipyards to smithereens, lit up as it was and actually producing something the Germans wanted to destroy. But the Nazis had no such weapons. What they had at the moment were Graf and Kittel, armed with a small handmade explosive device hidden in a metal lunch box, now on their way to set up their second act of sabotage.

"What can you tell me about the first explosion?" Ben said.

"It's classified," Nate said. "Need to know only."

Hammond looked over his shoulder at him, made a face.

"Okay, guess you need to know."

"Don't need to know that much," Ben said. "Did anyone die?"

"No. It blew up on the third shift. Five welders were slightly injured. Cuts, bruises, one guy lost some hearing."

"The explosion happened around welders?"

"Lots of welders in a shipyard," Nate said.

"I'm just thinking, they followed protocol for the first one. Tonight will be worse. Since they made it work, they'll probably choose the same setup, same type of target. But set it to go off so people will be killed. Not a lot, but enough to raise the stakes, get more workers beginning to wonder."

They came out of the city on President Street. "Okay, Ben," Hammond said. "Where to?"

"Turn left down this dirt road that runs along the outer fence."

"You don't think they'll just go through the gate? He's got clearance."

"Just Kittel does," Ben said. "The lady didn't mention them both working here, and I only saw Kittel this afternoon."

"So why bring the hard hat?" Nate said.

"I'm guessing it's a costume, in case someone spots them. Hope no one does."

"Why's that?"

"They'd slit his throat without batting an eye."

"And leave a murder scene? Won't that draw all kinds of attention?"

"You wouldn't find the body," Ben said. "Not until they were through with this target anyway. Hold on, could you stop right here?" The road and the fence dipped up ahead.

"Railroad tracks," Hammond said.

Ben saw a guardhouse next to a gate, two soldiers standing inside.

"The road doesn't turn in here," Nate said. "It's just for the trains."

"Drive a little farther," Ben said, "until we're completely in the dark. Got a flashlight?"

"In the trunk," Nate said.

"Can we stop the car and get it? I should have mentioned it before we got started."

Hammond stopped. Nate hopped out, came back a moment later. "Here. Brand-new batteries."

Hammond drove forward, over the railroad tracks. "You think they came in through here?"

"It's what I'd do," Ben said. He aimed the flashlight along the bottom of the fence. "Could you go slower?"

After they'd gone about seventy-five yards, Ben saw something. "Stop!"

"What is it?"

"There, look where I'm holding the light."

"I see more fence," Nate said.

"Let's get out here," Ben said.

Hammond nodded, then he and Nate followed Ben through a patch of dirt and grass. As they got closer, all three could easily see that a section of the metal fence had been cut, a clean slice about two feet high. It had been put back together and held in place by rocks lining either side. "They came in here."

"Then let's follow," Hammond said.

They kicked the rocks out of the way. Nate pulled it open and held it for the others to crawl through. When they stood on the other side, he said, "Maybe we should call this in, Vic. If these guys are in there somewhere setting up a bomb . . ."

"We do that, we'll lose them for sure," Hammond said.

"But look at all these buildings. How are the three of us going to cover 'em all? I don't think we've got much time."

Ben bent low to the ground, panned the flashlight a few inches above the grass. "They went this way. Look." The agents bent down to see. As Ben went back and forth across a certain section with the light, you could easily see a trail where their footprints had bent the grass down.

"That works," Hammond said. "Let's go." Both men pulled out their guns. All three ran diagonally across the field toward the river, then angled in toward a long metal building. The trail died where the grass ended.

Ben looked across the asphalt. "What's in that building? Either of you know?"

Hammond shook his head no. "Don't know exactly," Nate said. "But I do remember seeing a group of large propane tanks at that end." He pointed left, toward the far end.

"Any people work nearby?" Ben asked.

"Lots," Nate said. "On the first shift anyway."

"Let's start there," he said. The three men ran across the paved area to the back of the building, hidden in shadows.

One thing they didn't have to worry about, Ben thought, was making noise. The sounds of huge steel plates being hammered, riveted, and welded together was almost deafening. They walked around the corner into a well-lit open area. Toward the river, Ben could see the hull of three ships being assembled by dozens of workers.

"Think they might be down there?" Nate asked. "Those are some pretty big targets."

"I think we should go in here," Ben said, pointing to the building they stood next to.

"He's been right so far," Hammond said.

Nate checked the doorknob to a set of double doors. "It's unlocked."

He opened it, and they stepped inside. The area they entered was dimly lit. It had a high ceiling. Webs of metal trusses and pipes crisscrossed the span, as far down as Ben could see. Looked like a typical factory setting. But Nate was right, the area back here contained four large propane tanks, in rows of two each. The three men stood in shadows created by the nearest pair. Ben instantly tensed up. "Guys, this is where I'd set the charge, in here." The men lifted their guns.

"Careful when you shoot, Nate. Don't want to hit these tanks."

"We see them, we take them out?" he asked.

"Oh yeah," Hammond said. "Shoot to kill. Ben, you see them, you . . ."

Ben barely heard him. He had walked a few steps ahead and bent down, his eyes searching for the spies. He didn't see Graf or Kittel yet, but he was sure they were here. His eyes shifted to the two tanks on the other side of the building. It cast the entire area in shadows. But in front of the tanks, a group of twenty machinists worked on a variety of drills, grinders, and lathes. Ben lay down on the cement and looked at the space between the tanks and the floor.

There they were.

Two sets of legs, huddled close together in the shadows. One of the men was on his knees. Ben looked up at Hammond. "That's them. I'm sure of it." He pointed to where they stood. Hammond motioned to Nate to start walking along the back wall, across to the other side of the building. Ben got up and hurried to stop them.

"What's the matter?" Hammond whispered. "If we shoot them, will we set off the bomb?"

"Possibly. Not sure. They'd be setting it to go off by a timer. Depends how far along they are. Thought if I went over there, stood by the back wall, and called out to them, they might step away long enough to give you a decent shot. If it's not them, you don't want to shoot shipyard workers."

"All right, let's do it," Hammond said.

"How will we know it's them?" Nate said. "We'll only get a second. Pretty dark over there."

"How about this," Hammond said. "Speak to them in German. They answer in German, either one of them, we start shooting."

"All right," Ben said.

"Head shots," Hammond said to Nate. "Don't want to get anywhere near that bomb."

Ben led them across the cement floor and into the shadows cast by the second set of tanks. They walked behind the first one and paused. He felt panic rising up from his chest. His face became hot. *Stop this.* He took a deep breath. *Give me courage.*

He stepped out from behind the tank and looked down a dark aisle. Two silhouettes. One standing, facing the machinists, the other kneeling. *"Graf, Kittel . . . Ist das Sie? Es bin ich, Gerhard."*

The man standing turned. Ben still couldn't see his face. The kneeling man stopped what he was doing and stood also. He said, *"Gerhard, was tun Sie hier?"* Ben recognized Graf's voice.

"It's them," Ben said. He stepped to the left, against the metal wall.

"Speak English, fools," Kittel said.

A shot rang out, Kittel fell to the ground. Graf dropped to his knees, as a second shot flew over his head. "Traitor!" he screamed.

"I can't see him," Nate said.

"He's setting off the bomb," Ben yelled and ran down the aisle toward Graf.

"Ben, get out of the way," Nate said.

"Ben, stop!" shouted Hammond.

A brilliant flash. A loud roar. Ben felt himself flying back. He slammed against the metal wall.

Everything went black.

Chapter Forty

Ben opened his eyes. He couldn't see clearly. He was lying on the ground; he could feel the dirt and grass beneath him. In the distance, alarm bells were ringing. Someone shouted, "Get out! Everyone out!" Another man's voice, "The whole thing could blow any second!"

He rubbed his eyes and the night sky started coming into focus.

"He's coming to." It was Nate's voice.

Ben turned his head to see Hammond squatting down beside him. "You all right, Ben? Can you move?"

"I better get back there," Nate said. "What are we saying just happened?"

Hammond looked back at Nate. "Everyone in there is doing what we need them to, clearing the area. I'm sure all the guys on our team will be here in minutes. Put someone in charge of the crowd. We need that whole building isolated. Then get on the horn and reel in the rest of the team. Tell them we found the saboteurs here in Savannah, and mention they're dead." He looked again at Nate. "Well, you know what to say." Nate nodded and took off.

"How'd I get here?" Ben said, sitting up.

"We dragged you," Hammond said. "You remember anything?"

"Graf and Kittel."

"They're both dead."

"Anyone else?"

"Thank God, no. Thought you were. Don't know how, but there was no secondary explosion. Looks like the bomb in their lunch box was the only thing that went off."

"How long was I out?"

"A few minutes."

Ben looked through the opening at the rear of the metal building. It was hazy with smoke, but he could see the big tanks were still intact. "Amazing they didn't blow." More like a miracle.

"They still could. Are you hurt?"

"Help me up?" When Ben stood, he noticed a large crowd of workers hurrying across the yard from the ship assembly area, toward the action. "My head is pounding. My shoulders ache. Feels like my ears are plugged up, but I don't think anything else is wrong."

"You've got a few cuts on your face and neck," Hammond said. "But if you're not hurt too bad . . . Listen, Ben, things are going to start happening pretty fast around here. I don't know how much time we have."

"So . . . what are you saying?"

"I'm going to let you go."

"What . . . when?"

"Now. Actually, if you don't go now, it's going to get pretty complicated. No one but Nate and I know about you. I've got two dead spies in there. That's what we were expected to find. We'll be heroes for stopping them. It'll go down that they blew themselves up as we were closing in. Hoover will love it." He shook his head. "I hate doing this. You deserve the credit. But the only reward I can give you is this." He held out his hand.

Ben shook it.

"Truth is," Hammond said, "I wouldn't be surprised if none of this makes the papers. I don't think Hoover wants any more German spies in the country, whether they're here or not. But that's not my concern right now. Point is, you've got to disappear."

"Where should I go?"

"Up to you. But you can't go back to your old life, not in Daytona, not as Ben Coleman."

"But why—you just said you got the two they were expecting you to find. Nobody else knows about me."

"Everyone knows there's a fourth guy. We found your partner in the dunes. You guys move in pairs. Hoover knows that. Everyone on this team knows that. Graf and Kittel's deaths have bought us time, that's all. Nate and I talked about it, we're both fine with you getting that second chance you wanted. We think you deserve that. But there are a lot of sharp guys on this team, a lot of loose ends lying around for ambitious guys to find and run with. They're not going to stop looking for you. You're the fourth guy. You've got to disappear for good."

And Ben knew what would happen if they found him. "I don't know what to say."

Hammond smiled. "Say you're going to make something of your life. Do something meaningful. Cure some disease. Break some world record. Just don't do it as Ben Coleman, or Gerhard . . . whatever your last name is."

"What about the Richardses back in Daytona? What about Claire?"

"I'm going to say that was a dead end. They're in the clear. Nate and I will come up with something to explain how we found out about Graf and Kittel. But I wouldn't go back to Daytona. Like I said . . . I asked a lot of questions there, talked to a lot of people. One of these guys might pick up that trail. If you go back, they'll put two and two together like I did. You're gone, it all becomes just a rumor."

Ben shook his hand again. He wanted to hug the man. Hammond had just saved his life, and now, his entire future.

"Now get out of here."

Chapter Forty-One

Ben woke up the next morning in his hotel bed in Savannah after the first restful night of sleep he'd had in days. He felt like he'd been run over by a car. Moving slowly, he managed to get cleaned up, then grabbed his suitcase and headed down to the lobby to check out.

He'd left both the gun and his picture of Claire in the suitcase. He'd toss the gun in a marsh or creek on his way out of town. He was thankful he didn't need it anymore. He didn't think he could ever part with the picture of Claire. In the lobby the newspaper on a coffee table surprised him twice. First, it didn't say a word about the explosion last night at the shipyard. And second, that it was Saturday. Running for your life and almost getting blown up had a way of messing with your sense of time.

He walked the half block to his car and put his things in the trunk. Then he sat behind the wheel of his green four-door coupe, realizing he didn't have a plan. Didn't even know which direction he should head as he rode out of town. Didn't have a city in mind to go to, a place where he could take Hammond's advice for that "second chance." Ben had enough cash to pretty much do whatever he wanted, and enough ration coupons to live anywhere in the US for almost a year.

But what did it matter?

He'd trade all of it in a flash if he could have Claire back. He was, at least, relieved to know she and her parents were in the clear with the FBI.

An elderly couple walked by arm in arm on the sidewalk, the man staring at him the whole while. Ben smiled and nodded. The man smiled back. Ben started the car and turned left at the first intersection, onto West Oglethorpe Avenue.

It was such a beautiful scene.

He was heading toward the shipyards, the wrong direction, but he didn't care. The shipyard was at the other end of town. They had their hands full down there anyway, after all that excitement last night. He could at least enjoy the scenery for a few blocks.

Like these amazing oak trees. Had to be over a hundred years old, every one of them. Spaced about fifty feet apart on both sides of the road. He loved the way the gnarly limbs arched over the road and meshed in the middle to form a long tunnel. Specks of sunlight poked through here and there, but otherwise the road was totally engulfed in shade. He rode along, slowing down at each intersection to take in the historic buildings that lined the narrow roads.

If it weren't for all the trouble going on at the

shipyard and the swarm of federal agents coming into town, he wouldn't mind starting over right here.

How could he start over anywhere without Claire?

Hunger pangs reminded him that he should get something to eat before leaving Savannah. He turned down Drayton Street till he reached the intersection at Broughton, which looked remarkably similar to Beach Street in Daytona Beach. He noticed a McCrory's and instinctively turned toward it, then pulled into a parking space nearby. As soon as he looked through the five-and-dime storefront window, his heart sank.

He could almost see "the gang" sitting there at the counter. Joe and Barb, Hank, Miss Jane taking orders, and at the end, Claire herself, her beautiful smile lighting up the entire place.

"Does it say anything, Dad? Anything about Savannah at all?" Claire sat across from her father at the dining room table. Her mother was in the kitchen cleaning up the breakfast dishes. She'd insisted Claire relax with her father and finish her coffee. Claire didn't think relaxation was even possible at this point. Since Ben had left a few days ago, her only available emotions were heartache and anxiety, and then there were the various odd hours of the day where she'd sit staring at nothing, feeling nothing at all.

Her father flipped through a few more newspaper pages. "Not a word, Claire. There's nothing here. You keep asking, sweetheart, but I'm telling you . . . they don't report things like that, not in wartime."

She was at least glad to see him starting to resemble himself again. The day after their meeting with Agent Hammond, her father had been certain the Feds would rush in at any moment and arrest them all. At dinner that night and throughout the evening after, no one had said a word. It was tense and horrible.

But the Feds hadn't come. And then another day came and went. And another. Her father had told them both just a few moments ago that he didn't think anything bad was going to happen to them now. "Perhaps Agent Hammond wasn't lying after all," he'd said, smiling for the first time in days.

Her mother took that as a sign to return to living life the same way they always had. All morning, no one had brought up the subject of Ben escaping or returning or of Claire being free to leave with him if he did.

But it was all she could think about, in between the more terrifying thoughts of Ben being killed and never seeing him again. She wondered which was worse—that, or never knowing what happened to him.

Chapter Forty-Two

It was crazy what he was doing, but he didn't care.

After eating breakfast at McCrory's in Savannah, Ben had driven out to the edge of town and stopped at the junction for Highway 17. Thinking, praying, fretting. Left or right. North or south. He'd sat there at the intersection, must have been three or four minutes, till an angry farmhand driving an old pickup truck mashed down on the horn.

Ben just reacted, turned left, heading south.

That was it, then. He'd drive back to Daytona Beach one last time to see Claire.

The whole way down, he'd wrestled about it. That and the warnings Hammond had given him last night. Whatever you do, don't go back there, he'd said. But how could it hurt to return for a day, just one day? Ben would be there and gone before the G-men had even begun to get their hands around the mess at the shipyard.

The more troubling questions came from his last conversation with Claire, at the riverfront park across from Woolworth's.

Ben . . . are you saying . . . you're a German spy?

Ben, I do love you, but I don't know. This is so much . . . too much, I think.

Well, tell me . . . Gerhard Kuhlmann, what else? I want to know everything you haven't told me. No more lies.

You're not supposed to have to work hard at being honest with someone you love.

It was more than the words; it was the look in her eyes, the disgust in her voice.

But he had to go back, just one more time. To see her. Even if only to endure her rejection again. He'd assigned himself a higher cause, a more noble theme to this journey. He looked beside him at the wooden box. He had to return it to Mr. Richards; it was a family heirloom. Claire's father had only given it to him when he'd thought Ben would become part of the family.

Besides that, he decided he'd rather their last memory of him be something positive. He'd bring them the good news that they no longer needed to live in fear because of him, that Hammond had decided to leave them alone.

Driving thirty-five miles an hour had eaten up the better part of the day. He'd lost track of time but started to see signs of familiar Florida towns pass by his window. Saint Augustine, Bunnell, Ormond Beach, Holly Hill. He was getting close now. On his left was the beautiful Riviera Hotel, like something you'd expect to see in Beverly

Hills. He slowed as he approached Mason Avenue, driving behind a convoy of Army trucks driven by WACS.

He opened his window to take in the ocean breeze.

There was St. Paul's up ahead on the right. Maybe he should stop in and thank Father Flanagan. Ben owed him so much. The priest had gone out of his way to help Ben, and Ben wasn't even Catholic. But a number of cars were parked in front and a good number of people headed in through the front doors. Father Flanagan was probably hearing confessions.

After driving past Broadway, then Orange Avenue, Ben felt his heart begin to race. Claire's house, her big mansion-sized house, was just a few streets ahead. Dread filled his heart as it came into view.

He pulled into the driveway, but he couldn't find the strength to open the car door.

"Who could that be?" Claire's mother said, walking out from the dining room.

Claire looked up from her seat in the living room. They both heard a car pulling into the driveway. She tensed up. Couldn't be her father; he'd been home all afternoon.

Her mother looked out the window. "I don't recognize the car."

Please, God, don't let it be the FBI. Claire set

her magazine down and got up. "Can you see who's inside?"

"No, it's just one person. A man, I think. He's not moving."

Claire's father walked down the stairs. "What's going on?"

"Someone just pulled in the driveway," her mother said.

"What color is the car?" he said.

"Green."

He breathed a sigh of relief. "The FBI usually drive dark cars, black mostly."

"What are we going to do?" Claire said. "Is he still sitting there?"

"Yes," her mother said.

"Well, this is ridiculous," her father said. "I'll just go on out there and see who it is and what he wants."

"Wait," her mother said. "The car door is opening. Oh my goodness. I can't believe it!"

"What?" Claire said. "Who is it?" She walked toward the window.

"It's Ben." Her mother released the curtain.

"Ben," her father said. "Really?"

"Ben!" Claire shouted. "Ben?" She ran to the front door, threw it open, and ran out onto the porch.

Ben couldn't believe his eyes. There she was, standing on the edge of the front porch.

Claire.

Their eyes met. Tears instantly clouded his view of her. She was smiling.

"Ben," she screamed, then ran down the steps toward him. "You're alive! You came back!"

He ran toward her. She leaped into his arms. He swung her around and set her down. She looked up at him, her face beaming, tears streaming down her cheeks. "I love you, Ben. I've missed you so much. Don't ever leave me again."

They kissed, a deep and passionate kiss, longer than they'd ever kissed before. Ben's insides felt like they would burst with joy.

After a few moments, still embracing, he pulled back slightly and held her face in his hands. "I couldn't bear it, Claire. I had to come back. I thought you wouldn't see me. All the lies. But I had to try."

She kissed him again. "I don't care what your name is or how you got here." She kissed him again. "God brought you back to me, that's all that matters. I'll be Mrs. Whoever, I don't care."

The ring. He held up her hand. She was wearing the ring he'd given her at the park. He looked over her shoulder, saw her parents standing on the front porch. Mrs. Richards was crying; Mr. Richards had his arm around her shoulder. "What about them?" Ben asked. "What do your parents think?"

"They love you, Ben. We've talked it all out."

"But Claire . . . there's something else. Something you need to know . . . something *they* need to know."

"Whatever it is, Ben, it doesn't matter."

"Claire, listen to me." He pulled her back gently but kept his hands on her shoulders. "This is serious. It does matter. I can't stay here. I could get us all in trouble if I stay. I shouldn't even be here now."

"I know," she said. "They know." She turned to look at them then back at him.

"Do they understand what it means . . . for me and you?"

She looked into his eyes. "Ben, I love you. I will go with you wherever you go. I'll be whoever I have to be, if I can be with you."

Ben couldn't control himself. Tears ran down his face. How was this possible? It was beyond anything he dared to hope or dream.

She handed him a handkerchief then took his hand and led him to the house. "Let's go inside before any of the neighbors see us, and I'll explain."

Chapter Forty-Three

The next morning, Father Flanagan woke up early, as he had the last several mornings, with only one thing on his mind. He was worried about Ben. The other priests in the parish were scheduled to say Mass at every service this morning. He was glad he'd been relieved of this responsibility. He had decided to attend the ten o'clock service and planned to use the time between now and then to pray.

There was a knock at his door. He opened it to find Father Murphy standing on the other side. "Father Murphy, what a pleasant surprise."

"Good to see you, Aidan. Hope you slept well. I'm in a bit of a hurry, but I wanted to give this to you before I forgot." Father Murphy handed a thick envelope to him.

"What is this?"

"A young man dropped it off at the rectory last night. He said it was for you, asked me to make sure you got it."

"A young man?" Aidan wondered if it could have been Ben. "Did he seem troubled or upset?"

"Quite the opposite. He seemed very happy, and just sad that he missed you. I told him you had already gone to bed. Is everything all right?"

"I'm sure it is. Thanks, Father, for dropping this by. Do you need me to assist you this morning?"

"I'll be fine," Father Murphy said. "But thanks for asking. I'll see you in a little while."

Aidan closed the door and walked to a nearby upholstered chair. He sat down and opened the envelope. "Oh my goodness," he said.

It was filled with cash.

And a note.

He slid the note out and began to read:

Father Flanagan,

Things have turned out better than I could have ever dreamed. I wish I could tell you all the details. You have helped me more than you will ever know. There is no amount of money on earth that could begin to repay my debt of gratitude for your kindness, love, and advice. But please accept this donation to be used wherever you think it is needed most. Continue to keep me (us) in your prayers. I will never forget you.

An Anonymous Friend

Instantly, Aidan knew it was Ben. Had to be.

He hadn't signed it because he didn't want to get Aidan in any trouble. "Thank you, Lord," Aidan said aloud.

Somehow, some way, God had answered his fervent prayers. God had not only spared Ben's life and kept him from getting arrested, he had also allowed Ben and Claire to be together, if the reference in the note to "us" was any indication.

He was so grateful, and so relieved.

Later that afternoon, Ben and Claire, now as Mr. and Mrs. Whoever, drove north on US1 to start their new life together. To Ben, Claire's parents had been simply amazing.

Yesterday, after explaining to Ben how he and Claire's mother had reached the conclusion that God meant for them to be together—even though it meant they might never see their daughter again—Claire's father had gotten in the car and drove to his pastor's home to talk him into performing their wedding. Which he had done just one hour ago, after concluding this morning's Sunday service.

Since the war began, thousands of couples wanted to tie the knot in a hurry before the groom shipped overseas. The pastor had gotten used to performing last-minute weddings, and the local judge had waived the normal waiting period for couples to obtain a marriage license. Claire's father had told the pastor that Ben wasn't shipping overseas, but his reasons for getting married so quickly were definitely "war related" and "some-what classified." The pastor had said that if Mr.

Richards could vouch for Ben's character and approved of his intentions, it was good enough for him.

Mrs. Richards had let Claire use her wedding dress. It was a little big for her, but Ben thought she looked stunning. The hardest part of all was saying good-bye just before they drove off. Ben still couldn't believe the depth of sacrificial love Claire's parents had shown over the last twenty-four hours.

He had gotten an idea last night that he thought might offset their pain, a way he and Claire could communicate with her parents in the months and years to come. He'd typed out the procedures he'd learned in his Abwehr training. It was fairly sophisticated but something he felt sure Mr. Richards could grasp. It involved sending coded messages using classified ads in local newspapers. Ben had thought up an additional layer that would allow them to do this once a month, and how to make it work both ways.

The thing is, he'd said, "You have to memorize these instructions carefully, then destroy this sheet of paper." Mr. Richards looked it over and agreed. Ben heard Mr. Richards tell his wife that it wasn't as bad as families had it a hundred years ago. "They'd have to watch their married children head off on a wagon train or sail off across the sea," he'd said, "and they'd never hear from them again."

"And when Jack gets back from the war," Claire added, "you can teach it to him."

This idea may have brought Mrs. Richards some small comfort but did little to stem her flow of tears. All four of them cried as they kissed and hugged good-bye. Ben's heart ached for them. Still, it couldn't overcome the joy and happiness he felt inside, sitting next to the love of his life as they drove off on this romantic adventure.

Ben decided that the God he had learned to trust more fully had orchestrated things in an amazing way, beyond anything he could have dreamed. He would have to trust God to continue helping all of them in the uncertain days to come.

A Brief Epilogue

Over the next several years, Ben and Claire were very happy, enjoying their new life together. Still, every so often he would catch her staring off in the distance or crying quietly by herself. And each time, he knew what it was.

The loss.

The missed moments, the memories never made with her family. He'd wrap his arms around her and apologize all over again for the terrible sacrifice she'd been forced to pay by falling in love with him.

And each time, after her tears had run their course, she'd look up into his eyes and tell him how much she loved him, that he was worth the sacrifice she had made. And as hard as it was, she'd say that she would do it all over again.

And each time, Ben would quietly vow that he would love her with all his heart, and he would offer a silent prayer that God would help him become a man worthy of this beautiful woman, and her family, and the love that had come at such a cost.

Decades later, Ben would look back at these extraordinary times, and this thought would immediately come to mind: from the first moment he'd met Claire, through all the difficulties they'd had before getting married, through all the ups and downs in the years after that, he had known she was the only woman he would ever love. He never once doubted it. Never had a single regret. When God gives a man this kind of woman, he knows it deep inside. Almost at once. Like he knows his own soul.

A love like that is a gift you can never earn or ever repay.

THE END

17

I held the last manuscript page and sat back on the couch, thoroughly exhausted. Apparently, my eyes had adjusted to the diminishing light of the setting sun. The living room was dark. I hadn't moved since the moment I'd discovered I had been reading about Gramps and Nan. It was great as a book, riveting as a memoir. I had always loved Gramps, but now he'd achieved superhero status.

I read the last paragraph again, remembering the words Gramps had said that night out in the courtyard, when I'd asked if he'd ever had any regrets marrying Nan. He'd quoted from this manuscript almost verbatim.

Turning the last page over, I placed it on the stack, sat up, and stretched. I felt a strong urge to see his typewriter and the hand-carved wooden box, which had suddenly become priceless. They were back in his office—my office. I walked through the kitchen and flicked on the light as I stepped inside. There was the typewriter, still centered on his desk, the wooden box right beside it, right where I'd left them.

Had it only been yesterday? It felt like we'd traveled through time together.

Gramps had typed the entire journey I'd just taken on that old thing. I could see him sitting there, clacking away. Such a schemer, sly as a fox. It was what made his novels so fascinating. For some reason, he'd decided this was the way he'd unveil his story, this body of secrets he and Nan had sat on for sixty years. Written it like a novel, but not fiction. A love story, their love story. A spy story. A World War II thriller.

But what did he want me to do with it now? Was it just for me, for our family? Did he expect me to unveil it to the world?

I walked over and sat at the desk, spun the chair halfway around. He'd set up this scavenger hunt for me to discover. Did it this way on purpose, thought it all through. What did he expect me to find? Whatever it was, it certainly wasn't in this house; I'd searched it from top to bottom. Was it in the manuscript, in his journal? Something I'd missed?

I trust he'll know what to do with it, and with the package I've left in my wooden box.

I spun the chair back around and stared at the wooden box. "Gramps, you've given me too much credit. I was never good at puzzles."

Writing this memoir, he'd answered so many of the big questions we'd had about him and Nan, especially from my sister Marilyn. Where Gramps and Nan came from, how they'd met, how they'd fallen in love. Why he'd never talked about it before. Why there were no wedding pictures.

My grandfather was a German spy.

Who has that for their story? I thought of my good friend, Aaron Burns, one of the guys in my wedding. His grandfather had played in the NFL for the Packers, back when football highlights were done in black and white. I'd always thought that was something.

Wait a minute. I suddenly realized I was German. I'd always thought we descended from the British.

Whatever happened to the Richards family? My great-grandparents? And I had a great-uncle Jack, who'd fought in World War II. The only thing I knew about him was that he didn't smoke cigars. What about Hammond, the FBI agent? Had he and my grandfather ever met again? Were these names even anyone's real names?

So many questions. Given more time, I was sure the list would grow. Whatever the questions and the answers to them (if they could be found), I had already decided I'd never give up the typewriter or the wooden box. One day, I'd give them to one of my kids.

Of course, first we had to have some kids. I needed to call Jenn. She had to be off work by now.

When I got back to the living room, my cell

phone was glowing. I ran the last few feet but had missed the call. It was Jenn. I hit the send button, hoping she hadn't gotten into her car yet.

"It's you," she said. "I heard your message but you didn't answer. I thought, how can he do this to me again?"

"I'm sorry, hon. I just left it for a sec. You off work?"

"I am and I have some good news."

"What is it?"

"No way, you first."

"It's incredible, Jenn. It's all about him and Nan. It's not a novel. It's their story, how they met, where they came from. All the secrets Marilyn wanted to know. I should have figured it out sooner. Guess it was just too big to grasp. I'm dying to tell you all about it, but I know you're going to want to read this yourself."

"I certainly do."

"Already told you the ending," I said.

"Already figured it out."

"You did."

"I didn't want to say anything when you called last time, but I was pretty sure."

"It's so amazing, Jenn. I still can't get my mind around it."

"I can't wait to read it. So want to hear my news?"

"Definitely."

"I'm off for good this weekend. I can come

home. They were so great about it. Nobody thinks I should work the whole two weeks, including my boss. She said she couldn't even believe I came back at all."

"That's wonderful, Jenn. I can't wait to see you. You know, I just had an idea. We can do that now that we have money. Think of things and just do them."

"Maybe," she said. "What are you thinking?"

"How about I drive the Mini Cooper down."

"You don't have to do that, I can fly back. I bought a round-trip ticket."

"Don't you want to drive the Cooper?"

"Michael, I can drive it all the time when I get back."

"All right, I've got another reason. After reading this, I'd really like to see Daytona Beach. I can pick you up, we could drive over there from Orlando, stay at a nice hotel on the beach. You could read the manuscript, and I'll drive around, scout out all the places Gramps wrote about, see how many of them are still there. When you're done, I'll give you a tour."

She paused a moment. "Actually, that sounds pretty good. I still can't get used to our situation, that we can just do things like that. Have you thought about what to tell Mr. Samson, your grandfather's agent?"

"No, and I don't really want to right now."

"When's he expecting you to call?"

385

"He said a few days. I'm going to use the longer interpretation for 'few.'"

Jenn laughed. "Well, I'm in the car."

That meant she had to go. "I can be down there tomorrow, by the time you get off work."

"I can't wait. You're going to let me drive, right?"

"We're going to have to work out some kind of schedule," I said.

"It's that much fun?" she said.

"Yeah." The thing was, we both wanted this car, she way more than me, but that was before I'd gotten to drive it. "I love you, can't wait till tomorrow . . . Mrs. Kuhlmann."

"What?"

"You'll see."

We hung up. I reached down and gathered the manuscript together, carefully. First thing in the morning, I planned to make a hard copy and bring that down to Jenn. I'd put the original in a safe deposit box at the bank. Then I had another idea. I could buy a recorder, dictate it, and hire someone to make a digital transcript from that. When the time was right, I could email copies to the rest of the family. I wanted to talk to Jenn first, but I thought whatever we wound up doing with this thing, it should be a family-wide decision.

Back in the office, I opened the wooden box and laid the manuscript inside. A temporary home. I had no plans of bringing the box to

Florida. But I was starving. So my plans before turning in tonight were simple: get something to eat, buy a nice big envelope for the manuscript, and pack.

Before stepping into the kitchen, I turned off the office light. Barely a few steps away and I felt this nagging sense that there was something undone back there, something to do with the manuscript. I walked back, flicked the light on, and stood by the desk.

I looked down at the desk, at the typewriter. There was my grandfather's journal. Still nothing. I opened the wooden box, and it clicked.

Special Agent Victor Hammond.

Since this story was true, then Hammond must be a real person. So was his partner Nate. What if one or both of them were still alive? They'd be in their late eighties, maybe early nineties, but it was possible. What if my grandfather used their real names? He'd used his—he'd written "Ben and Claire" on the back of that picture.

Starving or not, I had to check this out. I grabbed my laptop and hurried to the couch. Didn't really know where to begin, but if Victor Hammond was somewhere on the earth, I planned to find him.

18

It was almost midnight. This late-night stuff was starting to get to me. I had just taken a week's worth of clean underwear and put it in the bathroom trash can instead of my suitcase. But I was happy—ecstatic might be a better word.

Something amazing had just happened. The kind of thing that fit perfectly with everything else that had transpired in my grandfather's tale. Left me thinking of that old familiar phrase . . . "the plot thickens."

Thirty minutes ago, after three hours of searching the internet, I received an email from a retired FBI agent who knew Victor Hammond and thought he might still be alive. "He was five years ago anyway," he'd said. "Golfed with him in Florida when we were down there at Disney World. Moving slow these days, but still kickin', I think." He didn't remember where Hammond lived. Said Hammond had driven over to golf with him "from somewhere on the east coast." I took that to mean the east coast of Florida.

I sent him a follow-up email, trying to verify that, but in the meantime I started looking online through the white pages for a "Victor Hammond" in the major beach cities, starting at the northern end of the state. No Victor Hammonds in Jacksonville. None in Saint Augustine. Then I came to Daytona Beach.

No way, I'd thought.

Typed it in. Yes way.

There it was: *Victor Hammond, 93 years old, Daytona Beach, Florida.*

I wasn't surprised to find that Hammond had retired to Florida. Having lived in the Orlando area, I knew all about the lure of the Sunshine State to retirees. But it was intriguing to see he'd picked Daytona Beach, of all places, to live out his final days. Not to mention that it saved me the trouble of flying off to who-knows-where to meet him, since I'd already planned to go to Daytona myself.

Initially, I had planned on calling him in the morning. Most elderly people I knew didn't stay up this late on purpose. Then I had the thought to leave him a voice mail. If he was asleep, it wouldn't matter, he'd just hear the message in the morning. Then I had another thought. Don't call him from my cell phone, call him from Gramps's house phone. Maybe he had caller ID, and in that case, he'd see my grandfather's name when he looked at it. For all I knew, the last time the two men spoke might have been that night in Savannah back in 1943, but what if it wasn't? I felt it was worth a try.

I don't remember the exact message I left. But

to my surprise, five minutes later, Victor Hammond called me back.

His voice was frail and weak, but I understood him clearly. "I've been expecting your call, Michael, ever since your grandfather's passing. I regret I'm too old to travel. I wanted very much to pay my respects in person at his funeral. He was one of the finest men I've ever known, and a good friend."

"Mr. Hammond, I can't believe it's you."

We agreed on a time to meet, the day after tomorrow, mid-afternoon, at his condo on the ocean in Daytona Beach Shores. I put my clean underwear in my suitcase, where they belonged. I was exhausted but wondered how I would ever be able to sleep.

19

Florida was living up to its reputation. It was a gorgeous October day, mid-seventies, surprisingly light humidity, a nice breeze coming in off the ocean, the sun high overhead and blocked only on occasion by a smattering of clouds.

The normally boring drive down yesterday didn't seem half so bad when traveling in a sporty little car with an outrageous sound system. I was thankful for cruise control or I would have undoubtedly averaged a hundred miles an hour. When I'd arrived in Orlando, I picked Jenn up from her last day of work, took her out to a lovely restaurant in Winter Park, then moved over to the passenger side to let her drive us both an hour east to Daytona Beach.

I had booked us in a five-star beachfront hotel that actually overlooked the historic Bandshell. It was too dark to see it when we checked in last night, and I had more important things on my mind. The room was fabulous, the hotel itself much fancier than where we'd spent our honeymoon. Jenn and I got to make up some valuable lost time. We had the kind of time that was . . . well . . . that was nobody else's business.

The next morning, after sleeping in and eating a late breakfast in our room, I'd left her out on the balcony reading my grandfather's manuscript.

I discovered that Victor Hammond's condo was only ten minutes south of where we were staying, but since we'd agreed to meet in the afternoon, I spent the time in between checking out the various places I'd read about in my grandfather's book. Starting with the Bandshell.

It was exactly as he'd described it, except the rows of wooden bench seats were gone. But I was very likely standing in the exact spot where Gramps and Nan had danced together for the first time. I walked along the "broadwalk" beside the Bandshell where they'd walked, and stopped along the railing to gaze out at the ocean. When I turned, there was the tall clock tower, next to the Bandshell, where they'd met that night, the time when Gramps first saw Nan reach out for his hand.

Not far from there I saw a Ferris wheel but, as it turned out, not the same one they'd gotten stuck on that night. I'd asked a gray-haired woman selling hot dogs in a stand nearby. She turned out to be a wealth of information. This Ferris wheel had been built a few years ago. The one Gramps and Nan had ridden on had been taken down in 1989. But still, standing nearby I could easily see them sitting up there in the gondola, aware of the romantic vibes pulsating between them. Gramps going crazy trying to behave. Nan pretending her feelings didn't exist.

Remarkably, almost the entire downtown area of Daytona Beach had been preserved. Woolworth's was gone. McCrory's too. But the original buildings were still there.

The beautiful riverfront park across the street had not fared so well. The grounds were still there, with nothing built on top of it. Even the walkways, little bridges, and ponds were there. But almost all the palm trees had been removed and all the gardens. I'd walked through it, tried to find the place where Gramps and Nan had first kissed, where they'd had that fateful conversation the day Jurgen's body had been discovered. The day Ben thought his world had just ended and he'd lost Claire forever. I stood there, surveying the area, trying to take it in. It was satisfying getting to see all these places, knowing they really did exist. That my amazing grandparents with their crazy-amazing love story had stood right here and had done all those things so many years ago. When they were crazy in love.

Like Jenn and me.

I took one last breath of the fresh sea air and worked up the nerve to get in my Mini Cooper, drive back across the river to Daytona Beach Shores, and hear everything retired Special Agent Victor Hammond had to say.

20

I parked in the visitor's section and easily found the security phone next to the front door. Hammond's condominium was nice but not nearly as tall as those standing on either side, nor as elaborately landscaped. He buzzed me through. I stumbled over the black floor mat just inside the door, grateful no one saw.

The elevator didn't respond the first time I pushed the button, so I stabbed it a few more times. *That doesn't help. Just calm down.* I was hearing Jenn's voice in my head.

Hammond's unit was 6A, a straight ocean view.

But it turned out to be at the far end of the hallway as I got off the elevator.

The door opened before I rang the bell. Someone who looked nothing like the Victor Hammond I'd created in my mind stood smiling in the foyer. I'd allowed for age. Apparently not enough.

"Come in. You must be Michael. You look just like your picture."

Picture?

"I am, and you must be Mr. Hammond?"

He closed the door behind me. "That's me, but call me Vic," he said as he stepped around me and led the way. We walked into a modest-sized living area with an amazing ocean view. On one side was a full-length sliding glass door that opened to a balcony, on the other a large picture window.

I stood in front of the glass door. "I don't imagine you ever get tired of this, Vic."

"No, I don't. God puts a new painting on display every day out there. Have a seat, have a seat. Care for something to drink? Got diet soda, beer, bottled water. Could make some coffee, if you'd like."

"Bottled water would be great."

"Well, I'll get it. It's so nice out, thought we might sit on the balcony."

"I would love that."

He walked into the kitchen, slightly bent at the waist. Maybe five-feet-eight-inches tall. Looked like he used to be close to six feet.

Totally bald, thick glasses. But he had a great smile. One wall was covered with family pictures in a variety of sizes and frames. I walked closer. He appeared to have three children, two daughters and a son. A number of grandchildren, maybe great-grandchildren. One row, scanning right to left, was like watching Vic and his wife marching backward in time. I could see the essence of the man in the kitchen getting younger and younger. The oldest photograph actually resembled the man I had pictured while reading Gramps's book.

"Here you go."

"Thanks. You live alone, Vic?" We walked toward the sliding glass door.

He sighed. "Yeah. Me and your grandfather had that in common. Angie passed away three years ago. Supposed to be the men that go first, right?"

"I guess so."

"My daughter lives in town, on the mainland. She checks on me once or twice a week. Makes me wear this thing around my neck." He held it up. "Supposed to fetch the cavalry if I kick the bucket."

Just then I noticed three dark bookshelves along a living room wall. My eyes fixed on the top two rows in the center. I couldn't be certain, but it looked like he had every single book my grandfather had written. All hardbacks. "Are those . . . first editions?"

He stopped and looked up. "Ah, I should have

guessed you'd spot those. My proud collection. Yes, every single one a first edition. And . . . all signed by your grandfather himself. Pull one out, have a look."

I did and opened its cover. My eyes almost bugged out. I recognized my grandfather's writing from all the books he'd signed for me. But in Vic's book, he'd written, "To my dear friend, Vic. A very special agent." Then his signature.

Gramps had a distinctive signature, pretty fancy. But you could still decipher his name if you knew what you were looking for. The thing here was, he spelled his last name with a "K" not a "W." Then I realized. "Is that . . . ?"

"Kuhlmann?" Vic finished. "Very good, Michael. Yes, it is. Your grandfather's little code. Just for me. I told him before he died, 'You know, you really screwed this up for me. How am I going to sell these as an autographed collection if some stupid Kraut wrote his name in all of 'em.' "

We both laughed.

"So you guys stayed in touch all those years?"

"A little. Hardly at all in the beginning. There was a very real danger of your grandfather getting caught, not just during the war. Really throughout the entire Cold War era."

"Really," I said. "That was going to be one of my main questions."

"How come he kept his identity hidden all these years?"

I nodded. "I can see why in the beginning. But I've been thinking about it a lot the last few days. Why keep this thing going so long after the war was over? Even from your family?"

"Let's go outside and I'll tell you."

He wrestled with the sliding glass door. I grabbed the part above his head and got it moving freely. In the middle section, the balcony was wide enough for a round white table and four padded chairs. He sat down, but I stopped to enjoy the view a moment. To the south was the stone jetty near the inlet. Somewhere around there is where the stock cars used to race in the thirties. At the northern end I could actually see the Main Street Pier sticking out in the ocean. In one of the hotels just beyond that, my Jenn was sitting on a balcony too, reading the manuscript.

"I imagine it would be hard for you to grasp, Michael. The way things were back then. 9/11 really changed the game quite a bit. Before that it was the Communists and before that, the Nazis. My partner Nate and I did something for your grandfather that would not only have gotten us fired, it would've sent us to prison, maybe for life. That was the atmosphere back then."

I sat down, opened my bottled water. "Vic, before we go on, I just have to say thank you for what you did for my grandfather all those years ago, back in Savannah."

"You don't need to thank me, Michael. Your

grandfather's already done that more times than I can count."

"Maybe he did, but I want to myself. I've been thinking about this. I wouldn't be here, none of my family would be here if it weren't for you and Nate, what you did all those years ago."

"Well, looking at what your grandfather did with his life, it was one of the best off-the-record calls I ever made. Way I figured, it really wasn't all that illegal. Not technically. Didn't have a witness protection program back then. I figured, that's really all Nate and I had done."

"I get that, Vic. But still . . . thank you."

"You are most welcome."

"Can I ask you something . . . was there really any danger of him getting arrested? I know there was in the beginning. But ten, twenty years later?"

"There's no statute of limitations on espionage, Michael. Even now. Technically, your grandfather could have been arrested right up until the day he died." He sat back. "Now I don't think that would have happened, not for the last ten, fifteen years. Government's got a lot bigger fish to fry. I suppose by then and, really, for all those decades, he *was* Gerard Warner, not Ben Coleman or Gerhard Kuhlmann anymore. The life he'd carved out for himself and his family was who he was, who they were. No sense in upsetting all that, opening up Pandora's box."

I took a swig of water. "I guess I can understand that."

"You remember that book he wrote, *A Rose by Any Other Name*?"

I nodded.

"It was like our little joke, that book. When I read it, I saw all kinds of clues in there about your grandfather. We talked about it the next time I saw him. Remember that line when the main character—I forget what his name is now—said 'A name? A name means nothing. A man is who he is on the inside. That's all that matters.' Laughed out loud when I read that."

I decided right then, I'd be reading that book again. "How often did you keep in touch?"

"Just every now and then. Like I said, not at all for years in the beginning. First contact was when his first novel came out. At first, I thought who the heck sent me this? Then something of a coded letter followed, and I began to connect the dots. At one point, after he'd become a bestseller, he'd gotten permission to spend some time with an FBI agent for research and mentioned he'd read about some of my cases."

"And they assigned you to help him?"

Vic got a big smile on his face. "After that, it was much easier for him and me to interact."

"Did he do something like that with Nan's parents? The Richards family?" I really hoped so. But Vic's expression instantly changed.

"That's the sad part of the story. First sad part was Jack, Mary's brother. He died in the war, in '44, I believe. He'd been married, but they didn't have any children. Your grandparents had this newspaper code they did with Mary's parents. Did that all through the forties and fifties. Worked pretty well, he told me. Then they found out her parents died in a car accident out west, 1961, I believe. After that, it was just the two of them."

This information instantly saddened me. I'd begun to hope there might be another whole side of the family yet to discover. "Vic, you said last night you were expecting my call. How did you know I—"

"Your grandfather came to see me, about a month before he died. I could see he wasn't well. He told me all about the book he'd written, telling about their story. The scheme he had in mind to get you to find it."

"Really? He mentioned me personally."

"Oh yeah. You're the writer, aren't you?"

"Yes. I hope to be."

"Well, he said he'd prayed and thought long and hard about it. Felt you were the one he was supposed to set all this up for. I asked him if he wanted me to call you after I heard he'd passed and he said no. Said he was sure you'd figure it out, even figure out the part about calling me."

I shook my head.

"You don't think too highly of yourself, do you?"

The question took me aback. "Why? I don't know—"

"He said you didn't see yourself the way he saw you, or the way God does. Not yet. Those were his exact words. Part of the reason he did all this was to help you begin to see yourself in a new light." Vic leaned forward and said, "He was very proud of you, Michael. By the look of things, seems he had good reason."

I found myself blinking back tears.

"And he brought me a package to give to you that day. A box. He said, 'Give this to Michael when he comes. He'll know what to do with it.' And he said there was a note he wrote inside it for you. I asked him what was I supposed to do with it if I kicked the bucket before you got here. You know, you get my age, it's a big deal each morning you open your eyes and still see the ceiling."

I laughed.

"He said to put it in my will, so it would get to you then. So I'm glad you came, Michael. Because I forgot all about that until this moment. I never did change my will. Now you saved me the trouble."

We sat there for a few moments. It looked like he was about to nod off. "So . . . where is this box?"

"Oh, shoot. I guess it's time for my nap, or else you just got real boring." He laughed. "I'm kidding, I'm just tired." He stood up. "Let's go get that thing. I've got it out on my bed."

21

I was back at our fancy hotel room with Jenn.

Vic had brought out the box my grandfather had given him for me. I'd opened it there on his dining room table. It contained three things. An old photo album, an old scrapbook, and a sealed envelope with my name on it, written in my grandfather's hand.

"That's a letter he wrote for you," Vic had said. "The photo album's full of old pictures from the Richards side of the family. The scrapbook's a collection of the coded newspaper ads they'd used back in the forties and fifties, to communicate back and forth."

I couldn't wait to dive in to both, but especially to read the letter. I hadn't wanted to do it there and Vic had completely understood. We shook hands, though I had a strong desire to hug the man. I told him he had to let me stay in touch. He said he'd like that but said it would have to be by phone. "Don't do any of that internet nonsense," he'd said.

I'd driven the ten minutes back to our hotel to

find Jenn still out on the balcony, flipping manuscript pages at the speed of light. It was a little breezy up there, so she used her cell phone as a paperweight. We'd talked a few moments. She wanted to hear everything about my time with Vic but asked me to hold off until she'd reached a "stopping place." I told her she wouldn't find any, but that I'd wait just the same.

We agreed I'd stay inside, read Gramps's letter, and maybe by then, she could take a break. Picking up my glass of iced tea, I walked back to a plush chair in the bedroom suite. The hand holding the letter was shaking, which was ridiculous. "Okay, Gramps, here goes."

I sat down and began to read.

Michael,

Well, I'm guessing that about now you know the whole story. I hope you don't mind the madness of my methods, but I thought as a fellow writer, if anyone would understand it'd be you. I'm writing this at my desk—your desk now . . . your office now (don't be so conflicted about this, I meant for you to have it all). I'm not sure where you're reading this letter, but I'm guessing if you got it from Vic, you wouldn't wait to get all the way back to Charleston to open it up (hope the old geezer lived long enough to give it to you personally, I really want you to meet him).

It's up to you what you do with this manuscript, my journal, and the two albums in this box. You need to know, I didn't write this story intending to publish it. I wrote it for the family. If you all decide you want to go public with it, I'm fine. My only request is that you agree, as a family, on whatever path you decide.

Oh . . . one big thing: if you do go public, better change Vic and Nate's names (sure don't want to create any trouble for these wonderful men).

Michael, I hope you and the family can forgive me for keeping this secret from you all our lives. But I had no choice. I am grateful for all that God did to allow your grandmother and me to live such an extraordinary life together. More than any fame or fortune we acquired, our children and grandchildren have meant everything to us. I was a young man without a family, without a country, without friends, but God has given me a rich heritage. Michael, you have every-thing. A true faith in God, a beautiful wife, a lovely home.

Michael, you are a gifted writer. It

would sadden me to think of you trying to live in my shadow. I've been listening and watching you for some time now. And I'm convinced, God has made you different from me. I love the way you see things, the thoughts you come up with all on your own. So write like that. Not as Michael Warner, the grandson of a bestseller. Write as Michael Warner, an author with his own stories to tell. It may take longer, may take years. But I think the world is waiting to hear what you have to say.

I know I would be, if I could be there.

Well, I keep thinking I should have some famous last words to tell you, since I know this will be the last time you'll "hear" my voice. I'm a writer, for crying out loud, I should be able to come up with something witty or wise at a moment like this.

But all I'm thinking about and aware of is this . . . I love you, Michael. Can't wait till I see you again and hear about all the things you've done with your life.

Gramps

"I love you, Gramps. Can't wait till I—"
The tears just flowed. Couldn't stop them. I sat

there with my eyes closed, I don't know for how long.

"Oh, Michael." I heard Jenn's voice speaking softly behind me. She bent down and put her arms around me. "Are you okay?"

"He was just so wonderful, Jenn. I miss him so much."

"Here." She handed me some tissues. "Do you need a little more time? We can go out later."

I stood up. "No, let's go. I need some fresh air . . . and some mahimahi." I set the letter on the end table.

"When do I get to read it?" she said.

I took her in my arms. "You can read it now, if you want, or after dinner. But I think you should wait until after you finish the manuscript. It'll mean more then."

"Then I'll wait."

She picked up her purse and we walked out into the living area, holding hands. We stopped to take in the view. "Will we ever get used to this, Michael? This new life your grandfather gave us?"

"I hope not, Jenn."

Three days later, Jenn and I were back in our new home in Charleston. She'd read the manuscript and my grandfather's letter, and we spent the better part of a day looking through the Richards family photo album and the old "secret code" news clippings they'd shared with Gramps and Nan. Gramps had typed out a sheet of instructions for us on how to interpret the code. At the bottom he'd written a note by hand: "Memorize then destroy." Beside that, a little smiley face.

I'd already called Rick Samson, thanked him for his interest in putting my grandfather's biography together, but informed him I had decided to pass on the project. I quickly added "at least for a few months." Didn't think I'd change my mind then but knew it would buy me some time to follow through on some of the things my grandfather had suggested.

Jenn and I had decided on a plan to inform the entire family. But we both agreed, one person in the family deserved to hear all about this first.

From me.

I sat in *my* office, looking out through the beautiful Charleston nine-by-nine windows into the gorgeous shaded courtyard and those lovely Adirondack chairs, and picked up the phone.

It rang three or four times.

"Hello, Marilyn? It's Michael. I found something here at the house, and I've got an incredible story to tell you. It's about Gramps."

Author's Note

The Discovery is entirely a work of fiction, and all the main characters are products of my imagination. But the setting and backdrop for the story are based on a number of fascinating historical facts. My inspiration for the book came as I thought about them and contemplated a "what if" scenario.

For example, everything I wrote about the original set of eight Nazi saboteurs who were rounded up by the FBI in June 1942 after landing onshore in Florida and Long Island, is based on historical fact. Their ringleader, George Dasch, wasn't a Nazi at heart. He actually despised the Nazis and used this "sabotage" mission as a means of getting back to the country he loved. He had no intention of following through. Shortly after he got here, he turned himself in to the FBI and told them everything he knew about the con-spiracy. He not only wanted to stop the mission from succeeding, he wanted to continue afterward to help our government fight the Nazis, divulging everything he'd learned while in Germany.

Without his help, it is doubtful the FBI would have ever known who the saboteurs were and what they were planning. Sadly, FBI Director J. Edgar Hoover broke his promise to Dasch and lumped him in with all the others. He wanted the FBI to get full credit for exposing the conspiracy and arresting the saboteurs. He then hoped to silence Dasch forever through a military trial and quick execution. You can read all about this amazing piece of American history in *Saboteurs: The Nazi Raid on America* by Michael Dobbs (Alfred A. Knopf, New York, 2004) or the book *Betrayal* (Hippocrene Books, New York, 2007) by David Alan Johnson.

One other historical work fueled my imagination: a scene from the HBO miniseries *Band of Brothers*. In one episode, shortly after D-Day began, members of the 101st Airborne are walking along a road toward a rendezvous point when they see several German POWs under armed guard. They mock them as they walk by. One of the German soldiers asks an American for a cigarette in perfect English. The American is startled and stops to chat.

He finds out the German was born in the US, even grew up there, not far from where this GI had lived. He said his parents dragged him off to Germany in the thirties, responding to Hitler's call for all good Germans to return to the Fatherland.

I found that fascinating.

I wondered how horrible it would be if that had happened to me. I think I would have done anything to get back to the US, especially when I learned the truth about the Nazis' agenda. The combination of these two scenarios became the foundation for Ben's story. Things began to snowball in my head from there. How would I handle the challenges and obstacles created by circumstances like these?

Such as . . . finding and falling in love with the woman I'd want to spend the rest of my life with.

A woman like Claire.

Acknowledgments

My esteem for my team continues to grow with the addition of this book. Starting with my wife, Cindi, who has grown to become quite the editor. She provides so much more than love, support, and encouragement. Her input into my work has become indispensable.

I'd also like to thank Andrea Doering, my editor at Revell. With each book my appreciation for you grows. Thanks for your insights and wise counsel, and for your friendship. And now it's clear I'm not alone in my assessments; congratulations on being named "Editor of the Year" by the American Christian Fiction Writers (ACFW) for 2011.

Thanks also to my much-loved agent, Karen Solem, with Spencerhill Associates. You have been with me from the beginning and every step along the way. Cindi and I feel we could not possibly be in better hands.

And to the management and staff at Revell who work so hard behind the scenes to get the book ready for the shelves, then into the readers' hands. Special thanks to Twila Bennett and Michele Misiak, and to Kristin Kornoelje for your keen eye with all the details.

Lastly, I'd like to thank the staff at the Halifax Historical Society in downtown Daytona Beach for their invaluable help with my research for this book. They helped me "see" the city as it was during the World War II years. If you visit the Daytona area, make sure you stop in and check out this museum on Beach Street.

About the Author

Dan Walsh is the award-winning author of *The Unfinished Gift*, *The Homecoming*, *The Deepest Waters*, and *Remembering Christmas*. A member of American Christian Fiction Writers, Dan served as a pastor for twenty-five years. He lives with his family in the Daytona Beach area, where he's busy researching and writing his next novel.

www.danwalshbooks.com